Witches and Warriors
Book 1

J. H. Wear

Published by
Melange Books, LLC
White Bear Lake, MN 55110
www.melange-books.com

ISBN: 978-1-68046-412-2

Cover Design by Lynsee Lauritsen

To my three sons, David, Ron and Trevor.
It is great to see that each of them has grown
to be a man that I can be proud of.

Chapter One

Terrowin swung a weathered tree branch at the thick vegetation skirting the main path of the forest. The journey was easy, but the destination to the Blackrain Cabins made him uncomfortable. He'd heard rumours that witches were also seen in the area but despite his occasional visit, he had never seen any.

His thoughts were interrupted by the cry of a large crow, sitting on a branch a few feet away, its yellow eyes peering back at him. His heart jumped when it screeched and flew off, the wings beating the air as it weaved between the trees. Terrowin stared at the shrinking black image and turned his attention to the branch upon which it had been sitting. The limb was thick but stunted, as if it just stopped growing and died. *A bad omen, his mother would say.* Slightly unnerved, he continued his walk, finding the sudden silence of the forest eerie.

The path led to the Blackrain Cabins, a trio of large cabins made of oak. Rumour was it turned black from a miscast spell the inhabitants used. Not much was known about those living in the cabins No one knew how many lived there or what they looked like. While they did do some magic, it was believed they had little to do with the witches. The occupants sold herbs and mild magic potions, and Terrowin's mother needed a potion from them to make the old bull fertile again.

An errant insect landed on his head, and he swept it away, pushing back his unkempt blond hair. Terrowin was worried over his appearance in attracting women. His height made him feel awkward, and his face held several red pimples making him self-conscious around mixed company, when the rare occasion arose. An angular structure to his face indicated he could be considered handsome as he grew older, but for now the frustration of being the only remaining male on a farm made him long for better times.

Following the memorized pathways to the Blackrain Cabins, the thick forest gave way to a clearing. Terrowin paused, apprehensive about his task. The cabins were composed of heavy, dark, square timber with the roofs made of thatch where a chimney poked through, always producing a dark, grey smoke. Taking a deep breath, he approached, reaching the largest by way of the worn pathway that angled over the grassy yard. Nervously, he knocked on the door and waited.

Terrowin jumped back when the thick rectangular door partially opened, showing only a dark interior. He held his breath momentarily as a musty, burnt smell escaped from the opening.

A tall figure wearing a black, hooded robe spoke in a deep voice. "What is it you wish?"

He stammered out a reply. "So-ome-something for our bull. He's not making the-the cows produce. He's not even in-interested in them much. Something for my mother, too. Her bones hu-hurt."

"Wait."

The door was pushed almost closed, and Terrowin could hear only muffled voices. The door crept open a minute later. A dirty cloth bag was thrust toward him by a thick arm covered with black hair and red scars. "This is for the bull. We have nothing now for your mother. Five bronze."

Terrowin swallowed. "I was told to pay only four."

Silence hung at the dark gap of the doorway. "Four bronze then."

He took the bag and passed over four tarnished brown coins. The door closed.

The inhabitants of the cabin varied prices according to their own needs, and it appeared he had arrived at a good time. Terrowin hurried away, pleased he had negotiated the price down. His mother had given him seven bronze coins, telling him he must try to pay no more than five for the bull medicine. If they had something for the aches in her joints, then he should obtain that as well. She stressed the bull potion was more important than her own pain.

He followed the weedy path back, hitting the occasional tree trunk with the stick, and returned where the stronger path presented itself. He was tempted to follow the path leading to a stream but turned the other way toward home. As he followed the path the noise of birds flapping away drew his attention, and he studied the blue and yellow gypsy birds darting between trees.

Two shadows emerge from behind the screen of branches and leaves, following the path that came from the stream. Terrowin dropped into a crouch next to a large tree and watched, barely breathing. The shadows turned into witches, women dressed in soft pastel gowns and unaware of his presence. While the dresses they wore were full length, they were also light in fabric, and their slim bodies could be made out partially underneath. He remembered a few years ago when he was with his family on a visit to the town of Drumclog where he saw witches for the first time. Both were also female. One wore a dark blue dress while the other a green one. At fourteen, he was fascinated with their supple movements and the hint of the female figure underneath. His older sister, Thea, had admonished him.

"Don't stare. If they see you looking too hard, they will put a curse on you. Witches don't want humans to know anything about them." She jerked his shoulder, forcing him to turn away.

At that time, he'd reluctantly stopped staring, occasionally casting a glance as they inspected some of the market goods, but he retained the vision of their beauty. Witches were usually tall, slim, and of good health. The women kept their hair long and walked with an easy grace. It became his idea of the ideal feminine form.

Those thoughts came back to him as they approached. When they were within a few feet of him, they turned off the path and into the brush. He carefully moved from his hiding spot and followed, keeping them just within his sight. They walked to one of the hills and stopped by a tree standing at its base where they stepped forward and disappeared.

Odd, he thought. He carefully made his way to where they'd vanished into the hill covered in grass, small bushes, and a large tree. *They went into the hill. A secret passageway or hideout.*

He turned to hurry away, suddenly aware he had discovered one of the witches' secrets. Blocking his way were six witches, all men, spread out in a semi-circle in front of him. Terrowin ran, seeking a path through the trees to make it difficult for his pursuers to follow.

The witches were quick, cutting off his escape. He pulled his knife from his belt, holding it in one hand while raising the stick in the other. The witches closed in on him, and he desperately swung the stick and jabbed with the knife. Both movements were ineffective. He was gripped by strong arms, disarmed, and dragged to the hill, him screaming. A leather bag was placed over his head, and in the darkness, he pleaded, "Please let me go. I won't tell nobody what I saw."

Resistance was useless. He was pushed and pulled into what he knew had to be inside the hill. It smelled of damp earth as he went down a spiral stairway. The hands holding him were gone, and as soon as he took off the hood, he found he was in a small bedroom. It contained a simple bed, a small table with a burning lantern on it, and a single stool. The walls and ceiling were made from stone blocks with grey mortar holding them in place.

Scared and, despite his resolve to be brave, tears ran down his cheeks, but his heart had slowly stopped thumping in his chest. Sitting on the bed, he thought back to how fate had placed him inside the witches' home. Long minutes passed, and he replayed the events that led him to the witches in the forest, until the wood door opened.

A female witch with long golden hair stepped inside and closed the door behind her. She smiled. "My name is Ululla. What is yours?"

He stared at her for several seconds. She was the most beautiful woman he had ever seen, exceeding even his fantasies. He replied in a shaken voice. "Terrowin. Please let me go."

She sat next to him on the bed. "Why did you follow the two witches here?"

"I don't know. I saw them and thought they looked nice."

"What is this?" She held up the dirty cloth bag.

"I bought it from the Blackrain Cabins. It's to make our bull want cows again."

"Was there anyone else with you?"

"No, I swear. Please, can I go now?"

She stood. "Please do not fear. I will return soon."

Terrowin looked at the door, sure it would be useless to try to leave by it. He hoped they would just let him go, but he remembered the stories of witches killing those who learned of their secrets. He regretted ever encountering them.

The door opened, and Ululla returned, carrying a tray with bread, a small vial, a cup, and a pot of tea. She gave him a gentle smile. "Terrowin, I don't want you to be scared. Try to accept who you are and how you are following a path of life." She placed the tray on the table and sat next to him on the bed.

"What's going to happen to me?"

"I think you know the answer already."

"Please…" Tears welled up at his eyes again.

"Tell me, Terrowin, have you considered where you were before you were born?"

He was surprised by her question and looked into her eyes, blue with gold sparkles. He lowered his head. "No, never thought about that."

She lifted his chin with her fingertips. "Witches believe we have many lives. This isn't the only life you have had or your last." She leaned toward him and gently brushed his hair from his face. "Would you like to know more about your other lives?"

He was surprised by the conversation and numbly nodded.

Ululla retrieved the tray from the table and passed him the vial with a dark blue powder in it.

"It tastes rather sour, but let it melt on your tongue."

"Is it poison?" He stared at the vial.

"No, just a means so you can remember the past. You will feel a bit light-headed, but you'll see part of your past. The powder will awaken your memories."

Terrowin placed the powder on his tongue. He waited as the bitter taste filled his mouth and was about to comment on it when he blurted out instead, "I remember being in a castle. I'm walking with others around me."

Ululla smiled. "What else?"

"I remember riding a horse." He grinned. "It was a big horse and well trained."

Ululla listened as Terrowin described a collage of memories. "I think I was important, maybe a nobleman, because others keep looking up to me. I know something about...spells, like I was a witch or something." Then he frowned. "They seem to be fading now."

"That's okay. They were part of your past life. We aren't meant to remember them normally as it would burden our new life. Sometimes we will see or hear something familiar and don't know why. It's a just below the surface memory of a previous life calling out to us." She looked at Terrowin in the eye. "Do you now understand we have past and future lives?"

"Yes."

"Good." She handed him the bread. "Please eat this now."

He took it from her hand. "Why?"

"It is to help you. Trust me."

He slowly ate the dark bread, and when he was done, she poured him a cup of tea. Unenthusiastically he took the clay cup in his hand, staring at the orange liquid.

"Drink it, please." She returned the tray to the table.

"Is it poison?"

"If you refuse to drink it, we'll have to use a less pleasant method. Please." She touched his shoulder. "I don't want you to suffer more than you have to."

"This will kill me, won't it?"

"Yes, your journey has come to an end. This life path is complete." She placed a finger under his chin. "When you awake again you will have a new life to begin."

"I don't want to die," he blurted out.

"We don't always have that choice. Your only choice is how you wish to go. I care for you and want you to make the right decision. Please drink the tea. Otherwise the others will have to do their job."

A tear ran down his cheek. "Will you give the magic in the bag to my mother? She needs the cows to produce calves and milk."

"I will."

"Will you tell my mother and Thea I died bravely? Let them know I love them?"

Ululla appeared to consider the question before finally replying. "For you, Terrowin, I'll do this."

He slowly lifted the cup and paused. "My mother has pain in her hands and knees. Will you please give her something to help her? I heard witches have magic that can help."

"That is not my decision to make, but I will ask this wish be granted for you."

He nodded. With a shaking hand, he placed the cup to his lips and swallowed the sweet tasting liquid. It burned in his stomach, although not too painfully. He handed the cup to her, and she placed it on the tray before climbing into bed next to him, pulling his head to her chest.

"The bread will slow down the effects of the tea. Don't be scared. You will get sleepy and not feel any pain. I'll be with you until the end."

Already he felt sleepy. As he moved his hand across her lap, the tingling in his legs and arms had already begun.

He croaked out a final question. "Why did you show me my past life?"

"I wanted to make you understand you will live again. I do care about you. You must understand the decision to end your life was done reluctantly, but I was glad I was chosen to be the one who you spend your last hour with."

He tried to move his arms, but the strength had left them. He wondered how he came to meet death this way and was curious as to why he wasn't scared anymore, though his heart thumped in his chest. Wondering how many beats it had left, his eye lids grew heavy, but he fought to keep awake as long as he could.

Terrowin gasped for air, his heart pounding. It wasn't as bad as he feared, his mind fighting consciousness for the final seconds. He closed his eyes, letting the warmth of the darkness take him.

Chapter Two

The chamber of altus had two entrances, each with curved tops at opposite sides of the room. One led to the hallway from which Ululla had approached; the other from the Hall of Sentential. The altus rector and others of high rank used the second entrance to enter the podium of the Hall of Sentential. Like most of the rooms located deep underground in the terradomus, they were without doors to the entrances. Doors were only for rooms being used for sleeping and needing seclusion. Coloured rocks made up the circular, high domed chamber of the chamber, the patterns of the rock designed to evoke peace, power, and obedience.

She bowed her head briefly and waited for the altus rector to acknowledge her.

"Step forward, Sister Ululla." His voice was deep but spoken lightly. Bealcrest was slim with short dark hair with hints of silver in it. He rose and gestured for her to sit at a simple chair in front of the heavy wood desk.

She nodded, sitting with her hands clasped on her lap, looked at his almond eyes, and waited as he sat again.

"These are turbulent times, Sister Ululla, and we have to be on guard against making errors. Thus, I was surprised when you made this request to visit the family of the male we killed to express he died bravely. Also, if I understand correctly, to give them what he purchased from the Blackrain Cabins plus a potion to help with the elder woman's joint pain."

He wet his lips before continuing. "You arrived here a several days ago, and in that time, you have shown us why the altus councillium has high expectations of you. This request seems out of character, and if it

8

was from some of the other witches, I would deny it without consulting them. However, I have decided to hear your explanation first."

"Thank you, Altus Rector Bealcrest, for your indulgence. On the day Terrowin died, he was given a task to do, a task to help his family survive. We interrupted his task, and he asked me to complete it. In our Book of Redemption, it states we are all responsible for completing the tasks appointed to us as individuals and as a group."

"Are you saying we are responsible for completing all human tasks?"

"Terrowin was taken into our terradomus against his will, and thus we interrupted his task. At the end, he accepted our judgement that he must die and freely took his life. Thus, he died in harmony with our thoughts and did not fight against them. In effect, he was in alliance with us, which means we share the responsibility to help complete his task."

Bealcrest pursed his lips. "You pose an interesting argument, Sister Ululla. It does have some merit, and I will have to reflect on that. Do you have a similar argument for speaking with his family and expressing how he died?"

Ululla smiled. "The Book of Redemption also tells in its commandants, whenever it is possible, one should bring harmony and peace of mind to all those we meet. Terrowin asked me to convey the message he died bravely. It was of particular importance to him, and I made a promise I'd do so. I ask you to grant me this favour as it'll help the family overcome their sorrow."

"The family may well be very angry to learn the witches and you were the cause of his death. I don't believe such knowledge would bring harmony in their lives."

"All they know is he is missing. Is it not better to know the truth than to not know? They cannot know peace until they know for certain he has passed on. Even today his brothers and sister are looking for him and calling out his name. If they are angry with us when they learn the truth, this is something we must accept rather than hide from what we did."

Bealcrest interlocked his fingers across his chest and looked upward as he closed his eyes. Seconds passed, and he took in a deep breath. "It's true we must be secretive in what we do. However, there is a difference between discrete in our doings and hiding from our actions. We have a responsibility in Terrowin's death and, as you pointed out, halting his final task. I thank you for bringing clarity to our ultimate goals. Your request has been granted, although I caution you not to go further on your explanation to them than necessary. You'll also take Brother Bruhamoff with you as protection, as well as he may learn from your application of our ways."

"Thank you, Altus Rector Bealcrest."

"This evening we will be addressing the discipline of Sister Yeerlin and Sister Angmar in the Hall of Sentential. Their failure to detect they were being observed by Terrowin ultimately caused his death. It would have been worse if he had remained undetected and told one of our secrets." He stood. "I believe it would be prudent for you say something at their hearing which will help towards a suitable punishment."

Ululla rose. "Thank you, I will do so."

* * * *

Ululla walked down the corridor, allowing intuition to guide her. Her mind was filled with questions on what had happened with Terrowin and with her purpose for arriving at Claireston Terradomus. Bealcrest had quietly accepted her explanation she had arrived only to rest for a few days before continuing her journey. She had told him the truth, for she was to continue to on to the city of Newharken where a new assignment awaited her. What she could not reveal to him was she was also to see if the rumours that a dark influence had seeped into Claireston. Forty-nine witches claimed Claireston as their primary residence, although it could accommodate another eleven. It was different from most witches' sanctuaries, being isolated from a major town or city. It was also the location where some witches went to hide from the authorities until it was safe for them to return to where the kings ruled. Claireston Terradomus was considered by the Whiterose witches to be of special importance, and its location was a carefully kept secret.

She noted the coloured stones marking her location, knowing she was reaching the hallway leading to the bedrooms and opposite to it, the ramp leading to the outside world. She slowed her steps and turned her attention to the first bedroom on the left. "Don't worry, Terrowin. I will fulfill my promise to you," she whispered.

She drew in a slow breath and continued down the corridor. The corridor dipped downward and turned sharply, leading to a lower level. The stone walls, floor, and curved ceiling were hundreds of years old in places, a testament to the long-range plans made by the witches. The oil lanterns gave a flickering light and were vented above, their smoke expelled efficiently to the outside.

Ululla reached the next level and the office of the Claireston Keeper. She saw the black-haired woman hunched over her desk, writing quickly on a piece of parchment.

Ululla entered the room, a chamber much like the altus rector, but smaller and with only one entrance. She waited a few feet within until the keeper acknowledged her presence.

"Keeper Elwendia." Ululla bowed her head for a moment.

Elwendia rolled up the parchment and smiled at Ululla. "Please enter, Sister Ululla. How may I assist you?"

Ululla stepped forward and sat on the chair in front of the desk. "I seek answers, Keeper Elwendia. A young man has been killed, and now two of our sisters are being considered in the Hall of Sentential for discipline." She paused for a moment, watching the fixed smile on Elwendia's face. "May I ask, Keeper, what happened?"

"Of course. I was in this chamber when I heard the alarm bells." She looked over at the pair of small brass bells attached above the entrance. Above the bells a cord ran up and into a hole in the wall. "I immediately went to the watcher on duty, Brother Ardziv, and he informed me that a man was trying to break in Claireston. I sent word for him to be apprehended. Unfortunately, they decided to bring him inside, and we had to make a decision on what to do with him. We couldn't risk the secret of Claireston's location being known, and it was suggested that we needed to end his life to ensure that. It was most unfortunate, and I later stressed to Sister Yeerlin and Sister Angmar how their failure to comply with our rules caused his death." Elwendia smiled. "Thank you for volunteering to do this difficult task. Otherwise, one of the brothers would have to use a more difficult means."

Ululla looked carefully at Elwendia. "I wish I had been there when the decision of bringing in Terrowin was made. Perhaps it wasn't necessary to have him killed."

"The council considered the alternatives, but sometimes the hardest decision is still the best."

Ululla stood. "Peace be with you, Keeper."

"And to you."

Ululla walked back up the ramp to the entrance to Claireston, the heavy oak door secured with iron rods into the stone walls. Above the entrance hung a rope ladder that led to the small cavity where the Watcher sat to observe the area around.

"Watcher Ardziv, are you available to speak?" she called up to the dark above her.

"I am."

Moments later a pair of legs dressed in a brown cloth emerged, stepping with assurance down the swinging ladder. When he stood in front of her, he was the same height as she was. His blond hair was cut very short, and he sported a small, thick beard. He looked young for such a thick growth of beard, and his blue eyes also gave the impression of youth. She knew ages were hard to tell among witches, and only someone with her experience could pick out the details on a face which told of the true age. On his face, there was a lack of the fine wrinkles around the eyes, and she concluded he was, in fact, a young man.

"I am Sister Ululla, and I would like to ask you about the intruder you saw yesterday."

Ardziv closed his eyes for a moment. "A sad happening, to be sure. I saw him approach the entrance shortly after the sisters entered. I don't know if he saw them enter, but he certainly had seen them approach. I rang the alarm and told Keeper Elwendia an intruder was at the entrance and seemed to be aware there was a doorway there. She immediately called the guards, ordering them to secure him and not allow him to escape. Keeper Elwendia went to speak to other members of the council."

Ululla thanked him and made her way back to the chamber of the altus rector. She stepped inside and waited until he acknowledged her.

12

"Sister Ululla, what brings you back here so soon? Do you have another request to make?"

"No, Altus Rector Bealcrest, just a question if you don't mind. When you met with Keeper Elwendia and other members of the council, who first suggested death for Terrowin was the best option?"

Bealcrest thought for several seconds. "I am afraid several suggestions were made at once, and I can't recall who first spoke the need to kill him. I do remember Keeper Elwendia speaking out in agreeing death was the only method to ensure our secrecy."

"What were your thoughts at the time?"

"Being the altus rector and making the final judgment, my role is to not make suggestions but to either agree or dismiss their suggestions. I try not to interject my own feelings into the matter, unless there is a stalemate. No one seemed to be pleased about the decision to kill him, but I accepted it as necessary."

Ululla nodded. "I understand. It must have been a surprise someone was trying to break into Claireston."

"Yes, not merely walking around the area but trying to force his way in. I find it most unfortunate it came to killing him, but as Keeper Elwendia pointed out, the secrecy of Claireston must be paramount." He gave a tight smile and placed his fingers on her shoulder. "Sister Ululla, I can fully sympathize with your feelings of unease. A young man had to die, but perhaps you're tormenting yourself about a situation not of your making."

"Perhaps you're right, but I can't help but wonder if he truly needed to die."

He withdrew his hand from her shoulder. "Then I do hope the truth you seek will bring peace to you."

"Thank you for your sentiment and your indulgence with my questions."

"Not at all. Please let me know if you discover anything new."

Ululla nodded as she retreated out of the room. *I already have.*

* * * *

Ululla wanted to talk to Sister Yeerlin and Sister Angmar and located them preparing food in the kitchen. She smiled as she approached them, softly calling out their names. Both women had red eyes and looked tired and nervous.

"This must be a terrible ordeal for you both."

Sister Yeerlin nodded. "Indeed it has been. We feel…" A tear fell down her cheek.

Sister Angmar spoke up. "We understand we made a mistake. Keeper Elwendia has made that quite clear, but she made us also quite worried about what will happen to us."

"Tell me, what were you doing outside yesterday?"

Sister Angmar put her arm around Yeerlin's waist. "Sister Yeerlin is a novice, so I was showing her around the area and took her where a path led to a stream. We had a nice walk and when we returned, we used the path Keeper Elwendia suggested. I thought it was a bit too close to the entrance but the Keeper suggested it was best to vary our paths from the usual longer route."

"I understand. What did Keeper Elwendia say to you that worries you?"

"The Keeper told us we will likely face discipline for causing his death."

Sister Yeerlin broke in. "She told us the punishment should be severe." She began to cry.

Ululla squeezed her hand into a fist. "That will not happen, I assure you." She took in a slow breath and spoke carefully. "Please understand while you feel guilty for a young man's death, the responsibility lies with many of us, including Keeper Elwendia. I am particular heavy in the heart over his death. However, punishment will not accomplish anything, and there's no need to add more pain to what has already happened."

She left the kitchen, after bidding the two witches peace.

I know of you now, Elwendia. You will be held accountable for your sins.

Chapter Three

Ululla entered the Hall of Sentential from the lower level. Bench seats without backs circled the chamber. She looked at Yeerlin and Angmar, who sat together at the front on a separate bench. It was similar to all the Halls of Sentential at the various witches' terradomuses with curved walls and domed ceilings of coloured stones that spelled out messages. In some, the Hall of Sentential was much larger, with several entrances, while others were barely large enough to seat more than a dozen. This one contained two copies of the Book of Redemption held on two separate small tables.

She sat down on one of the open spots on the bench seats, nodding to some of the witches she recognized. She waited with the others in silence, save for a few quiet whispers from the two dozen witches watching. A small copper plate was struck and five witches entered from the altus rector's chamber. Altus Rector Bealcrest led the way, followed by four other high witches including Keeper Elwendia. They sat on a mezzanine that reached out far enough to hold a single long table with five chairs.

"We are here to determine the possible discipline of Sister Yeerlin and Sister Angmar. Would they please stand before the council?" Bealcrest spoke, his voice carrying easily within the chamber.

The two witches stood with their heads bowed before slowly looking up at the council.

"You have been accused of negligence of your duties and thereby compromising the security of Claireston and the death of a young man. What do you have to say in your defence?"

Sister Angmar spoke. "We are sorry for the harm we caused. We ask only for your understanding and forgiveness."

Bealcrest pursed his lips, preparing to speak, when Ululla rose.

"May I speak as their advocate?"

Whispers sounded around her and the two witches as they turned to her with looks of surprise.

Bealcrest spoke and leaned forward on the table. "Go ahead, Sister Ululla, I believe your input will be valuable."

"We seem to be looking for a suitable punishment for Sister Yeerlin and Sister Angmar when I doubt there's one for their supposed sin. It is true they didn't use a reveal spell to determine if anyone was watching them, but that in itself isn't a sin. If it is, then, are we to punish anyone who ever fails to make each task perfect? Remember the reveal spell is only used when we believe someone is observing us undetected. That wasn't the case here.

"I would like to point out the reason they were detected entering Claireston was Keeper Elwendia asked them to use a different path to return here, which, was the reason they were seen. Secondly, it was Keeper Elwendia who ordered the intruder to be brought inside. If he was merely detained outside, perhaps his life could've been spared."

Ululla paused and turned toward those sitting behind her. "I submit to you that we as a group must share in the responsibility for Terrowin's death and not try to relieve our conscience by punishing one of us. Sister Yeerlin and Sister Angmar have been punished enough by their own feeling of remorse and now should be forgiven."

Ululla turned back to the front and looked up at Bealcrest. "That is all I have to say, except to acknowledge my own participation in his death."

Bealcrest slowly nodded. "You've made a strong argument. Does anyone wish to add or refute what she has told us?" He scanned the room. "Very well, I wish to confer with other council members before announcing the decision."

The council members left the room with Bealcrest leading. Ululla sat on one of the bench seats again, noticing the time to arrive at a decision was extraordinarily long.

Bealcrest returned with the other council members, minus the keeper, after the long delay. He looked confused as he looked back into his chambers and addressed the assembly. "As Sister Ululla pointed out, there isn't any sin here to punish. If there is, we could all be guilty of one infraction or another. Sister Yeerlin and Sister Angmar, you are free to go and are absolved of any sin in the death of the intruder. Go in peace."

Ululla hurried out of the Great Hall and up toward the chamber of the altus rector. She entered his chamber just as he was about to leave.

"Forgive my intrusion, Altus Rector Bealcrest, but where is Keeper Elwendia?"

"I don't know. She left when we adjourned, indicating she would return momentarily. Before we returned to the Hall of Sentential, I had her office checked, but it appears she has disappeared. This is most unusual."

"I am afraid I must inform you Keeper Elwendia is likely a member of the Darkrose. I believe she purposely had Sister Yeerlin and Sister Angmar use a route where they would more than likely be detected and had Terrowin brought inside when she knew it could result in his execution. She may have also used a spell of confusion when the council was trying to decide what to do about his fate, allowing her to push forward the need for his death."

Bealcrest placed a hand on his doorway to steady himself. "She was a member of the Darkrose and worked against us right in our midst? This is horrible news."

"She was clever and tried to spread darkness here. Do not despair, for she has been found out."

"True, but I agreed to his death. If I had only known the truth."

"Altus Rector Bealcrest, Terrowin's death was the correct decision once he discovered the secret location of Claireston and was brought inside. All Keeper Elwendia did was to cause more turmoil with that judgment."

Bealcrest nodded. "I assume she has left Claireston. Perhaps we'll find her someday." He looked carefully at Ululla. "I'll not ask you to reveal who you really are, but it is obvious you're not just a sister travelling through here."

Ululla smiled. "Thank you. I'm not comfortable with too many secrets. I'm a member of the altus councillium's singular sect and am to arrive at Newharken to learn of my next assignment."

"I understand. I thank you for your assistance here. Peace be with you."

Chapter Four

Brother Bruhamoff, a tall, young man with a face unable to grow a proper beard, followed Ululla past the small farms which faced toward Drumclog. The narrow road was muddy in places and while Bruhamoff took to stamping his feet to shake mud off his sandals, Ululla carried her sandals in her hand. Occasionally he walked next to her but usually kept far enough back to make conversation difficult. She understood his unease and allowed them to travel in silence.

Ululla wiped her feet on strands of grass and put on her sandals when they arrived at the farm where Terrowin had lived. She entered past the small wood gate set in the middle of the fence made of tree branches intertwined together. Near the front was a modest stone and log home with a roof made with a thick blanket of grass.

Bruhamoff stayed outside at the gate while Ululla knocked on the only door. A minute passed before a heavy-set woman, leaning on a cane, opened the door. Her face, red with grief, froze at the sight of Ululla.

She gasped. "Thea, come quick. Witches are here!"

Ululla smiled. "Please don't be alarmed. We bring no harm to thee."

Thea stepped next to her mother and stared at her. "What do want with us?"

Ululla looked at her mother and at Thea, seeing the resemblance of the two in their faces. Thea, she noted, was taller and of a fuller figure. "I've come to give you information about Terrowin."

Moments passed, and Thea stepped aside. "Please enter then."

Ululla followed them into the kitchen. The only other rooms in the house were taken up by small bedrooms. She sat on one of the simple backless chairs and waited for the other two women to sit.

Cool air swept over her, and the old woman gave a small shudder.

"My brother, what has happened to him?" Thea asked.

"I'm saddened to tell you he has passed on from this life."

The mother covered her face with her hands. "No! My boy cannot be dead. Please say it isn't so."

"It pains me to see your grief for him." Ululla watched as Thea rose and hugged her mother. "Terrowin passed on without any suffering. He was very brave at the end."

Thea looked at her. "How do you know of this?"

"I was with him."

Thea shook her head. "He was just a boy, full of so much promise."

"Terrowin died as a man, but his journey is not yet complete."

Thea looked puzzled. "Explain."

"Did you not feel the cool air in here when we sat down? That means his spirit is here with us now. Tell him you love him and say goodbye, for he needs to move on to the next part of his passage."

The old woman wailed, sobbing out words hard to distinguish. Thea bowed her head and whispered. She looked at Ululla. "What was your part in his death? Did you kill him?" Anger seethed out of the words.

"I was part of his departure, but I never held any ill against him. I cared for him very much." She stood. "I am to give you this." She placed a small bag on the table. "It's for the bull at the back."

"My brother is gone, my mother can barely walk with her bones hurting so, and all we've to replace him is a bag of powder for our old bull. How do we survive when the oldest brothers have already left us?"

"I don't know what your future will bring. I'll say this, the dark clouds now above you will move on. I'll now leave you in peace."

"Peace?" The old woman spat out. "Me so useless as not to do work, my son gone, and you say that?"

"I am sorry to hear the pain in your voice. May the sun tomorrow bring you warmth." She paused before asking, "Was he named after King Terrowin?"

Thea nodded, not bothering to wipe the tears falling freely. "He was a king known for his intelligence and kind heart. Our Terrowin had the same virtues."

"Know this. Like the king, your Terrowin was a man of courage and strength of being."

Ululla walked back to the front gate where Bruhamoff stood stiffly. "Wait."

Ululla turned to see Thea running after her. She clutched Ululla's wrist.

"You said my brother was a man. You also said that you were with him when he died."

Ululla smiled. "A man can be defined by many qualities, courage, strength to do what is required, and concern for those he cares about. By those definitions, Terrowin died as a man."

Thea finally gave a trembling smile. "Terrowin thought witches were so beautiful. He was fascinated with them. I am glad he spent his final minutes with you."

Ululla took both her hands into hers. "Your brother was a good man. Be calm with that thought."

Thea nodded, the tears finally stopping. "He'd have been so happy to be with you." She tilted her head slightly. "You're truly beautiful."

"Thank you." She released Thea's hands. "Terrowin loved you and the rest of your family. Please be happy for him." She turned and walked away to the waiting Bruhamoff.

* * * *

Once again, she took off her sandals and spoke after a few minutes of walking. "Brother Bruhamoff, what is bothering you? You seem to have many questions on your mind."

"I'm trying to understand why you went to the farm and talked to them. Are we not supposed to be as secretive as possible? This seems to be breaking that rule."

"It's not a rule, but one of guidance. There're two kinds of secrets. One you know and no one else suspects is a secret. The other type is one you know as a secret and others know you have a secret. That type can be dangerous and sometimes harmful as it leads to speculations.

"In this case I did have a secret, but my knowledge in keeping it a secret was causing Terrowin's family harm. I also made a promise to him to talk to them. I was willing to break that promise if it was for the greater good, but truly it served no purpose save to make others suffer by keeping silent."

"It is okay to reveal ourselves and some secrets? Are there no rules or guidance for that?"

"You misunderstand part of the Book of Redemption. The scriptures are for interpretation, inspiration, and guidance. You must think for yourself, and when in doubt, follow your heart and do what you believe is right. Do you understand what the ultimate goal of the Book of Redemption is?"

"Yes, to bring peace, happiness, and contentment to all people."

"Very good. Now I ask you, how do we accomplish that by always hiding what we know? If you believe what we know is the way, then isn't it a contradiction to not give peace when we can?"

Bruhamoff shook his head. "This seems so confusing."

"Decisions involving life are not always easy. We must make decisions not just for today but for many years in the future."

"I understand. You're helping Terrowin's family because it will also help our goal of peace to everyone."

"In a way, yes." She smiled. "You're taking your first steps to understanding what we need to do."

Her thoughts returned to the uneasy feeling she had about Terrowin's death. She wondered if being at Claireston when the decision was made that he had to die and she'd felt compelled to volunteer for the task was a coincidence. She felt destiny was pulling her forward as if she was caught in a powerful stream, unable to do much more than slow down the certainty of her fate. Her encounter with Elwendia was also unnerving, and she was certain the Darkrose witch had recognized her for who she was when they first met. It helped to explain Elwendia's hurried and almost desperate attempt at causing as much havoc as possible in her final days in Claireston.

I suppose in the end it was Elwendia and I who caused Terrowin's death. It is a sad thing to have in common.

"Ululla, are you all right?"

22

She turned and smiled at Bruhamoff. "Yes, thank you." She wiped the solitary tear from one eye. "It was an emotional visit with his family."

"You've helped them, haven't you?"

"Yes, I hope I have done enough. Tell me, Brother Bruhamoff, do you know where you're going after your stay at Claireston?"

"No, I was told I'd know when it was time to leave. I've lived here for over seven years."

"I'm leaving for Newharken in two days' time. Perhaps you'd like to accompany me."

"Really? Can I do that?"

"I think it's meant to be. It can be dangerous for a single woman to travel alone, and your presence would make me feel safer. It would also give me an opportunity to explain parts of the Book of Redemption."

He was silent for several seconds. "I'd enjoy travelling with you very much."

* * * *

Thea slowly picked up the small basket she found at the front door. Morning had barely broken, but she awoke from the noise of their old bull chasing the cows around the pasture.

She looked at the orange powder inside the clay cup and the note lying next to it.

> *To be taken at the mid of night when the moon is at*
> *its highest to remove the pain deep in bones and bodies,*
> *so one can once again feel useful. Peace be with all.*

Thea bit her lower lip. *Maybe Terrowin was right about the witches after all.*

Chapter Five

Ululla entered her sleeping quarters, her final night at Claireston before leaving. She closed the door and opened the clasp at the back of her dress. She paused, closing her eyes deep in thought.

"Terrowin, why are you still here? Your time here is over, and you should be going to the next plane."

She felt the change in the air as his spirit moved around the small room. "Don't you know it isn't polite to watch a lady undress uninvited?"

The air changed again and suddenly she felt alone. *Terrowin is either still feeling confused or he needs to tell me something.*

Ululla undressed and slipped into bed, folding her hands across her stomach. Her eyes fluttered closed, and she fell into a deep sleep.

* * * *

Ululla led the way along the path that snaked between the forest trees. Occasionally, along the wider portions, Bruhamoff walked by her side. When he did, he would often lower his head without speaking.

"Don't be nervous, Brother Bruhamoff. This will be an opportunity for you to understand more about the world of humans outside of witches. You shouldn't be worried about this prospect. Ask me questions if you're curious about anything."

After a moment, he answered. "I know so little I don't even know what to ask, but I'll try to learn as much as I can from you during our journey."

"Let's start with what we do know. Do you understand why Claireston and some other terradomus are built deep within forests?"

"To hide from others?"

"That's one reason, and one which helps preserves our secrecy, but there's another reason, a profound part of being a witch and our philosophy."

Bruhamoff quietly considered before answering in a quiet voice. "Is it because the terradomus brings us closer to Mother Earth?"

Ululla turned to him and smiled. "You know the answer, and yet you reply in a question. You're a smart young man who has studied the Book of Redemption, so you should be able to answer without reservation. Please try again and tell me why many terradomus are built deep within the forest."

He took a deep breath and stuttered out the first few words before his voice gained confidence. "It-it's be-because we are part of Mother Earth and by living within her we can find peace, calm, and fulfilment. This is the source of our strength from which we can reach out to others."

"Excellent. The second line tells us to reach out to others. What do you suppose that means?"

"To help enlighten those within our community and those who are lost."

"Close enough. Others does mean all witches, humans, and even animals. Any creature that can feel emotions can be helped."

"Is that why you wanted to help Terrowin's family?"

"It's one of the reasons. I made a promise to Terrowin that I wanted to keep. Although he appeared to be a young man, I sensed his spirit was older, and perhaps even powerful. I wanted to appease him as he could still have an influence on our journey."

"How so? I don't understand."

"Terrowin is still with us. I can feel his spirit as we walk. I don't know why he's accompanying us. I suspect he doesn't know either, but it seems he has a task to do, otherwise he would've already gone on to the next plane." She pointed to a small clearing off the path. "Let's stop here for nourishment."

Bruhamoff stretched out his legs on the grass and quietly ate a dried berry and pastry mixture. After a drink of water, he spoke.

"I've much to learn. It never occurred to me Terrowin's spirit would still be around and following us."

"I'm still learning as well. I hope we both shall learn every day."

He nodded slowly. "Tell me, yesterday you took off your sandals to walk on muddy ground. Why did you do so? It puzzled me, but I was afraid to ask."

Ululla smiled. "Perhaps you know the answer already. How do you think I was feeling that day?"

"Sad, perhaps anxious about going to Terrowin's family."

"Yes, I was feeling upset about what had transpired. Thus, I needed to bring calmness and strength back into my being." She waited for him to respond.

His head lifted up. "Oh, by walking barefoot, you came into contact with Mother Earth." He dug his fingers into the soft ground and lifted up the fragments. "From here comes our strength, peace, and contentment."

"You see, you did know the answer. You know more than you think you do."

* * * *

Ululla's shadow stretched out in front of her. She paused on the hard-packed dirt road, wide enough to allow two wagons to pass each other. Since they had left the forest path for the road, they had encountered people, horses, and wagons slowly making their way to and from the town of Equisurbem, the midway point to Newharken. Most of those passing them reacted to their presence, casting a careful look as they retreated to the far side of the road. A few other brave souls acknowledged them, murmuring, "Peace be with you."

"I can smell smoke and animals. It seems we'll reach the terradomus just before sunset."

"It's better to sleep there than on the side of the road." He looked at the thick bush to either side of them. "It may not be safe out here at night, and it's difficult to find flat ground where one can rest."

"True, although we'd be in less danger because we're witches if we camped here. Still, it will be nice to have a bed to sleep on."

Ululla continued the journey. The town took over the forests and farmland. The stone and wood structures were normally small dwellings, some for storage. She also glimpsed at the upper story of a nobleman's home, imitating the style of a lord's castle without daring to challenge its size. She guessed many of the smaller dwellings around it paid rent to occupy his land and the right to grow a small garden for their needs.

"All terradomuses have at least two entrances. This terradomus has three. One of the extra entrances is in a dwelling much like the ones we are passing but at the other side of town. The other additional entrance is actually in the forest, away from the main road. However, we don't have to hide our visit here. We will use the main entrance. As you travel, it's important you memorize the additional entrances or exits for each terradomus."

"That's a lot to learn."

"Being a Whiterose witch means you'll have to constantly study. Besides the Book of Redemption, each terradomus has a library of scrolls and books to study. It might be prudent to look at the maps when you visit any new one. It'll show all the entrances, tunnels, and other details. The maps will also show where the Umbravox temples are located."

"You mean the Darkrose. Why should we care where they've their temples?"

"They are in many ways part of our family, despite our differences in beliefs. You cannot ignore what you don't approve of. Remember at one time all witches belonged to the Umbravox, the name the Darkrose still like to call themselves. I suppose they still believe we will eventually rejoin them." She paused a moment. "Do you know why we call them the Darkrose?"

Bruhamoff stammered, "Be-because they practice dark magic?"

"No, they rarely use dark spells. A rose, whether it is dark in colour or not, is beautiful and a gift from the earth. The Darkrose, like we do, believe in the Mother Earth and hold what she brings to us sacred. The Darkrose, you may know, wear clothing dyed in earth tones of dark brown, dark green, and other deep colours. We wear earth tones too, but because we also place an importance on the Sun and the Moon, we change the colours to a lighter shade. Think of a tree leaf dark in colour. That's what the Darkrose wear. Now think of sunlight shining through a leave. This is what we would wear for colour."

"Oh, I never thought of it like that."

"Do not be fooled by names or titles. The Darkrose also has less than complimentary terms for us."

The rutted, hard packed dirt road gave way to one paved with flat stones. The traffic increased with people, horses, and carts. The closely placed buildings provided some illumination with flickering yellow light from windows while people hurried to reach their destinations before night fell.

Bruhamoff spoke quietly to Ululla. "It doesn't smell very good here."

Ululla smiled over the smell of food being prepared, garbage, and smoke saturating the air like a blanket. "You have lived too many years in the clean air of the forest. You'll get used to the smell of towns."

"I suppose so, but it cannot be healthy to live here."

"No, but these people have little choice. Remember one of the objectives in the Book of Redemption is for all people to live healthy lives. We have much work to do." She pointed to a street that forked to their right. "We go this way. The terradomus is two hundred and fifty-six steps on our right."

"You have memorized their location even to the steps to reach it?"

"Yes, all terradomus can be found by counting steps from a specific landmark or by measuring from a specific point. This terradomus is measured from the fork in the road and is a multiple of two to the power of eight. It is an easy number to remember because Equisurbem Terradomus is the eighth terradomus to be built."

"How about Claireston Terradomus?"

"Claireston is the tip of an equilateral triangle with the other two points at the ends of Alcedonia Lake."

"I should've known that."

"Don't judge yourself harshly. That brings negative energy. Instead, look at this as an opportunity to study and learn something new. You should always look forward to increasing your knowledge."

"I do. It's just that I don't know where to start."

"As you become experienced in life, you'll understand that questions and answers often travel together in circles. Like a circle, there isn't a beginning or an end. Therefore, it doesn't matter where you start, but it's important you do start."

* * * *

The Equisurbem Terradomus stood out from the smaller surrounding rectangular buildings. The sides of the building were slightly sloped with rounded corners, and the roof consisted of overlapping circular sections. Like the neighbouring buildings, stone and wood was used as a construction material, but the terradomus also had clay tile on the roof. The imposing structure sported several tinted glass windows at the roof line.

Ululla and Bruhamoff walked the stone path to the single heavy wood door and pulled the chime cord. Ululla knew they had been observed walking up and wasn't surprised when the door immediately opened.

The elderly man was heavy for a witch and also on the shorter side. Like many male witches, he wasn't entirely clean shaven but wore a well-trimmed white goatee. "Sister Ululla, it's wonderful you have come to visit us again."

"Keeper Jerod, it has been too many years since I've seen you. My companion is Brother Bruhamoff."

"You're both welcome to stay with us as long as you like." He stepped to side of the door.

Ululla passed through the doorway, remembering the high, curved ceilings and the catwalk which followed the roof line. "We also have a spirit travelling with us, although I believe there isn't any cause to be concerned."

Jerod looked around. "A spirit? You didn't use a banishing spell?"

"No, he means no harm. I believe we're travelling parallel paths as he completes his journey."

"Very well. Please come with me. You must be hungry and tired after your journey."

He led the way across the open floor. Circular benches faced a stage furthest from the entrance. Jerod stepped on the slightly raised stage easily, crossing it to where two overlapping dark oak walls left a gap in the middle. Behind the walls a staircase led to the upper catwalk and a small office. Jerod took a second staircase to a lower floor.

Ululla recalled the library along the curved walls and the half dozen long tables that served as desks and places to eat. An enclave to their left featured a pedestal holding a copy of the Book of Redemption left open to the carefully handwritten words.

To their right another room held a pantry of prepared food. A young woman assisted an older one, folding dough on a stone counter next to a heavy cast iron stove.

Ululla smiled at the older woman when they entered the lower floor. "Sister Hollyn, you're looking well."

Hollyn grinned, creasing her pale, smooth skin. "They say hard work keeps you healthy, so I must be very healthy. I miss your presence, Sister Ululla. Welcome back."

Ululla followed Jerod to the back wall of the library where another set of stairs took them to the sleeping quarters.

"Please choose a room you desire, and then come upstairs for some refreshments." He indicated the two rows of doors facing the hallway. Ululla knew at the end of the hall the last bedroom had a set of stairs hidden under the bed which led to the stone walled tunnels.

"Thank you, Keeper Jerod. It feels good to be back here, even for a short time."

Ululla led the way to the bedrooms. "Pick a room you like, Bruhamoff, although I believe all of them are identical in size. It's best that you don't mention to anyone a spirit is with us."

He nodded as he cautiously opened a bedroom door. "I understand. I won't tell anyone."

Ululla picked a door that didn't have a wood slide in the occupied position. She set her bag on the chair and whispered, "Terrowin, you may stay here tonight, but you must not disturb the others in the terradomus. Some will be aware of your presence and may not react well to it."

Cool air passed by her face. Ululla relaxed, closing her eyes as she twisted her head to follow his spirit. She opened her eyes and smiled.

"Very good. Wait by the bed and I'll be back later."

Chapter Six

Ululla met Bruhamoff in the dining area. After she was greeted by several of the other witches, she took a seat next to him where he sat quietly by himself.

"You should try to meet others here. Don't feel inhibited. You may be new, but I assure you many of the witches here would like to meet you." She paused and lowered her voice slightly. "Especially the women."

He blushed. "I don't know how to begin a conversation."

"Just turn to the person next to you and say hello and your name. The conversation will start by itself."

Bruhamoff took a deep breath and turned to the woman next to him, stuttering his introduction.

Ululla smiled at his attempt, knowing the woman next to him would make up for his difficulty in speaking. A minute later he turned to her and whispered "Gloriana is very nice."

"Of course she is. She is a witch after all." *And she will help you learn how to talk to women.*

Ululla mingled with the others after the meal, noting Bruhamoff was in quiet conversation with Gloriana at a far wall. She wandered to where Watcher Jerod stood.

"There appears to be a larger number of inhabitants at the terradomus than I was here last."

"Yes, there has been a lot of activity here in recent weeks. I'm just the keeper, but even I can perceive there's urgency in some of our guests."

Ululla smiled. "Even you, Keeper? You've always had an attention to detail. What can you tell me of what's going on?"

Jerod gave the smallest of shrugs. "It's not my place to say." He paused and lowered his voice slightly. "It would seem a conflict is brewing between the human kingdoms, and it has special interest to Altus Rector Montagu."

"I am to meet with him tomorrow. Perhaps he'll have some information for me on the conflict."

"No doubt he will. I have also noted an increase in the Darkrose in Equisurbem. The coming conflict seems to be of interest to them as well."

"The Darkrose caused us a problem at Claireston Terradomus, one that may still not be resolved." She thought of Terrowin. "The Darkrose may have made a miscalculation there."

"Has this something to do with the spirit that's accompanying you?"

"You are very perspective, Keeper Jerod. I believe there's a destiny for the spirit, and I need to help guide him there."

Ululla went to her room. After closing the door, she paused, searching out the room and spoke. "It is good you remained here, Terrowin. I shall sleep now, and I hope you don't mind waiting until I know more of what is going on here."

A coolness slid by her face, and she smiled.

"Goodnight, Terrowin."

* * * *

Ululla ate a light breakfast, sitting across from Bruhamoff. As he ate his bread, he kept looking over his left to the entrance.

"Are you looking for Gloriana?"

He looked back at Ululla, looking surprised by her question. "Yes, she said she would see me at breakfast."

"Don't be worried. Sometimes a woman takes a bit longer to get ready in the morning, especially if she wishes to look nice."

His expression changed as he thought over the new information. She smiled at him, understanding his nervousness. It occurred to her he was possibly still a virgin. The Claireston Terradomus didn't have many younger women, and it wasn't likely he'd had sexual relations before he moved there. That didn't rule out an older woman seeking his company, but witches were very careful about the emotional state of others. Most likely the witches would consider he wasn't ready for a sexual relationship. She thought Bruhamoff was best off starting with a woman near his own age, such as Gloriana. She appeared more confident than him and seemed to have had experience with men.

Ululla looked over and saw Gloriana approach the table.

"I've finished my breakfast and must go to a meeting. I'll see you later."

He nodded rapidly and stood as Gloriana greeted them.

"You may have my place, Gloriana. I was just leaving."

"Thank you. Good day to you, Sister Ululla."

Ululla returned to her room.

"Terrowin, I have a meeting to attend, but afterward I'm going for a walk. You're welcome to come with me as you must be bored waiting here."

His spirit brushed against her.

"In time, you will learn how to communicate. I can feel your presence, which means you're able to exert a small amount of physical force. While I'm at the meeting, try to move something small."

She looked in her bag and produced a small glass vial containing a green powder. She placed it on a desk that also served as a dresser. She stared at the vial, and it began to wobble slightly before sliding a few inches.

"You see. I can move it without physically touching it. Now you try. Not as if you are pushing it, but rather envision it moving to a new location. Let the natural forces do the work for you."

She left the bedroom, hoping Terrowin could learn how to use the turpis force, something that took her years to learn. She knew some spirits could learn to use the turpis force quickly and considered they may be actually made up of that energy.

* * * *

Altus Rector Montagu stood up from his desk as Ululla entered. The desk reflected the importance of his office with carved symbols on the legs and the front of the top. Unlike the Darkrose witches, the Whiterose witches decided some of their terradomus would not be hidden from the rest of the human population. Four terradomus were chosen to be built in larger towns and cities. Their purpose was for the population to see and meet witches without fearing them. The terradomus served as a place where people could learn about the Book of Redemption and ask to be trained as a witch as well. The terradomus also would provide food to those in dire need of nourishment, in particular to families with small children. Once a week, the terradomus would open the front doors and give sermons about the Book of Redemption. Attendance was normally low, but always a few individuals came to hear what the witches believed in.

"Thank you, Altus Rector Montagu, for seeing me." Ululla sat in one of the two chairs in front of the desk and faced the tall, blond man.

Montagu nodded and sat. "Not at all. I understand you're passing through here, but you used to call our terradomus home."

Ululla smiled. "Yes, I did. I recognized a few of the witches here."

"I believe Sister Emeline was the altus rector during your last stay here. She, of course, is now with the altus councillium, and she sent me a message, stating you've been given a special assignment and discretion should be observed in asking questions about your journey." He sighed. "I'm curious as to why you decided to travel with a spirit but will not press for an answer." He raised his eyebrows. "With the upcoming conflict between the human kingdoms it is those details which cause me to wonder about a larger pattern."

"If it makes you feel any better, I'm not sure of the role the spirit might have, either, but a Darkrose arranged the circumstances that ended with us killing a man. Now his spirit is travelling with me. Rather than banish him, I believe it's best I find out what his new journey involves."

"The spirits can be our guides as well. Perhaps he will help you on your own course of travels or give us information we can find useful. I assume he's not here now with you as I don't feel any spirits with us."

"True. He's waiting for me in my room. What can you tell me about the conflict?"

"King Hadrian is the source of conflict. He's ambitious and wants to increase the size of the Kingdom of Dwykath. He's also not sound mentally and has fits of rage, in particular to witches. I believe he is ready to launch an assault at a neighbouring Kingdom of Kireland."

"Kireland is a small kingdom. Unless they can form an alliance with another kingdom, King Hadrian will prevail in a contest."

"True. King Briebeth has been negotiating with two other neighbouring kingdoms, but he does not have much to offer in return. His army is small, and to get the protection from the larger kingdoms will likely mean paying a stipend."

"Is this the conflict that has the altus councillium worried?"

"I fear it's only the beginning of a larger conflict."

* * * *

Ululla walked along the streets of Equisurbem, occasionally stopping at the shops. The road was old, located in an original part of the town. Some of the flat stones were broken or missing, but the hard-packed clay-like soil filled the empty spaces. She touched a roll of green cloth with her finger tips at one of the tables sitting outside a store, accepting the stares of those who recognized her as a witch. Some stares were curious, some friendly, a few with fear, and the odd one with loathing.

The Equisurbem Terradomus had made it possible for the population to be comfortable with contact with witches there. However, a distinction wasn't usually made between the Whiterose witches and the Darkrose witches, including when a negative spell was used by the Darkrose witches.

She wondered if those passing by her knew there was a spirit next to her. She had seen earlier he had managed to move the vial, finding it on the floor. So far it appeared he was content to follow her and not cause any disturbance. She left the market area and entered the next block where tea shops and small cafes were clustered. Ululla froze for a moment when she spotted Elwendia.

"Terrowin, please wait here. I want to talk to Elwendia, but I don't want her to know you're around as a spirit."

She walked quickly to the woman, calling out her name.

Elwendia turned slowly, giving Ululla a smile as she recognized her.

"I'm not surprised our paths have crossed again, although this is sooner than I expected."

"Perhaps we've a common journey." Ululla gave her a weak smile. "I doubt it's a coincidence we're in the same area."

Elwendia slowly walked with Ululla. "Are you still angry with me? I was wondering if you might try to put a spell on me. I'm prepared for such an attempt."

"You were hiding within the Claireston Terradomus long enough to know we don't use spells to cause direct harm to others. The Book of Redemption, which I'm sure you had time to study, is specific. A spell or curse to harm another living thing will result in a backlash to those who use it. You, Sister Elwendia, are not worth it."

Elwendia turned to look at her. "You're still angry with me."

"No, not angry. Feeling disappointment in that you were willing to cause death to an innocent young man. I don't understand why you and the Darkrose Order abuse your power so."

"We prefer the term Umbravox. The Book of Destiny tells us in order to accomplish the ultimate goal of peace and harmony for all people, some sacrifices must be accepted. Our altus councillium has given me a task. I follow their direction without reservation. However, I'll confess to you I felt sadness at Terrowin's death. I don't wish any harm to you or anyone, but it was a duty I had to perform."

"Was Terrowin the specific target, or was he just in the wrong place?"

Elwendia was silent for several steps as she thought out her answer. "I'm sure your altus councillium must know that Terrowin could have become the center of events. We saw him as a strong force that didn't move in a direction advantageous for us and thus had to be stopped."

"The death of Terrowin will not stop an event from happening. It's like trying to block a stream from flowing. The water will eventually find a way around it."

"The teachings from The Book of Redemption. I won't argue the merits of it, but will remind you it was written by a witch with a guilty conscience from tasks set out for him when he was a member of the Umbravox. Eventually the Whiterose will understand they need to return to the fold of the Umbravox. The Whiterose is too passive in human affairs and will only prolong the road back to harmony."

"The Whiterose has been apart from the Umbravox for hundreds of years. Our numbers are growing, even at the expense of the Umbravox, as more witches accept our way. Harmony built on deceit and dark spells sit on a false foundation that will not last."

They walked in silence, and Elwendia finally stopped. "Perhaps we best part ways here, before we argue too much." She touched Ululla's hand.

"Sister Elwendia, you've done evil and caused Terrowin to die earlier than he should have. I suggest you ask for forgiveness. I don't wish to see harm done to you by the latent negative energy of your sin." She gave Elwendia's hand a small squeeze. "Peace be with you."

"And to you, Ululla."

Ululla watched her walked to a side of the building where she disappeared from view.

* * * *

Ululla sat at the patio of one of the cafes with a cup of tea. The proprietor was a short, portly man with his only remaining hair grey. He gave her a warm smile and refused payment for the tea.

"I have visited the terradomus and listened to a sermon there. The words spoken have had a profound effect on me."

"Thank you. That's good to hear."

As he walked away Ululla considered how allowing the terradomus opening to others was a bold but clever decision by the altus councillium. She felt a pressure on her arm and smiled at Terrowin. Her talk with Elwendia had revealed how they had considered him to be an important factor in shaping human affairs, but death had not stopped his journey.

If they knew his spirit still travelled among the living, what would they do? The right spells could contain a spirit or force it out of the plane of the living. How far would they go to stop him? Could he be stopped from completing his journey? My early analogy about stopping a stream of water was pertinent in this case. He accepted death so easily,

I wonder if part of him must have understood that death was going to free him to go to his next task.

"Terrowin, I sense you're growing stronger." She spoke in a whisper.

Her tea cup slid a few inches on the table.

Like the flickering of leaves in a breeze, an almost inaudible sound touched her ear, *"Yes."*

Her hand froze as she reached for her cup. She took a deep breath.

"You have to be careful you do not reveal yourself to others. If the Darkrose knew your spirit was here, they may take action against you." She took a drink of her tea and stood. "Perhaps it's best we return to the terradomus. We need to talk about your journey."

Chapter Seven

Even though her sleeping quarters were underground, Ululla heard the deep rumble of the thunder. She judged it was still early morning, but decided sleep was not likely to occur again.

"Good morning, Terrowin." She felt it odd to stand naked in front of a ghost, and she wondered if he felt any attraction to her or if she had simply become a friend.

She felt his presence move in front of her, and a whiff of cool air cross her face.

"I need to have breakfast, and I'll return here later. We can talk then." She quickly dressed and left the room, thinking how to best convey her concerns to him and how she could help him.

She sat with several other witches, with most of the conversation settled around how the thunder storm made sleep near impossible. The porridge was thick, hot, and filling and, with the tea, helped her fully wake up. Ululla noted Gloriana and Bruhamoff were not present. He normally was up early to eat, and she assumed he hadn't slept through the thunder, concluding he was likely sharing a bed with Gloriana.

He'll be acting different during the rest of the journey.

Ululla took a pot of tea, a cup, and a map back to her room. She unrolled the thick leather skin map on the desk, poured herself a tea, and settled down on the chair.

"Terrowin, this is a map of the area." She touched a point on the map. "We're here in Equisurbem, and will be travelling to Newharken next." She traced the road on the map. "There I'll find out where I'm to go next." She went to her bed and found a small feather protruding from her pillow. She gently placed it on the map near Equisurbem.

"Show me your path."

Slowly the feather tumbled along the road to Newharken, paused, and continued to move.

Ululla followed the trail that led past streams, rivers, several cities, and across a small range of mountains. It entered the Kingdom of Allisure and moved to the capital, Knavemire. There it stopped.

"The Kingdom of Allisure. One of the better run kingdoms with a king known for his good judgement and temperament. It's also the kingdom where King Terrowin, whom you're named after, ruled for many years. He was a great king, perhaps the best king to have ruled in any kingdom. His assassination caused a traumatic upheaval and halted the great progress he was making to bring peace to all." She paused. "Your journey to Knavemire cannot be a coincidence. Do you feel you are returning home?"

"Yes."

"Do you know why you're returning there?"

"No."

Ululla nodded. She knew spirits sometimes liked to visit places that give them the most comfort before moving on. Sometimes a spirit needed to come to terms, which caused them great emotional turmoil. Being assassinated there would certainly cause that, assuming Terrowin and King Terrowin were the same spirit. It seemed quite possible to her. Both were tall and slim with a strong jaw. Perhaps her true task in going to Newharken was to help ensure his safe journey.

But why did the Darkrose consider Terrowin so important as to have him killed? How much harm could a farm boy do their cause? She frowned. *It has been known peasants sometimes revolted against tyrannical kings, if one among them had the courage to lead. Perhaps Terrowin would have been that man. If so, they would've stopped a revolution before it even got started. Of course, that leads to why they would want to keep the current king in power.* She sighed. *It's useless to speculate, but it seems my task is at least partially to help Terrowin find his way as far as Newharken.*

"I shall help you reach Newharken. If the Darkrose are aware of your wish to go there, they may use a spell to prevent your spirit from proceeding. If so, then we may be able counteract such a spell with one of our own, but it's important they don't learn you are with us. If they detect your spirit, they may be able to do other things to isolate you."

She felt him move close to her.

"Scared."

"Do not fear. Together we'll get you to where you need to be."

* * * *

Ululla watched the rain pour down through the windows in the upper catwalk. Occasionally sheets of rain came blistering down, and a wave of cold air blew at her through the cracks between the panes of glass. She hoped the rain wouldn't turn into hail, damaging crops, and property. She had asked Terrowin to remain in her room as she wandered about the terradomus, not wanting to draw attention to herself by staying in the room during normal waking hours.

No doubt a Darkrose could infiltrate here as they did in Claireston. I don't need anyone to speculate why I'm staying in the room. Any comfort I bring to Terrowin in the room will jeopardize his safety.

The rain began to wane, reduced to a mere drizzle. Ululla open the window, peering down on the street below. Water flooded the street, unable to find a place to run off. A horse and rider galloped past, spraying water.

Ululla waited, staring at the sky as the sun broke through the evaporating clouds. She smiled as a rainbow coloured the sky, glowing in the sunlight.

"Ululla, are you still searching for rainbows?"

She turned to Jerod. "You know me well."

"When you were younger, I recall you recited a poem every time you saw a rainbow."

She laughed. "I suppose I still do in my head, although my wish has changed. It always brings me comfort to see the rainbow." She blushed, remembering the first time she sang out the poem, not noticing Jerod quietly listening. She was much younger then, and her spoken wish caused her much embarrassment.

Oh, rainbow of colours in the sky,
may you see me as I see you

full of beauty, hope and strength,
bringing joy and peace everywhere.

Oh, rainbow of colours in the sky,
you bring me comfort and courage,
but if I may ask for one wish,
give me a man to love.

He placed his hand on top of hers. "I do hope all your wishes come true."

"I really shouldn't be wishing for anything. My life has been very fulfilling."

"You have given much to others, and you deserve to have what your heart desires."

"Thank you."

He turned to the window, staring at the now double rainbow. "You know, Ululla, you're a beautiful woman with much purpose in your life. A man meeting your needs may not be so common and will take time to find. Have patience. His journey will take him to you."

"I do hope so, but if it's not meant to be, then it's not meant to be."

"Now, I'm only a keeper, but I do see things others miss. I see someone who will meet the love of her life, when the time is right. You still have a task to complete before you'll be ready to settle down."

"It seems I have been given a lot of tasks to complete first. It's hard to meet a man when you aren't able to stay in one place for long."

"You'll know when your tasks are done. Then you'll meet your mate."

"Thank you. That makes me feel better."

* * * *

The following morning came with the sun peeking between clouds. Ululla took a deep breath of air smelling fresh from another late-night shower.

She hoped the rain didn't return as she prepared to leave the Equisurbem Terradomus. She glanced at Bruhamoff hug and kiss Gloriana goodbye and reluctantly pick up his pack to join her. He was silent as they made their way down the streets, the morning sun promising a hot day ahead.

"Gloriana was a very nice girl. It was nice you were able to spend time with her."

"Yes. I shall miss her." His voice sounded distant.

"She will miss you, too. I understand how you're feeling. Sometimes our tasks take us away from people and places. It's a sacrifice we have to make, but I know that doesn't make it any easier to accept."

They walked in silence, reaching near the edge of town. Gradually his steps became lighter, and he held his head up higher.

Two young women carrying baskets approached them on the road as they travelled.

"We have bread to sell. If you're on a journey, it'll help fill your stomach."

They stared at Bruhamoff, smiling, barely acknowledging Ululla.

He turned to Ululla. "Do we need more provisions?"

Ululla grinned. "I've seen you eat. I suspect you could eat the whole basket of bread by yourself." She gave the required coins to one of the women.

After the exchange of bread, the women waved goodbye, still smiling at him.

Ululla laughed. "My, they were certainly interested in you."

"They were just being friendly."

"To witches? Bruhamoff, if I wasn't here, they would've dragged you back to their farmhouse and given you more than just bread."

He blushed. "I don't know about that."

"I do know women see you as a very handsome man. Try not to let them take advantage of you."

* * * *

They came across several large boulders off the road, one of them flat enough to sit on. The ground was still damp from the rain, and the boulder provided a place where they could eat. As Ululla suspected, Bruhamoff didn't have any problem eating almost a whole loaf of bread by himself.

"Newharken is a large city, isn't it?" he asked between bites of bread.

"Yes, and there are several roads that lead to it from other cities. It also sits on a large river that feeds to the sea with a lot of boat traffic."

"Is the terradomus in the open there like in Equisurbem?

"No, but it isn't hidden, either. At one time, it was meant to be in a secret location, but with so many people moving about the city, eventually the location became known to many people. However, we do not open the doors there to the public. The Newharken Terradomus has extensive tunnels under it, being one of the oldest terradomus."

"Is the Darkrose's terradomus known also?"

"Yes, it is, although they are more secretive about its location. They also inhabit several other dwellings to confuse the location of the real terradomus. The Darkrose's terradomus is also old and has many tunnels under it. Some of our tunnels come in close contact with those of the Darkrose tunnels."

Bruhamoff thought over the information. "Are the inhabitants of Newharken aware there are so many tunnels under their feet?"

"No, they're aware of underground buildings and tunnels, but have no idea of their extent. You know how careful we, and the Darkrose, guard our secrets. The tunnels and structures are hundreds of years old, and even today, most people have little knowledge of them. Armies have tried to invade the terradomuses in the past, but strong spells have repelled all their attempts."

"The spells made them ill and unable to fight. I've heard death will result if they venture too far inside. The Darkrose don't reveal what they know about us to others, do they?"

"No and we don't reveal their secrets to outsiders. In some respects, we're still part of them and would never betray them, nor do they wish to destroy us. They still believe we'll return to their fold and won't admit our numbers are now almost their equal. Few Whiterose witches join the Darkrose, but we have accepted many of the Darkrose to ours."

* * * *

The road for long stretches became empty of travellers. By the time the sun became blocked by a dark cloud in the late afternoon, they came across another town. Mayathorp was a busy town, where many travellers spent the night before going on to Newharken or Equisurbem.

"Are we going to stay here tonight?" He looked at the various inns as they walked down the main street.

"Yes, I believe there'll be a storm tonight, and it's best we be indoors." She turned down a side street, studied the few dwellings on either side.

"What're we looking for?"

"The terradomus here is marked by a tree with open arms to witches." She pointed ahead. "That appears to be it."

They studied the oak tree for a moment. The tree trunk was wide enough it would take four men with outstretched arms to circle it. Two of the branches on either side of the tree pointed toward the road, forming a giant U.

Satisfied it matched the description, they continued to follow the path to the stone dwelling with a door and a single window at the front. The roof consisted of thatch woven together with a brick chimney that was releasing white smoke. After they knocked, the door was opened by a male. He gave a smile and gestured for them to enter.

"Welcome to our terradomus. It's not large, but we'll do our best to make you feel comfortable."

"Thank you." Ululla saw the cabin was as small as it appeared on the outside. The male witch was average in height and walked with a limp. There were three other witches, two males and a female sitting inside the main room. "We're concerned about spending the night outside as it appears a storm is coming."

"I believe you're correct. Our sleeping quarters are full, but I shall give you my room." He looked at Bruhamoff. "We can sleep below in the tunnel. Not ideal, but we will be dry."

Ululla thanked him, not arguing his offer to give up his room. Witches believed offers should always be sincere and to refuse an offer without a valid reason would be insulting. In the past, she had slept in tunnels and, although not fond of the cold, hard stone, knew it was for only one night. As she suspected, he was the altus rector after introductions were exchanged. Every terradomus had an altus rector, and in the smaller terradomus, often it was a male. Besides having extensive knowledge of the Book of Redemption, the altus rector in the smaller terradomus was also responsible for the wellbeing and protection of those who lived or visited in the terradomus. While spells were often effective against armed assaults, sometimes the physical presence of a man would prevent a deterrent to those who wish to do harm. Ululla suspected Altus Rector Osred's limp may have been the result of a confrontation.

In the larger terradomus, the altus rector would designate many of the tasks to others, such as defending the terradomus. Thus, there were as many females as males in the higher positions in the larger facilities. Ululla was offered the opportunity to be an altus rector on more than one occasion, but turned them down, feeling she had other tasks to do first.

* * * *

Bruhamoff sipped at his red wine, the first alcohol he had in his life. While witches did not believe in an excessive consumption of alcohol, nor did they believe it was wrong to have an occasional glass of wine or beer. It seemed to him this altus rector had a slightly more liberal view of occasional, although he returned the clay bottle to a cupboard after a single pour to everyone.

Osred spoke after taking a drink. "I trust you understand we don't always have a drink of wine, but sometimes a bit of wine helps sleep come easier in the tunnel. Besides, I wish to make your stay as positive as possible."

Bruhamoff was curious over the sensations from the wine, the flavour of dark fruit followed by a burn down his throat. His mouth had an odd dryness in his cheeks after the second sip, and he wondered what it would be like if he drank more than one serving. By the time he finished his wine, he felt warmer and more relaxed.

"Come, Brother Bruhamoff. It's time for us to prepare for the night."

Bruhamoff carried two blankets with him to the last sleeping quarters, where under the bed a trap door swung open to reveal a stone staircase. Osred carried a torch he used to light an oil lamp at the bottom and led the way to cool interior.

The tunnel was a semi-circular oval shape and twice as wide as a man was tall. It was tall enough for Bruhamoff to walk near the sides without bumping his head. The small bricks were overlapped and placed tightly together. One of Bruhamoff's tasks at Claireston had been tunnel work, digging and placing the bricks. The tunnel he'd worked on was to eventually connect to the Equisurbem Terradomus. Although the labour was hard, he'd enjoyed seeing the slow progress over the months from where he had first laid a brick. Like many other witches first employed in tunnel work, he scratched his name on the first brick he put down. He looked around the tunnel, and in flickering yellow light, saw evidence of other similarly marked bricks.

The tunnel was kept clean, dirt and other foreign objects swept away regularly. The result was a lack of insects and small rodents, as there was little in the way for food for them. Bruhamoff still inspected the floor before placing his blanket down. He stretched out on it and used the second blanket to cover himself.

"Brother Bruhamoff, I hope you're able to find some comfort so you can sleep. If it makes you feel any better, when you get as old as me, the bricks seem to get even harder."

"I'm sure I'll sleep fine, Altus Rector Osred."

"If I may inquire, how did you end up travelling with Sister Ululla?"

"I guess it was my time to leave Claireston Terradomus, and Sister Ululla was preparing for a journey. She invited me to travel with her."

"Do you know what your destination is?"

"No. I hope to discover that."

Silence stretched on for several moments.

"You're aware a spirit is travelling with you and Sister Ululla?"

"Yes. He means no harm. It seems he has a journey to complete as well and is travelling the same path as us. Perhaps he doesn't know exactly where or what he must do."

"Ah." Another moment of silence. "It would seem Sister Ululla and a spirit who don't know their final destination are travelling with you."

"Yes, although I never thought of it that way."

"That's not likely a coincidence. You and the spirit are intertwined somehow. Your destination may be the same."

Bruhamoff lifted his head. "How may that be?"

"I don't know, except to say you may have an important role to play for the spirit. Be prepared for a door that opens before you, for it may be a turning point for something important for the spirit and others."

"Then where is Sister Ululla going? The same place as us? She was told to go to Newharken for her next task."

"I suspect Ululla has her own path, but at least part of her journey is to guide you and the spirit. I believe she is a moderor."

"A moderor? One who guides in the spirit world?"

"That's only part of the definition. A moderor also guides spirits and beings on the physical plane, often without knowing they're doing so. They're a conduit for a journey."

"Sister Ululla just happens to be going to the same place the spirit and I are heading?"

"As I said before, I don't believe it's a coincidence. She's entangled with you and the spirit."

Chapter Eight

King Hadrian threw the partially eaten apple across the throne room. It bounced twice before sliding and landing near the arched doorway. Guardsman Alric saw a servant scurry across the throne room to retrieve it, knowing the consequences for any perceived negligence of duties. Alric watched the king pace, his purple cape flowing behind him.

Serving the king as one of the guardsmen was never an ambition for Alric. He wasn't impressed by the king's rule, his regal appearance, or expensive clothes. Although tall in height with a full head of dark hair and a reddish beard, King Hadrian had poor posture accented by a pear-shaped body. Alric knew the king had made ill thought out decisions in the past, something he reflected on as he waited with the other high ranking men of the king's army. They all stood near the long table, not even whispering as they waited for the king to make an announcement. Alric was the tallest of the soldiers present and with his red hair and blue eyes, stood out from the rest. Unlike most soldiers, he kept himself clean shaven, and so far, was free of serious scars.

"We need to prepare for an assault on the Kingdom of Kireland." He pointed at Alric. "I want you to lead the horse charge. Since Blacson was killed in the last battle, we're in need of a replacement. I believe you're more than capable of taking over his leadership."

"Thank you, Sire. I'll do my best to live up to your expectations."

"Of course, you will, or you will die." King Hadrian smirked. "As for the rest of you, you already know your duties. Be certain I will not tolerate anything less than the complete domination of Kireland." He stared at the men around the table. "In battle your lives may be at risk, but I assure you, failure to win the battle will certainly result in your death. If not then, then later when I review your actions. I trust I made myself clear."

* * * *

After the officers were dismissed, Alric headed to the weapons room, to get the best sword he could if he was going to lead a charge. The weapons room was an addition to the blacksmith's shop, and Alric nodded at the apprentice working on a sword.

"Where is the head weapons clerk?"

The teenage boy pointed at the back wall. "He be there."

Alric made his way past the wood racks holding different weapons, finding the weapons clerk behind a heavily built wood table examining a sword for flaws along the blade. The heavy set, older man wore a black streaked tan apron and barely glanced up at him.

"I'm in need of a sword." Alric announced.

He finally paid attention to Alric. "We have plenty for you to choose from, sire."

"I want your best." Alric flipped a coin to him.

The clerk took a moment to glance at the coin before it disappeared behind the apron.

"May I suggest this one?" The clerk produced the sword hidden moments before from under the table top. He smiled, showing a picket fence row of teeth.

Alric took the sword and hefted it, gripping the silver and black carved handle. "Nice weight."

"The blade, I tempered it myself. It is sharp, true, and will cut through a knight's armour."

"Then it will do." Alric turned and left the weapon's room, knowing when a bribe was done it was best not to linger.

I won't be making the same mistake Blacson did. He not only led the charge, but stayed in front during the whole battle. The right thing to do is drop back after the troops engage and live to lead again. At least going to battle will be better than listening to the king going on one of his rants.

Alric was confident with his ability in a sword or knife fight and knew he rode a horse better than most men. Those abilities provided him with quick promotions among the ranks and being noticed by the king himself. Despite his success as a soldier, Alric was not a content man. He didn't enjoy fighting, and killing a foe left him feeling remorseful.

I wonder if I should've followed in my father's footsteps and become a woodworker. He had learned the skills needed to work wood, but as he entered adulthood, decided the excitement of being a soldier appealed to him. He soon learned the glamour of being in uniform didn't make up for the duties a soldier had to perform. *Okay, I should've become a woodworker.*

* * * *

The following morning, with a light drizzle falling, Alric mounted his horse, Darkian. The dark-brown steed occasionally showed a bit of temper. He liked the horse's attitude of refusing to give in easily to commands, although eventually he gained the horse's respect and could control him.

The parade of soldiers, horsemen, and other troops moved across the border to the Kingdom of Kireland, where the town of Billige stood. Alric knew Billige was a medium sized city, and its importance to Kireland was significant. The town manufactured most of the metal goods for the kingdom, including weaponry for the army. The town was also part of the trade route to the port city of Styrnovo in the Kingdom of Cadyvia, and was a concern to Alric. He hoped the attack on Billige wouldn't cause a reaction from Cadyvia, although he considered it unlikely. Kireland had not managed to solidify a relationship with the neighbouring kingdom, nor did it provide vital goods to Cadyvia.

"You look deep in thought, Alric."

Alric turned to see that Commander Willis had moved his horse alongside of his own. Willis was a gruff looking man with a wild beard and hair. He was average in height but heavyset.

"Just thinking about the battle at Kireland. I hope it goes as quick as we planned."

"That depends on everyone doing what they're supposed to. I've seen you in battle. You're good with a sword, but I've concerns about you just the same."

"Why do you say that?"

"You hesitate in killing your opponent. Someday it could cost you your life. In battle, you must show no mercy. You must kill any enemy within reach of your sword. I'll tell you why. Fear. You must make the enemy believe we are ruthless and will kill anyone in our path. If we've that reputation, then we already have an advantage for the next battle. Is that understood?"

"Yes, sire."

"Just so you know where we stand, if I see you jeopardizing our battle, I'll kill you myself. The king appointed you to lead the horse charge. You certainly weren't my first choice. Blacson was fearless. Death didn't concern him. He's the type of man I like to have by my side."

Alric stomach turned into a knot as he watched Willis ride away. *Either the enemy kills me or he will.*

* * * *

Morning came as the sun fought to break through the fog. The rain during the night left the ground muddy with small pools of water. The chill of the air didn't stop insects from buzzing around as Alric packed his horse. He ate a small breakfast, despite his stomach not being in a mood for any sort of food.

This may be the last day of my life, and what do I wake up to? Fog and a chill in the air, not a good sign from the gods.

He swung his leg over his horse and settled in on the saddle. He looked up, and the sun burst through the fog, accompanied by the chirping of birds.

Well, maybe the gods were listening.

He patted his horse and urged him forward. "Come on, Darkian, it's time to get ready for battle."

Alric ignored the splashing of mud and water as they travelled, as well as the chatter and chants of soldiers as they prepared for combat. The humid air was heavy and smelled of horses and unwashed men. He found the soldiers' preparation for battle at odds with his own feelings. He preferred quiet to collect his thoughts, knowing he would soon be killing men he didn't know, and then the guilt afterward.

The commander called a halt just before the rise of a small hill to address the troops.

"Kireland and the enemy are on the other side of the hill. We shall kill any man holding a weapon or standing in our way." He fixed his eyes on Alric. "No mercy will be shown."

After the soldiers were separated into groups, with Alric's horsemen behind the archers, he spoke to his men before the battle.

"We don't need dead heroes, and we won't have any if everyone follows what we talked about earlier. Stay in your positions and remember we hit the front line at the same time." He pointed at the direction of Billige. "We shall win this battle and live to see the end if we all do our jobs."

He went to his own horse and waited for the signal that the battle was to begin. Minutes passed. Alric raised his sword in the air, waiting for the last volley of arrows to be fired. He lowered his arm and yelled, "Charge!"

Alric barely heard the thunder of the hooves and the yelling of men. Mud and water flew in the air as they raced to the enemy, badly outnumbered and likely making any resistance short lived. The clash of the horses, men, and swords brought forth screams of anguish from the injured and dying. Alric engaged another soldier, slightly smaller than himself in height but of the same weight. The horses pivoted around each other as the men attacked with their swords. Alric saw an opening and brought his sword across, slicing open his opponent's arm. The man screamed and dropped his sword, slumping on his saddle.

Alric raised his word to finish off his adversary. The injured soldier, leaning forward on his horse, turned his head to look at him. His eyes locked on Alric, pleading. Alric hesitated and turned his horse. He glanced once more at the wounded soldier as he tried to steer his horse away. He hoped the man survived and directed his horse from the main battle, yelling encouragement to his men.

Time to step away from the battle. I don't care what the Commander thinks. I'm planning to survive this battle and fight again.

As the battle drew to a close, Alric pulled alongside Commander Willis.

"It looks like we have almost defeated the enemy and just have to take the lord's castle. Billige will be ours soon."

Billige was a moderately wealthy city, but King Briebeth preferred to live in the larger city of Trontta, that could be defended better.

"True. Send your men into the town and search for any of the enemy hiding. Go through shops and homes and kill any soldiers. I'll lead the rest of the troops into the castle and raise the banner of Dwykath."

Alric nodded, dreading the order to kill the survivors. He met with the horsemen and directed them to search for the enemy remaining and to execute them.

What have I become? Ordering others to kill in a war that's of our own making.

He went into homes, some made of wood, and others of brick and mud. Women and children huddled as far as they could away from him. He didn't say anything, hoping they understood he meant them no harm, but not trusting his voice to give them assurance. A few old and crippled men had also retreated to the homes. There were also a few men that could have been in the army, but chose instead to put their efforts in other work. He ignored them and other civilians.

Methodically he went from door to door. He didn't look too closely in other rooms, not wanting to find anyone. Occasionally he saw his men pull a struggling soldier from hiding and taken away to the town centre. To his grief, he also saw a man with a wounded arm dragged out of a home, believing him to be the same soldier he'd injured in battle.

He opened the door of a small dwelling, watched a woman wrap her arms around a boy a few years from adulthood. He saw her eyes flicker to the next room, likely used as a bedroom. He raised his sword and entered the room, hearing a gasp from the woman.

A man in a warrior's uniform stood in front of a younger version of himself, holding a sword in front of him. The younger man held only a knife.

Alric frowned. The soldier's posture and positioning was poor for any sword fight, obviously unskilled in the matters of battle. *No doubt the father and son accepted the position in the army for a small amount of coins to help make ends meet. Now that meager amount of money could cost them their lives.*

He cleared his throat. "Get rid of those weapons and uniforms. The next time anyone comes in here they better only see civilians, or it will mean your lives." He turned and walked out of the house, feeling better he may have saved two lives.

The captured soldiers were forced to the town square where they kneeled with their heads down. The townspeople crowded around, some of them wailing as they waited for the horror to begin. Among the captured were the noblemen who represented the King of Kireland.

Alric couldn't hold back his tongue and approached Commander Willis.

"Commander, some of these men could be absorbed into our army. Is there really a need to kill them all?"

"I don't want our army to be known to have any sign of weakness."

"To spare the life of a good soldier is not a sign of weakness. He may even be more loyal to those who spared his life than the army he's in now."

Willis stared at him, and Alric plunged on.

"We need to secure Billige after we leave for Trontta. If we kill all these men, there'll be deep resentment against us, and we'll need to leave more men to secure Billige."

"I admire your courage for speaking up. Another commander might have you executed for voicing those opinions." He rubbed his beard. "You have a good argument, but I'm not entirely convinced. I'll offer them a chance to pledge their loyalty to King Hadrian. The last ten to do so will be executed, along with all the noble men. Anything else?"

"No, sire. Thank you for listening to me."

In the main courtyard, the remaining prisoners were gathered. Their hands were chained behind their backs, and they were forced to kneel on the cobblestones. The noblemen who maintained the administration of Billige joined the kneeling men. Four swordsmen walked behind the soldiers who were slow to pledge their loyalty to King Hadrian.

The townsfolk gathered around to see the final moments of the men in the centre of the courtyard. Many were weeping and a few cried out to spare them their lives. Soldiers stood in front of them to prevent any from rushing to their aid.

None of the men moved from their kneeling position. They had known this could be their fate and refused to let cowardice enter their final moments. A few prayed before their life was ended, but none resisted or screamed. Several soldiers stood behind the prisoners and on command, sliced off their heads.

Alric turned away at the bloody carnage and hoped Willis didn't see him, thinking of the action as a sign of cowardice.

* * * *

"Your men did well. The horse charge was effective and helped in our victory." Commander Willis took a drink of his ale as Alric stood stiffly in front of his table.

"Thank you, sire."

"I didn't see you in action, but then again, I didn't see you avoid battle, either. I shall assume you provided honour to our king and land and fought bravely." He waved his hand toward the exit of the room he had commandeered after the takeover of the castle. "You may go now, but send the serving wench in here. I've need of her services."

"Aye, sire."

He walked out of the room and beckoned the young woman waiting in the hallway.

"He wants you." He jerked a thumb to the room behind him.

She closed her eyes, taking a deep breath before walking slowly to the room.

Alric walked in a daze to a tavern, finding the dark clouds above him matching his disposition. There he consumed ale after ale. He didn't participate in the singing, fighting, or socializing. Several women tried to engage him, but he spurned their efforts, preferring to sit by himself. After the ale finally had the intoxicating effect, he stumbled out past the boisterous crowd to the cobbled street. Cold rain poured on him as he walked. He made his way to his sleeping quarters, hoping the rain could wash away more than just the dirt clinging to his clothes.

* * * *

Following breakfast the following morning, Commander Willis called a meeting for his officers. After they assembled in a spare dining room, he growled at his officers around him. Alric knew that despite the successful capture of Billige, he didn't want any of the men to believe he was satisfied with the mission so far. He believed in putting fear into his subordinates, never giving too much credit when they did well.

"We'll be leaving a small contingent behind to maintain order in Billige, but in the morning, we'll be leaving for Trontta, where King Briebeth will make his last stand. We will take all of the soldiers who surrendered here to Trontta, as we don't need them to have any temptation to help free Billige. When we attack in two days' time, make it clear to your men there must be no lack of resolve to kill any who oppose us. Whether it be soldiers, women, or children, our swords must find their mark quickly. Are there any questions about this?" He glared at Alric.

Alric shook his head and was glad when another officer spoke up.

"Sire, do you expect them to battle or surrender?"

Willis frowned. "I prefer a battle. It makes sure our men will know how to fight when we take on other, better prepared opponents. However, there's a good chance they will attempt to negotiate a surrender. In that case, I will make the surrender unconditional."

* * * *

Alric left the room with a heavy heart. He knew there wasn't an escape from the upcoming battle or his conscience. If he attempted to leave the army now, he would be tortured before being executed. There wasn't any escape except death.

He walked the quiet streets, ignoring the hostile stares of the town folk. A stone bounced off his leg. He turned and caught a glimpse of a woman quickly dragging away a boy by his arm as he yelled at him. A hand grabbed his arm, and he stared at the eyes of an old man, hunched over and using a walking stick for support. There was strength in the knurled fingers, and the reedy voice spoke without stuttering.

"Please, the boy meant no harm. His father was killed in the battle."

Alric frowned. He touched the cold hand of the old man.

"I won't do any harm to those who cannot fight. I understand his anger and have no argument with him."

"Thank you, sire." The old man turned and hobbled away.

Alric continued his walk, occasionally seeing soldiers among the market stalls. He guessed they were getting similar treatment from the population and hoped they kept their heads cool. He stopped at a food booth and placed a coin down for a leaf filled with rice and goat meat, obtaining a look of surprise from the woman tending the black pot on the counter.

"I pay for what I eat."

"The other soldiers didn't."

"That's their choice. This is mine."

He walked a few steps away to eat. Presently, he became aware of a slim figure standing next to him, wearing dark, earth tone coloured clothes.

She spoke quietly. "You're a troubled man. A woodworker wearing a soldier's guise doesn't suit you."

He looked at the dark-haired witch, much shorter than himself. She looked to be still short of adulthood, but he knew better than to try to guess a witch's age.

"I'm trapped in the path I'm on. I'm a soldier now and shall die as one. Why do you say I'm a woodworker?"

"I see things I cannot explain. Fear not, when the soldier who covers you is dead, you'll have a chance to be the woodworker again."

"I have to die first. That's cold comfort."

"No, I said the soldier dies. I didn't say you did." She walked away, disappearing into the crowd.

Alric puzzled over her message, wondering exactly what she meant.

* * * *

The castle belonging to King Briebeth came into view. The road was deserted, and there was little sign of any peasants toiling in the fields. The surrounding city spread past the castle walls was nearly empty. A few brave souls, a few crazed ones, and witches made their way among the empty streets.

Willis halted his men near the drawbridge preventing access to the castle. The king's soldiers pointed their longbows at him and his troops from high above on the castle walls. He sneered and turned to an officer at his side.

"Fire a few volleys to get their attention."

A few minutes later, a few hundred arrows soared in the air, arcing over the castle walls. The castle's soldiers returned a volley of their own, but fewer in numbers.

Willis laughed as he stood behind a protective wood wall, well away from any danger. "Pathetic. Now let's hit them with a bit of fire and cannonballs."

He heard the thudding and whistling sound of the catapults as their arms hurled weapons into the sky. Black smoke trailed some of the objects. Another volley of arrows followed, peppering the sky with dark slivers. Willis wasn't surprised when an officer came to him with news King Briebeth wanted to talk.

"Damn." He sighed. "Very well, bring me his messenger."

The messenger was a young man, nervous as he stood.

"Sire, we wish to end the hostilities. King Briebeth invites you to meet with him to discuss a mutually acceptable conclusion."

"Of course, he wants to end the hostilities. There'll be no conditions to his surrender, save for one. His life will be spared, for we'll be taking him and his heirs to Dwykath, where King Hadrian will decide his fate."

Willis would have preferred not to spare King Briebeth's life, but protocol protected royal families from death during battle. King Hadrian reluctantly followed that protocol, believing it would save him in the remote event his kingdom came under attack and lost.

The messenger nodded and quickly backed away.

Willis turned to Alric. "I'm sure you're hoping he'll surrender, but I want my men to get more battle experience. The outcome of the battle is not in doubt, but how we accomplish it is important."

"I understand what you're saying, Commander."

"But you don't agree with me."

"I don't disagree with your logic, but as one who faces death in battle, I prefer the aspect of surrender."

Willis laughed. "You're well-spoken for a soldier, and I suspect a bit of a thinker. Unusual qualities for a man also well versed with a sword."

"Thank you, sire."

"However, that may not make for the best soldier. As I said before, I want men who aren't scared of death. You think too much about life."

He sat on a chair, causing the wood to creak. "I still don't believe you should've been made leader of the horsemen, but you have changed my mind about one thing." He took a drink from a tankard. "You have courage."

* * * *

When the news of the surrender was announced, the majority of the men cheered. A trumpet sounded, indicating Alric and other officers were to report to the commander's tent. Alric breathed a sigh of relief and made his way through the groups of soldiers and tents facing the castle's drawbridge to where the commander's tent was located. He didn't cheer at the news of the surrender, but reflected on what the commander had said.

He didn't say it directly, but made it clear enough he doesn't think much of me as a soldier. He's right. I'm a sword wielding woodworker, who thinks too much. Willis is also right about the men still needing to learn how to fight.

The air smelled of too many unwashed bodies, smoke from fires, food, and ale. Flies and other insects buzzed around lazily under the hot sun as Alric pushed past men wasting time until the next order came.

Willis was sitting in the only chair when Alric entered. Two other officers were already in the tent. After Alric arrived, the last three arrived.

Willis stood and spoke directly. "The surrender is official. Today we'll take King Briebeth and his heirs, plus his high-ranking officials to Dwykath. I won't have them stay in Trontta any longer, in case they inspire some sort of resistance. Next, we need to secure the kingdom with our own men and administrators. Finally, we'll be leaving for the city of Stranor to secure it. Afterward, we can assume Kireland is absorbed into the Kingdom of Dwykath."

Alric listened to Willis divide up the responsibilities among the officers. He paid little attention to some of the objectives, save for his own tasks. He was slightly surprised he was assigned to secure Trontta and not part of the force to take Stranor.

After the meeting, he waited behind to talk to the Commander.

Willis stared at Alric and scowled. "You've had your wish, Alric. They surrendered."

"I'm sorry you're disappointed, Commander. I understand why you wanted a battle."

Willis nodded. "Good." He pointed a finger at Alric. "I don't think less of you as a man, but my preference is to have men in my army who enjoy a fight."

"Circumstances have put me here. I assure you I would fight hard in a battle."

Willis grunted, but didn't speak.

"May I ask why you decided to have me stay at Trontta instead of going to Stranor?"

Willis frowned, "I don't need to see a man wrestle with his demons every time he has to kill." He sat in his chair. "I don't enjoy ordering men to kill, but as commander of King Hadrian's army, my job is not to be concerned with anyone's life, save for the royal family and my own. I must prepare the army to be ready to attack or defend. If it means men have to die so the army is better prepared for the next battle, then that's what I must do. I ordered the execution of men in Billige, not because they deserved to die, but to put fear in those who thought about opposing us."

"You do indeed make difficult decisions, not something I'd want to do."

"I very much doubt you could make those decisions. You have too much of a conscience, and it can break a man in my position. Fortunately for me, I can make those decisions without reflecting on it. Where my conscience once resided is now hollow."

* * * *

Alric wandered through the streets, thinking about his conversation with the commander. *Although he said he had lost his conscience, he still felt compelled to explain why he did things. He's a troubled man. No wonder he drinks as much as he does.*

He spotted a soldier, with an arm wrapped in a bloody bandage, scanning the crowd as he made his way through the market stalls. Occasionally he would stop and look around before resuming his search.

Alric approached him. "Were you injured at Billige during a horse charge?"

"I was."

"I think I may've been me who battled you."

The dark-haired soldier stared up at him for a moment, appraising him. "Then I should thank thee for not killing me when I was in a vulnerable position."

"There wasn't any need to strike you again. You were no longer able to fight."

"Still, another soldier would have been tempted to finish me off. My name is Tybalt."

"Alric. Who are you searching for?"

He frowned and lowered his voice. "Witches. My arm is in pain and has little movement. If I cannot repair it, then I surely will die in the next battle. The witches may have some magic that can heal me."

"I shall help you look." Alric understood why Tybalt didn't ask anyone if they knew where the witches were. Some of the people believed witches to be evil and refused to acknowledge their presence. Others would refuse to help soldiers who had taken over their city by force. The witches also kept a low profile in the city, and unlike the terradomuses maintained by the Whiterose Witches in large cities, they disguised their places of residence in the smaller centres.

They walked the length of the market road and turned down one of the smaller streets. The vendors sold less food and concentrated more on tools and clothing. At the end of the street a tavern did a brisk business of selling ale during the warm afternoon. Alric considered an ale would be welcome when he spotted a pair of witches near a store selling leather goods. One witch with long black hair wore a light green dress, while the other, with red hair had a soft yellow skirt with a white blouse. Both walked casually toward Alric and Tybalt.

Tybalt spoke quickly, "I think those are witches coming toward us."

"Yes, you're right. What're you going to say to them?"

"I'm not sure."

Alric understood Tybalt's concern. In many kingdoms witches were treated as undesirables by soldiers. It was only the fear of the witches' use of magic and spells which kept them safe from too much harm.

"Allow me to speak to them first."

Tybalt nodded. "Please do. I'm not feeling well. I believe my arm may be infected."

Alric raised one open hand as he approached the witches. "Excuse us, we wish you no harm. We only want to ask you for your aid." Alric waited for them stop.

The two witches halted in front of them by an arm's length. The one with red hair gave an amused smile. "Soldiers asking for assistance from witches? Will wolves be playing with lambs next?"

"My name is Alric and my friend, Tybalt, has an injured arm. Can you help him?"

The redhead looked at the other witch and then at Tybalt' arm. "We might be able to, but why would we do this for you, even assuming you have enough coins?"

"I thought witches believed in peace, contentment, and harmony with the earth."

"We do."

"Is the belief only for witches and others must suffer?"

The red-haired witch frowned. "Clever words, warrior. Follow us, Alric, and we'll see what we can do for your friend."

Alric and Tybalt walked behind the witches as they went through less travelled streets, turning at various intersections.

"May I ask you your names?" Alric called out.

The redhead turned briefly around to answer. "I'm Ysmay. She is Catrain."

"Thank you for helping him."

"We haven't helped him yet. Perhaps we won't be able to heal his arm."

"I believe you can, otherwise why would you have us follow you?"

"Again, you're being clever." She stopped in front of a stone walled dwelling. "Wait here."

Alric, Tybalt, and Catrain waited while Ysmay entered the building. A few minutes later she returned, beckoning the others to enter.

As Alric entered the door, Ysmay spoke to him.

"Don't speak to the other witches inside, unless spoken to. You may sit in the main room while we tend to Tybalt."

Alric nodded and chose one of the three unoccupied wood chairs in the room. He watched as Tybalt was taken across the room and through a doorway. Minutes passed, and other than the occasional witch peering at him, he was left alone. The room was almost bare, save for the chairs and one table. He examined the chair he sat on, frowning at the workmanship. *Father would be able to do a better job blindfolded.*

A male witch, tall and slim, entered the room carrying a clay mug and a biscuit.

"Sister Ysmay suggested we offer you some refreshment while you wait."

Alric slowly reached for the mug and biscuit.

The witch smiled. "They're safe to drink and eat. We decided not to poison you."

Alric grinned at the witch's joke. "Thanks." He sniffed the tea. "Smells good. How is Tybalt doing?"

"I'll check for you." The witch walked away.

Alric drank the tea, ate the dry biscuit, and waited as he stared at the stone walls, wondering how long he would be waiting. Time passed, and Ysmay returned to the room.

"Wolf, you have been patient." She walked up to where he was sitting. "Your friend was very ill, but he's getting better now."

"That's good. Are you finished with him then?"

"No, he's still healing." She moved closer to him, placing a knee between his legs to rest it on the edge of the chair seat. "I admire your courage. You surprised me when you approached us to help your friend. We have had only unpleasant experiences with King Hadrian's men before."

"I'm not the usual soldier, I guess. Another witch told me I was really a woodworker and not a soldier. Maybe she was right."

Ysmay reached forward, touching his head with her fingertips. Her fingernails pushed past his hair to his scalp.

"A witch told you this? When? What was she wearing?"

"A few days ago. She was wearing a dark brown robe."

"The Darkrose." She pushed her fingers through his hair.

"They're different from you?" Alric kept his hands on the arms of the chair, not sure what to make of the close contact with Ysmay. She was, like most female witches, slim and beautiful, but he'd heard rumours if you made love to a witch, she took part of your life force with her. He didn't really believe it, but this wasn't the time he wanted to test those beliefs.

"We're the Whiterose."

"What's the difference?"

"The Darkrose believe in destiny and prophecy, and the future is fixed. The Whiterose believe paths will take us to a time and place, but we still have free will to make a choice."

"In other words, my path led me to speak to you, and it was your choice to heal my friend?"

Ysmay withdrew her hands. "Alric, you're a most unusual warrior with a kind heart, very clever, and a handsome face. It makes you very tempting to bed, but circumstances aren't right tonight." She took a step away from him. "Tybalt will sleep here tonight. We'll send him on his way in the morning."

Alric stood. "How much do we owe you?" He removed a handful of coins from a leather pouch tied to his waist.

She closed his hand with her fingers. "Consider the debt paid. Your path will lead you back to the witches again, and you'll have the opportunity to help us."

"Thank you. He's going to be all right then?"

"Come." She took his hand and led him through the next room, to a narrow hallway with two doorways on either side.

Alric quickly glanced around in the first room, deciding it was a kitchen with the usual wood counters for preparing food and a small table with four stools to eat. It also held a rack on a wall that contained various clay jars, holding unknown substances.

Ysmay pointed at the first doorway in the hallway. "You can see he's resting, but still needs to recover."

Alric peered inside the small bedroom, barely big enough for the narrow bed and a table. He was shocked to see Tybalt naked on the bed, eyes closed as he took in slow breaths. His skin had a pink glow to it and gleamed as if it was wet.

"His body is expelling the infection that had invaded him. He would've died if you had not brought him to us." Ysmay took his hand and led him back the way they came.

Alric stood at just outside the doorway that led to the street. "How do I find my way back?"

"Simply turn left. It will take you to the main market."

Alric smiled. "So, you took us on a convoluted route to make it difficult to find you in case we meant harm."

"It's very rare for a warrior not to want to get rid of witches. You can be trusted. Go in peace, Alric."

He looked at her, feeling tempted to give her a kiss. Instead he replied, "Peace be with you." He turned and walked slowly to the market in the evening sun, replaying the events of the day.

Chapter Nine

Ululla was amused by Bruhamoff's head movement as he stared at the buildings when they entered the main road into Newharken. The prosperous city boasted tall buildings, several up to four stories. Horses with riders and others pulling carts filled with goods moved down the road in the centre, while men pulling smaller carts kept to the outside of the road. Sidewalks were bustling with people moving with a purpose.

"This is amazing, Ululla. So many people and high dwellings."

Ululla laughed. "Those are called inns and boarding houses. There's a lot of commerce here. Many trade routes pass through Newharken."

She weaved her way between people on the sidewalk and occasionally had to quickly dart across the busy streets.

"How much farther to the terradomus?"

"We still have a ways to travel. The terradomus is in the oldest part of the city, near the centre."

Bruhamoff didn't make any comment on the smells of the city, despite the increase in density of people, animals, and buildings compared to Equisurbem. She decided he was too excited to notice the heavy air.

They crossed another street and went down a narrower road. Sidewalks still existed on either side, but they were only wide enough for a single person. The cobblestone street was just able to accommodate two passing horse drawn carts. The businesses were primarily boarding houses, inns, and a few merchants selling specialized goods.

Ululla heard yelling and the rumble of wheels bouncing on hard stones. She turned back, and saw a dark brown horse within a few steps of her, galloping down the sidewalk. A hand hit her on her shoulder, thrusting her into the small doorway of a merchant shop. She slammed into the corner of the entrance, turning as her hip gave a jolt of pain.

Stunned, she watched as Bruhamoff's push at her shoulder left him in the path of the charging horse. The driver in the cart yelled at the horse to no avail, desperately pulling at the reins. Bruhamoff turned away from the horse, his eyes closed.

Ululla cringed at the impact as the horse hit him at its flank and heard the thud as he was slammed into the wall of the shop. His legs fell away from the building, but the cart's wheel lifted off the sidewalk and floated mercifully over his legs.

Ululla hurried over to Bruhamoff, lying still on the sidewalk, blood seeping from his head. She carefully touched him, feeling for a pulse, finding it weak. She carefully touched his torso, feeling for broken bones, and noticed his shoulder sat at an odd angle.

"Bruhamoff. Bruhamoff! Can you hear me?"

People gathered around them, and a man pushed his way through to her side. "I'm sorry, so sorry. She's never done that before. Just took off on her own. Is he all right?"

"I don't know. I hope so."

Bruhamoff groaned and slowly raised his head.

Ululla used the hem of her dress to blot the blood on his forehead. "Tell me where you feel pain."

"My head. Shoulder."

A voice spoke from the crowd. "He needs a doctor."

Another voice spoke. "There be a surgeon up the road."

Ululla considered the information for a moment. Witches preferred to use their own methods for cures and injuries, but she knew they were still some distance away from the terradomus, and Bruhamoff was not in a condition to travel. "Please get him."

Minutes passed. Bruhamoff cried out in pain when he tried to move his arm. Ululla and the others convinced him to lay still. Gradually she became aware of the pain in her back and hip, but didn't consider it serious.

The doctor arrived on a horse and quickly examined Bruhamoff. "Head should be okay. I need two men to help me tend to his shoulder."

At the doctor's direction, two men held Bruhamoff, and he used a quick movement to force the arm back into place. Bruhamoff cried out and gradually relaxed.

Ululla paid the doctor as the crowd dispersed. She didn't hear any comments that they were witches.

The man whose horse hit Bruhamoff spoke softly. "I don't have many coins and couldn't pay the doctor, but I can give you a ride to where you need to go."

Ululla looked at him, dark, grimy clothes on a small frame. His face was pockmarked with a thin, black beard.

He continued. "Horse is fine now. Hilda never do that before. Something spooked her."

Ululla looked at Bruhamoff, who looked to be in pain and not likely able to walk too far without resting. "That would be welcome. Thank you."

Bruhamoff sat on a bed of bags of potatoes, while Ululla climbed on the front bench with the driver. She found out he knew the general area of the terradomus, although he didn't know if she was a Darkrose or Whiterose.

"Can't say I know the difference between them. You do, but to me they're just both witches."

"We're more similar than different. It seems you and the other people aren't concerned about witches."

"We've a lot of people here, soldiers, seafarers, farmers, and witches. They just have their own reasons for doing what they do. One group is no better and no worse than another. We are used to witches being around. They be here since the city first came to be."

Ululla considered that the larger urban centres were more comfortable with the presence of witches than the more superstitious rural areas. The rural areas were also where the Blackrain Order was located. Neither the Darkrose nor the Whiterose knew much about the Blackrain, considering them warlocks who had their own plans and were not pleased when they sold spells and potions to make money.

The driver stopped the horse and cart in front of a large dwelling made with stones. It looked old, and the surrounding lot stretched in the back, testifying it was built on farmland before the city enveloped it.

Unlike most of the other original inhabitants, the witches never sold the surrounding land it was built on.

"This be your place? The other witches' are down the street some."

"This is our home. Thank you for the ride." Ululla climbed off the wagon and helped Bruhamoff climb down. Her hip hurt, and her leg was stiff to move, but he was in worse shape. Besides his shoulder, he pressed a hand to his back. He staggered slightly as he walked.

"Are you dizzy, Bruhamoff?"

"Yes. Headache, too. I don't feel very good."

Ululla whispered to the air. "Wait here Terrowin, until I can inform the altus rector of your presence." She put her arm around Bruhamoff's waist and helped him to the front steps of the witches' terradomus. The door swung open before she could knock. Two male witches stepped forward and helped Bruhamoff inside and to a bedroom. Ululla followed, quickly glancing at the witches in the common room, and stood at the bedroom's doorway as a female witch began to check his condition. She realized they had been taken to a set of bedrooms reserved for special guests. They were larger and on the main floor near the common room and kitchen.

"What happened to him?" the female witch asked as she looked at his shoulder.

"He was run over by a horse pulling a cart." She described the sequence of events and how he pushed her out of the path of the horse.

"Really? A horse suddenly bolted and charged in your direction? That doesn't sound like an accident. More like someone used a spell to scare the horse. The question is who was the target? You or him?"

Ululla shook her head as she looked at the blonde-haired petite witch. "I don't know. This doesn't seem to be something the Darkrose would do, if it was a spell. They don't usually do something violent and are more subtle in what they do."

"There are others who perform spells, but we can speculate on that later. I better examine him. Can you help me undress him? It appears he has suffered additional injuries."

Bruhamoff watched her as she approached the bed. He didn't offer any protest, and she decided he was hurt worse than she first suspected. His shoulder had turned a dark blue, and his side looked red.

"I wonder if his ribs are cracked."

The witch frowned. "I hope not." She gently touched his side. "They seem okay."

Bruhamoff groaned and turned his head away.

Ululla touched his forehead, startled how warm he was. "Is he going to be okay?"

"His body is fighting his injuries. I need to check his back, but I believe the more serious concern is his head."

Ululla helped remove the rest of his clothing, grimacing at the bruise on his thigh. Blood seeped from several minor cuts around it. "He really did get a jolt from that horse."

"He did. Now, could you make some tea with capsicum and penny royal? It should help him stay awake."

Nodding, she pulled a blanket up to his waist, making a point of not looking at his naked body. He was good looking, but too young for her. She didn't want to take advantage of him, although there was a part of her who saw him as a man.

Ululla hurried to the kitchen. An older female witch observed her opening a cupboard door and quickly offered to help her after hearing why she was looking for a particular tea.

"Thank you. I'm Ululla."

"Eabae. It's good to meet you, Sister Ululla. I'll take the tea to Brother Bruhamoff. Perhaps it's best you talk to Altus Rector Muriel. I believe she's expecting you."

* * * *

The dark wood floor showed signs of repair and the wear of thousands of steps as she walked to the back of the terradomus. She took the wide, stone stairs down and entered a round chamber where several open doorways led to other rooms and walkways. As with all terradomus, the stonework was carefully done with coloured stones indicating the different passageways beyond. The ceiling was high and each doorway featured a curved top. Despite being underground, a clever arrangement of vents ensured a supply of fresh air. She took a deep breath and went to the doorway which led to the chamber of the altus rector.

She paused at the entrance until she was acknowledged by Altus Rector Muriel. The room was large with square walls and two other doorways on opposite sides. As soon as she saw Ululla, the altus rector stood from behind a large, dark wood desk dominating the room.

"Welcome to the Newharken Terradomus, Sister Ululla. Please enter and sit down." She turned to another doorway. "Sister Guinevere, would you please bring in a cup of tea for Sister Ululla?"

Ululla returned a smile to Muriel. The altus rector was tall, even for a witch, and had long, thick silver hair hanging in waves. Her pale complexion had fine lines around her mouth and eyes. Ululla sat on the armless chair in front of the desk.

"I understand you and Brother Bruhamoff had an unfortunate incident on arriving at Newharken. Have there been any other problems on your journey?"

"Yes. The Claireston Terradomus was infiltrated by a Darkrose witch. We don't know what her ultimate goal was, but she managed to have a young man killed for discovering one of the secret entrances."

The Altus Rector nodded. "A very sad circumstance. It was fortunate you were able to discover her presence."

So, she knows already of the details of what happened at Claireston. "I did come across the Darkrose witch again, Elwendia, at Equisurbem, I don't know where she is travelling to, but it may be on the same path as myself."

"We shall have to watch out for her."

Ululla waited as a young woman placed a cup of tea on the desk in front of her and departed to a side entrance. Ululla knew the larger terradomus would have a helper for the altus rector and in this case, the assistant had a small side room to do work. "Altus Rector Muriel, the spirit of the young man we killed at the Claireston Terradomus, has been travelling with Brother Bruhamoff and myself. As far as I know, the Darkrose are not aware of his spirit. The spirit may have another task to accomplish, and I want to try to help him. I would like permission to bring him inside the terradomus."

"Are you certain he does not mean to cause harm? Is there a possibility he would seek revenge on those responsible for taking his life?"

"I trust him, but there's never any complete certainty when it comes to how people will act. I believe he will have a special influence on future events. I don't know why his journey is parallel to my own, but he told me he feels he is being pulled."

"I'll allow him to enter and trust your judgement on this matter. Sister Ululla, the altus councillium wants to meet with you tomorrow afternoon. They will summon you after lunch. I'm not aware of the reason for the meeting." She frowned. "Sometimes my task as an altus rector is made more difficult with their presence, as I'm restricted in what I may ask some visitors." She raised her eyebrows.

"I understand as I'm restricted in what I may say and don't always receive all the information I want. However, I do understand the difference between my curiosity and what I'm required to know to complete my task."

Muriel slowly nodded. "Well said, Sister Ululla." She stood. "I won't hold you any longer, as I'm sure you've things to do."

Ululla bided her good day and immediately went to the bedroom where Bruhamoff was sitting up in bed. Two pillows helped to prop him up against the wall. A single blanket covered him up to his hips as he drank tea. He looked pale, and his hand shook as he took another sip. The witch who treated him earlier sat on the edge of the bed.

"How is he?"

"I think he'll be okay. I'm Malkyn, the doctor for Newharken Terradomus."

"Ululla. I'm thankful you are able to provide care for him, Sister Malkyn. He looks cold. Should I get him another blanket?"

"Not yet. I want him to stay awake a while longer and being cool will help. I need to be sure his head injury isn't serious."

"Where else is he injured?"

"His ribs are bruised, and his right leg has a large discoloration and cuts I bandaged. He lost a bit of blood there. His back is quite tender and has had muscle spasms a couple of times." She smiled. "Other than the concussion, he's in great shape."

Ululla smiled at her joke. "Can I bring anything?"

"You can bring me a tea. So far, he's received all the attention. Some of the young females have come to inquire how he was doing. I suspect he won't have trouble getting volunteers to give him a back rub later."

Faint colour crept into his cheeks, and although he had a boyish face, his chest and arms were of a man. He still hadn't developed a lot of hair on his body, but his muscles spoke of strength. "I suspect you're right. I'll get you your tea."

When she returned, another young female witch stood at the doorway. *Word of a good-looking man needing medical help got around fast.* She passed the tea to Malkyn. "I'll check up on him later. It seems he's in good hands."

Ululla went outside and walked around in the front yard. Near the gate, she felt Terrowin's spirit.

"Come with me, Terrowin. You may stay inside the terradomus." She led the way downstairs and chose the hallway leading to the bedrooms designed for temporary guests. She knew a different hallway led to bedrooms meant for those staying for an extended time. In all, the Newharken Terradomus could house close to three hundred witches. The huge structure was almost entirely underground, with four different levels below the surface.

She picked a bedroom along the long hallway that made a series of right angled turns, taking it to the end, back to the beginning. After unpacking her belongings, she spoke to Terrowin.

"Terrowin, you've permission to be in the terradomus, so you can move around here. However, I want you to be careful about the witches. It's quite possible the Darkrose have infiltrated and are spying here."

"Do we spy?"

"No." She thought about her answer. "Not as far as I know." She suddenly wondered if the Whiterose did place witches inside the Darkrose terradomus. "It's important you keep away from people when you move around and not give them an opportunity to know a spirit is near them."

"I'll be careful."

"Good. Did you see what happened when the horse ran over Bruhamoff? What caused the horse to do that?"

"Spell by man. Didn't follow him."

"Did he dress like a witch?"

"No. Dark clothes."

Ululla nodded. It seemed to her the man was likely a warlock and not someone from the Darkrose.

"Thank you, Terrowin. Please be careful when you're around anyone. There are spells that can do harm to spirits or banish them from our plane. We need to make sure you complete your journey, wherever it takes you."

Ululla returned to the upstairs and went through the common room to the kitchen, very hungry. Her hip was sore, but she felt it was no more than a bruise. She was certain if Bruhamoff hadn't pushed her away, she could have easily been killed.

As she opened a cupboard door, Eabae came into the kitchen. "Sister Ululla, you have been through an ordeal after a long journey. You must be tired and hungry. Please sit while I make you something to eat."

"Thank you." Ululla smiled and sat at the table in the kitchen with four simple chairs. A second entrance to the kitchen led to the dining room that held long tables with bench seats on either side.

"Brother Bruhamoff seems to be doing better. Sister Malkyn is a very good healer and is making sure he's comfortable."

"That's good to hear. I'll check on him after eating."

"I don't wish to pry, but are you in a relationship with him? Several witches are interested to know if he's free of commitment."

Ululla laughed. "I'm afraid he's too young for me. Brother Bruhamoff is not committed to anyone."

Eabae turned from the stove to look at Ululla. "You don't give yourself enough credit. I don't see a problem between you and Brother Bruhamoff as far as age is concerned."

"Thank you, but I see myself more as a teacher for him about the Book of Redemption."

"Very well, but another reason I asked about you and Brother Bruhamoff is there were some inquiries made about your status as well. Both male and female witches, I might add."

Ululla blushed slightly. *So, Sister Eabae is the one who feeds gossip and obtains personal information. Most terradomuses have at least one, but she seems very dedicated to the task.* She didn't have a problem in attracting others to share a bed, but the right man had not appeared for

75

anything more. She would like to meet some men during her stay at Newharken, but with Terrowin always nearby, that made it impossible. If she was to show signs of being interested in another man, it might make Terrowin jealous, angry, sad, or cause him to leave. She had to hold off on her own personal needs and wants until her task with him was complete.

"I'm afraid I'm in a relationship. It only appears I'm alone."

Eabae set a plate of steaming food in front of Ululla.

"I understand. Sometimes our journeys take us away from our loved ones for periods of time."

Ululla began to eat. *Except I have no loved ones to go home to. I don't even have a home.*

* * * *

After eating, Ululla wandered through the backyard, admiring the rows of vegetables and the fruit trees which grew far back. She took off her sandals and walked between the rows, feeling the soft dirt with each step as she recalled passages in the Book of Redemption.

By the time she had reached the fruit trees, she felt lighter in spirit. She continued to recite passages she felt were appropriate to how she was feeling. When she reached the terradomus again, her shoulders were straight and her head held high.

In the common room, she saw Malkyn, who was drinking tea.

"How's Brother Bruhamoff?"

"Resting. He asked me if you were okay. Apparently, he thought you may've been hurt, too."

"Just a bruise. It was more of the shock of suddenly being pushed into the wall. I'm fine, thank you."

"His door is closed, but it'd be all right if you wanted to check on him. I just didn't want all those other women to be bothering him with endless cups of tea." She smiled. "They were all concerned for his wellbeing, of course."

Ululla smiled. She liked the doctor, who had a sense of humour along with excellent healing abilities. Most healers she met were too serious. "Have you been at Newharken Terradomus long?"

"Over a decade. I have four children of my own, and my husband is a farmer. We have a farm just outside the city."

"Your husband is not a witch?" Ululla knew some witches married ordinary people. It wasn't too common for witches, who often moved about in their earlier years of training, and usually formed a relationship with other witches.

"No. He did attend some of the training to understand what I did as a witch, but said it wasn't for him. Two of my children are interested in joining the Whiterose, but I try not to put any pressure on them. How about you? Anyone special?"

"No, not yet." *I guess Malkyn hasn't been around Eabae today, or she wouldn't have a need to ask.*

"Your time will come, likely when you least expect it. I need to go home and make dinner. It's a good thing our farm produces a lot of food. Growing children and a hardworking man can finish of a table full of food quickly." She carried her empty cup to the kitchen.

Ululla went down the hallway to Terrowin's room. She lightly tapped on the door, but didn't receive any response. She slowly opened the door, allowing her eyes to adjust to the yellow light given off by the single lamp mounted on the wall above the bed. The bedroom featured a desk and a separate chest of drawers. On top of the chest rested a wash basin and a towel.

Next to the bed was a small table with six full cups of tea. She smiled, remembering Malkyn's comment.

Bruhamoff lay on his back, with his arm bandaged to his chest. His upper thigh was also bandaged and even in the dim light she could make out the dark yellow and blue bruise. She felt his forehead, finding it warm and slightly damp.

That explains why he's kicked off the blanket. She wondered if covering him up with the blanket would make him too warm, and then compromised by bringing the blanket up to his waist. *A bit of modesty for him. When he wakes up, he may figure out why all the tea was sitting on the table.*

She touched the side of a few cups and found one still hot. She carried it out of the room, gently closing the door. *No point in wasting all that tea.*

She made her way to the common room, drawn by the sound of dozens of voices and the smell of cooked food. She followed the sound and aroma to the dining room, surprised she felt hungry so soon after eating.

She took a bench seat and helped herself as she joined in the conversation with those next to her. She heard a few witches at the table behind her comment about Bruhamoff. Between their giggles, she summarized they were the ones depositing cups of tea as he lay naked on the bed. She smiled as she thought of his possible reaction if he could hear their comments.

After dinner, she helped carry plates to the kitchen where a line of other witches began the task of washing them. She remembered having to do the same in her younger years.

Ululla decided to take a cup of wine to help relax. The events of the day were putting too many thoughts into her head. She wondered who was the target of the attack by the horse. Bruhamoff? Herself? Both? And why? She hoped her meeting with the altus councillium would clarify her mission and not leave her with even more questions. Their last instructions to her were to stop at the Claireston Terradomus, where she was to correct a problem. She was then to travel with a companion and stay at Equisurbem before going back to Newharken. The companion wasn't specified, nor the reason for going to Equisurbem. They told her she would know when the time came and to trust her feelings.

She believed she had done well so far, but wished she could have had a confirmation before she had arrived at Newharken. A second thought creeping in her mind was Eabae's questions on her relationships. She was feeling frustrated at not being able to seek even a temporary bed partner with Terrowin around.

The wine began to have the desired effect. She yawned. It was earlier than she normally went to bed, but knew she would sleep easily. Ululla went downstairs and to her bedroom.

"Terrowin, did you have a good day?"

"*Yes.*"

"Is there anything new you discovered you want to tell me?"

"*No.*"

"Good night, Terrowin. I need to sleep now." She took off her gown and climbed into bed. She felt too warm, but pulled the blanket over her, knowing Terrowin was still in the room.

I guess in a way I do have a relationship with a man.

Chapter Ten

Alric found Tybalt the next day in the afternoon in the courtyard of the castle. He was surprised to see him looking hale and hearty.

"Come with me, Alric. Allow me to buy you a few drinks."

Alric grinned. "Sounds good on a hot day."

They made their way to a noisy tavern that took up the lower floor of an inn.

Tybalt raised a tankard to Alric, "Thank you my friend for taking me to the witches."

Alric returned the gesture and drank the heavy tasting ale.

"What do I owe thee? The witches said you paid for my treatment."

"They refused payment. I believe they decided to do us a favour."

"Odd. Perhaps my thoughts about witches were all wrong before."

"Indeed. What do you remember of what they did?"

Tybalt let out a sigh. "I hardly remember some of it. I was tired and with a headache when we arrived at the witches' house, and they gave me tea to drink. After a couple of swallows of that stuff, I was barely awake. Couldn't feel my limbs, which was good because they used a hot knife to clean out the cut in my arm. I think I passed out. Anyway, I woke up naked with all these witches rubbing this oil onto my skin."

"That doesn't sound unpleasant."

Tybalt laughed a deep chuckle, "Maybe not to you, but remember I could hardly move my arms. I didn't entirely trust the witches. I have to say whatever they did, worked. They even washed my clothes. I feel like a new man."

Alric raised his tankard. "To the witches then."

Tybalt leaned forward. "Alric, if it wasn't for you, the witches would never have healed me. I owe you my life. If ever you want anything, you can count on me."

* * * *

Commander Willis spoke to his officers, giving them instructions to make sure Kireland was secure. "The royal family has been taken to Dwykath, but we need to continue to secure Kireland. If we see any signs of the former king such as the family crest, they must be removed immediately and destroyed. Let us make it as if Kireland was always part of the Kingdom of Dwykath. Any questions?"

Alric spoke. "Our men are taking liberties by not paying for food at the market. If we're to be seen as rightful rulers of Kireland, then we need the respect of the population."

Willis nodded. "Good point. All our men must act in good faith, or they'll have a meeting with me. Make sure you spread the message to the troops."

Alric left the meeting feeling good. He had done something right. He walked down the cobblestone streets to the market area, looking for witches and one in particular.

Unlike the time he was with Tybalt, Alric soon spotted witches. They moved slowly and quietly in the market, usually in pairs. He also saw the two different factions wearing either the dark or lighter shade of clothing. He watched a pair of the Whiterose witches approach three Darkroses. There was only a short acknowledgement and little conversation.

He walked cautiously toward where the pair of Whiterose witches were inspecting vegetables. He hoped they knew where Ysmay could be found.

Alric moved past a counter, actually part of the front wall of a building folded down. Inside the building, two women replaced food on the wood platform as soon as a customer took an item. A portly man took payment from the side of the counter. Alric thought it was an efficient way to do business. At the end of the day the wall was folded back up and the dwelling became a place where they could live and sleep.

"Were you looking for me?"

Alric turned and met the still face of Ysmay.

"Yes, I wanted to ask you something."

Two other witches stood a few steps behind her. Ysmay turned to them. "I'll meet you back at the terradomus." She motioned at Alric to walk with her.

"The terradomus is where you cured Tybalt?" he asked.

"It's part of it."

Alric heard the witches built deep underground structures and tunnels beneath the dwellings they inhabited. They also strongly protected their secrets, and Alric knew it was best he didn't ask too many questions.

"I want to ask you something. Do you know something of my future? The Darkrose witch said that I'd become a woodworker again, and you said I'd have a chance to help witches."

"Alric, the future is hard to foresee, even for those most gifted in the art. I mentioned to you free will, and it's not easy to predict what people choose to do at crucial moments."

Alric recalled how he almost ended Tybalt's life in the battle instead of sparing him. If he had killed him, he wouldn't have come in contact with the Whiterose witches. "It would be difficult to take into account each decision one makes."

"Except we don't have to take account of all decisions we make. I told you, you have a kind heart and are smart. Those qualities would sooner or later lead you into contact with the witches. There is a pull between people of similar minds." She took his hand. "You have come in contact with us because the universe seeks the harmony of similar souls."

"I'm not a witch."

"Yes, but I suspect our beliefs are very similar. For example, we both seek peace."

"Since I've come in contact with you, what does that mean? Does it change my future?"

Ysmay was silent for a few steps. "Our altus rector believes you have moved down a path where you will keep in contact with witches, a spiral path will draw you closer to us. Does that frighten you?"

"When I was growing up, I was taught to avoid witches, for they could put a spell on you. I suppose I feel cautious about approaching witches, but you make me feel at ease."

"That's good to know."

"You still haven't told me if you can see my future. I suspect you can but won't tell me."

"You're correct. If I told you the future, you may wish to avoid it or even try to make it happen too soon."

They reached the witches' dwelling.

"Come inside for a tea."

Alric nodded. "You called this a terradomus. Do the Darkrose witches also have one here?"

They entered into the house. "Yes. Their design is a bit different, but both serve as a home for witches. A select number of our terradomuses are open to the public. None of theirs are. We normally don't allow outsiders in here, but you have permission."

"Thank you."

He sat in the main room with Ysmay. Shortly afterward, a female witch brought them tea and departed.

"Why have you invited me inside for tea?"

"I thought you wanted to talk, and I want to know more about you."

"I do. I think you know something is going to happen to me."

"Have you heard about the Book of Redemption?"

"I've heard witches use a book for spells to guide them." He glanced at the far wall where a large leather-bound book lay open on a pedestal.

"The Book of Redemption guides what we do. It doesn't contain any spells. Those we're more secretive of."

"What's the Book of Redemption about?"

"The Book of Redemption was written by Altus Rector Bercthun when he broke away from the Darkrose with his followers."

"Why did he break away?"

"The Darkrose believe to do good for all, sometimes a sacrifice has to be made. I don't mean a ritual sacrifice, but one of principles. Altus Rector Bercthun, who later became Altus Councillor Bercthun for the Whiterose, disagreed. He believed you cannot have true harmony and peace if it is accomplished by using evil and deception."

"That's interesting. So, is this a book of his beliefs?"

"Let me show you." She walked over to the pedestal with him.

Ysmay turned a few pages, stopping at a chapter titled Truth.

Alric read a few lines and stopped. "There's a lot here on truth and honesty."

"Truth and honesty are important qualities."

"Obviously not easily conveyed."

Ysmay gave him a smile. "The Book of Redemption teaches while we must always strive to speak the truth, we must understand what's true now, may not be true later. For example, if we state it's raining, but within minutes the rain stops, then the truth has changed. Another thing the Book teaches is the truth depends on the point of view. You may see the rain in the east, but I may be looking to the west where the sun is shining. The truth is if it's raining depends on who is asked."

She took his hand and led him back to the chairs.

"The Book of Redemption also tells us when we speak we have to consider its effect. When we speak the truth, we must ask who gains from it. Will it cause more harm than good? Are we only trying to make ourselves sound important? The truth can be a weapon, and we must be careful how we use it."

"Is that why you don't want to tell me of my future?"

"Yes. By telling you the future, you may decide to change it."

"A paradox."

She raised her eyebrows. "Such odd words coming from a warrior. In a past life, you must have been a scholar."

Alric laughed. "I think that's very unlikely. My father taught me many things when I was growing up. I would sit by him as he worked wood."

"Your father sounds like a very smart man to teach you so well." She touched his hand. "I cannot tell you the future, except for this. The path in front of you is long, and you'll leave the seeds of change in this world before your time is up."

She stood. "Thank you for coming in for tea."

Alric moved toward the door, understanding she had revealed to him what she had planned to and no more. "I don't know if we will meet again, but it has been very interesting to have met you."

She stood on her toes and planted a kiss on his lips, her hands clutching his shoulders. "My warrior friend, I just might seek you out someday."

* * * *

Alric was getting bored with patrol. His biggest concern was addressing the behaviour of the men in the taverns after they consumed too many drinks. When the commander announced in two days' time he and others would be returned to Hardoff, the capital of Dwykath, he confided to Tybalt he was looking forward to being bored in a different kingdom.

Tybalt chuckled. "A horse of a different colour but rides the same. I've never been to Dwykath. Something new for me to see. Perhaps you can introduce me to a few of the taverns where the serving wenches are friendly."

Alric clapped him on the back as they walked down the market streets. "It seems to me you'd have no trouble finding a few pretty women by yourself."

"I can find them, but they do play hard to get."

"Patience, my friend, patience. Women do like to be noticed and then wooed."

They entered a tavern and settled down at a long table, acknowledging the soldiers sitting at the other end.

"How about you, Alric? I'd thought you'd have a few lady friends. They sure seem to notice you, but you spend a lot of time alone. Needlessly, I might add."

"I do a lot of thinking." He shrugged. "I guess I'm not happy being a warrior, but don't know what else I can do."

"A woman can help you forget your troubles." He gave him a wink.

"True, or cause you even more."

Tybalt joined Alric in laughter.

Alric drank slowly, not wanting to set a drunken example to the men in the tavern. After a few tankards, he bid goodnight to Tybalt, who was getting along well with one of women in the bar.

He walked down the quiet streets, past the market, and to his quarters in the castle. As an officer, he was given a private room, and he looked forward to a good night's rest. He opened the door to his chambers and was startled to see Ysmay waiting for him, standing by the open window.

"Hello, Alric. I understand you'll be leaving soon for home. I want to spend tonight with you before you go."

Alric closed the door behind him. "How did you get past the guards of the castle?"

She laughed. "Does it matter? You have me in your bedchambers. Are you going to ask me to leave?"

He shook his head. "No, you just surprised me."

She reached behind her neck and untied a string. "I thought I gave you a hint that I'd find you." She smiled as the gown dropped to the floor.

Alric took in a deep breath as he gazed at her naked body.

She walked over to him, and kissed him slowly.

"I promise I won't steal your soul."

He picked her up in his arms, hearing her give a sigh of satisfaction as he kissed her neck. Carrying her to his bed, he gently lowered her to the straw mattress and smiled. "Was your visit to my bed predicted by the witches?"

"No, not at all, but I knew the first time I met you I wanted to bed you."

He pulled off his clothes. "I never knew witches would make love to a warrior."

"Not witches or warriors, but a woman to a man."

Chapter Eleven

Soon after eating breakfast, Ululla went to see how Bruhamoff was doing. She felt she'd had her best sleep in days, feeling energetic as she went down the hallway. The door was closed, but her knock was answered by Malkyn.

"Who is it?"

"Ululla."

"You may enter."

Ululla pushed the door open, Malkyn worked on his back with a dark cream. He was naked, and she hesitated a moment as she approached.

"His lower back muscles are still acting up, but this should help them heal. I also used a healing spell on him, so he should be able to get up and walk around after this." She looked up at Ululla. "He's sensitive about being naked in front of others, but I told him part of being a witch is accepting who you are and a human body doesn't always have to be hidden. As a healer, I cannot do my job if he wants to stay covered."

"I'm sure he understands. How are you feeling, Brother Bruhamoff?"

He twisted his head to look up at her. "Much better. My headache is mostly gone."

"That's good to hear. You saved my life. I believe that makes you a hero."

He gave a smile. "Thank you. I was so glad to hear you were okay."

She looked at the small table. It was empty save for one tea cup.

Malkyn answered her unasked question. "I had nine cups of tea removed this morning." She shook her head. "Sometimes I wish we could lock these doors."

"I'm sure the visitors meant no harm. Brother Bruhamoff, you're okay that visitors came in to see if you were all right?"

"I suppose so. It feels a bit odd though. I don't know who they were."

"Sometimes a bit of a mystery is okay. I'm sure some of them will let you know who they are at the right time."

Malkyn wiped her hands on a cloth. "Okay, turn around. I need to check your shoulder."

Bruhamoff frowned but rolled over.

Ululla moved so Malkyn's body blocked her view of him below the waist. She headed toward the door when Malkyn asked her a question.

"Do you know when you're to leave Newharken? I don't believe Brother Bruhamoff will be able to travel for at least two days. His body needs time to rest and heal."

"I'm meeting with the altus councillium this afternoon. If I need to go, then I must go. However, I doubt they'll ask Brother Bruhamoff to travel before he's ready, and I could likely return for him later."

"His shoulder is fine, better than I expected." She turned to him. "I suggest you get dressed and try walking around a bit. Don't stress yourself. Aches are okay, but let me know if any sharp pain occurs or the headaches return." She stood, picking up her cup of tea.

Ululla watched him sit up with some effort, but he planted his feet firmly on the floor.

"I'll have breakfast waiting for you. Come to the kitchen after you get dressed."

Malkyn walked with Ululla down the hall.

"He's a very nice young man. I'm glad you're travelling with him. He needs someone like you, giving him wisdom without making him feel stupid. I think he sees you also romantically, although that's a difficult line to cross if you're also his mentor."

"It shall have to remain that way. He needs to find a companion closer to his age and maturity as I need to find a companion closer to my own needs."

"Wisely spoken, Sister Ululla. I've been around Newharken Terradomus for a long time and have heard your name spoken many times in the highest regard. You were here before, but because of my duties I didn't get a chance to talk to you. I'm glad of the opportunity to have met you now."

* * * *

Ululla watched Bruhamoff finish of two helpings of breakfast before he was done.

"I guess I was a bit hungry."

"Healing takes energy. Now, I suggest you go for a walk and try to get the stiffness out of your muscles."

He stood. "I think I'll take a walk down the street. I've never been in such a big city before. There're buildings everywhere."

She smiled. "Don't go too far." She looked in the common room and saw several witches sitting or walking around. She walked over to a young female witch who had a pleasant face with long blonde hair and trying to be discrete in showing interest in him.

"Excuse me. Brother Bruhamoff wants to go for a walk around town, but isn't familiar with the area. Do you think you could act as his guide?"

She smiled quickly, her eyes flashing toward him. "I'd be happy to show him around."

Ululla watched as she took him by his arm and smiled to herself. *Best he doesn't go out alone, and it'll be good for him to have female companionship. I wonder if she was one of tea cup bringers to his room.*

At lunch time, they returned, and Ululla was certain Bruhamoff had enjoyed his walk. She settled down in the common room. The blonde witch sat with Bruhamoff during the meal and after lunch escorted him to his bedroom. A few minutes later she returned, saw Ululla, and sat next to her.

"I'm Sybbyl. I know you and Brother Bruhamoff are just visiting here. It's nice to meet you both. Brother Bruhamoff spoke highly of you, and I want to thank you for introducing me to him."

"You're welcome. Brother Bruhamoff is a fine young man, and I thought it would be good for him to have a friend here as he recovers from his injuries."

"He told me his back was the worst." She glanced down the hallway where the bedroom was located. "I offered to put some ointment on it for him after he had a rest."

Guinevere approached Ululla. "Sister Ululla, the altus councillor would like to see you now."

* * * *

Ululla went downstairs and entered a doorway indicated by marked stones embedded above a curved top. The hallway had various rooms along the side which she ignored. At the end, a second set of stairs, broad and with a low riser for each step, curved downward. It was quiet, although she passed two other witches going the opposite way. She entered another wide hallway with a high, curved ceiling and followed it to the middle where she turned to enter a chamber. It appeared it could hold a hundred people but now merely held a semi-circular dark wood table. A single chair faced the table on one side and on the longer curved side sat seven witches. She waited at the entrance until the middle witch, a tall, grey-haired male beaconed her to enter.

"Please enter, Sister Ululla." He smiled as she sat. "It's good to see you again. I hope your travels have treated you well."

"Thank you, Altus Councillor Alchfrid. My travels have been enlightening." She quickly looked at the other councillors, identifying a few from her travels when they were altus rectors. In particular, she recognized Councillor Emeline, who she met years before at Equisurbem. Emeline gave her a short acknowledgement by a nod of her head and a faint smile. All of the councillors had grey hair, and it was unlikely any of them would speak to her. That was the job of the altus councillor, and he had earlier conferred with the other councillors. Ululla knew they rotated the job of altus councillor, but was unaware of the term. She also knew they reported to a higher authority, but such information was kept from those in lower ranks.

"You have completed your tasks well so far, and we are pleased with your success. You have managed to find out who the Darkrose was

90

at Claireston Terradomus and prevented her from causing more confusion. You have also brought Brother Bruhamoff here, whom we will be talking to later."

"Thank you." Ululla sat still with her hands on her lap.

"What do you know of Terrowin?"

"He was a farm boy, whom we killed when he learned of the secret entrance to the Claireston Terradomus. His death was very sad, in particularly because we allowed the Darkrose witch, Elwendia, to use us to accomplish it."

He nodded. "Do you know why Terrowin was targeted?"

"No, I assumed he was in the wrong place at the wrong time. I believe he was innocent of any intent to do harm to us."

"The Darkrose are fearful of any reference to the name Terrowin, a powerful king, one who was poised to do much good for all people. Unfortunately, he was killed too soon in his life."

"I have read the legends of him. He was a great man."

"He was strongly connected to the Whiterose." He watched her reaction.

Ululla's jaw dropped, and she recovered. "I wasn't aware of his connection."

"Few are. We thought such information was best kept hidden until an appropriate time. The Darkrose know he was affiliated with the Whiterose, and their writings spoke of his return. Thus, they believed the farm boy Terrowin may have been his reincarnation. As we have seen in the past, sometimes a peasant can rise and become a leader. They were worried he might have been able to do so."

"Terrowin's spirit has been travelling with us since we left Claireston. He's here at Newharken."

"We're aware of the location of his spirit. We will do our best to facilitate his travels and the path he is on. We believe he may indeed be the spirit of King Terrowin. If so, his memories of his past life will be surfacing."

"That is good news. Terrowin is being pulled in the direction of his old kingdom then."

"True. I wish you to accompany him on his journey there. Terrowin trusts you and has strong feelings for you." His eyebrows rose slightly. "That is a good thing." He smiled.

"I'm fond of him as well."

"You're to take Brother Bruhamoff with you when you travel to Allisure, specifically to Jital. We understand that Brother Bruhamoff is still recovering from his injuries, so wait until he is able to travel. He has a task there as well. Now do you have any questions?"

"I do have a concern with the Darkrose having spies around us. I fear they'll learn of Terrowin's spirit."

"It cannot be helped. We know of three Darkrose witches here who believe they're undetected by us."

"May I inquire why you allow them to stay among us?"

"What will they learn from us? We preach honesty, peace, and caring for the earth. We hide little from any stranger who asks us. After a few weeks, we take them to a room, and as punishment for spying, make them read out loud one hundred pages of the Book of Redemption. Afterward, we send them away." He smiled. "We hope some of them will see the light and want to join the Whiterose."

Ululla licked her lips. "May I ask how the Darkrose treat spies we may have sent?"

Altus Councillor Alchfrid sat up straighter. "Sister Ululla, are you trying to trick me into admitting we use spies against the Darkrose witches?" He shook his head. "A very poor attempt, if it was."

Ululla blushed and stammered out her apology. "I ask for forgiveness. I didn't think, I merely..." Her thoughts spun out of control.

He held up his hand. "Sister Ululla, we believe in honesty. This is one of the first lessons in the Book of Redemption. If we were to send spies against the Darkrose, it would involve telling a lie to get inside their terradomus, being dishonest. No, Sister Ululla, to answer your question, we do not spy. We will do the right thing each time to the best of our abilities. We shall not waste our time and energies on doing wrong."

Ululla nodded, feeling the same as if she'd been given a stern lecture after being caught stealing an apple.

"Before you go, I want to tell you your journey to Allisure with Terrowin and Bruhamoff is more than just you being a moderor. It's for your benefit, too. The council cannot tell you all we know, but know this, your journey is near an end."

She stood. "Thank you, Altus Councillor Alchfrid."

"Peace be with you, Sister Ululla."

Chapter Twelve

Elwendia continued to lean with her back against the stone building long minutes after her conversation with Ululla. Although her eyes remained closed, tears continued to find a way down her cheeks.

Ululla was right. I cannot escape from what I've done. I tried to block out what I did, tried to pretend it was for the greater good, but my heart tells me different. Dear Almighty God, forgive me for my sin. I shall never knowingly do anything that will lead to the death of others— unless it's my own.

She took deep breaths to calm herself and wiped her tears with the sleeve of her dress. Slowly she made her way to the Darkrose Terradomus, walking the memorized path between buildings and eventually came to a modest stone home. As required by the altus rector, she continued past the home and used a second entrance in the field next to it. Stone steps went down to a strong wooden door braced with iron plates. She pulled the chain cord, knowing a bell sounded on the other end. Moments later, the door opened outward to allow her inside.

"Welcome, Sister Elwendia." The tall, male witch spoke in a clipped voice.

She gave him a smile he barely returned. "Thank you, Watcher Bertwald." She didn't take offence to his lack of pleasantries, knowing he recently suffered the loss of his wife and only child to robbers. She heard he had longed to go after those responsible, but was told by the altus rector personal vengeance was not permitted.

She walked down the long hallway barely wide enough for two people to pass. The short tunnel to the house was one of the oldest to be built and predated the separation of the Whiterose from the Umbravox.

The stone was rough cut, compared to the smooth surface of more recently made tunnels, and gaps between some stones were filled with a clay mixture. The worn floor of the tunnel was uneven with small dips. Still, it provided the witches with basic knowledge on cutting stone into shapes and the making of a tunnel. Newharken was the original home of the Umbravox that later split into the Darkrose and Whiterose witches, and had the most complex and longest tunnels.

The hallway came to a circular foyer, with several exits, including two sets of stairs. One led to the lower levels, but Elwendia choose the one to the main level of the dwelling. The main floor consisted of a kitchen, a dining room, and a few small bedrooms. The common room had been overtaken by tables and chairs, an overflow from one dining room. A second, larger dining room was located on one of the lower levels. Elwendia thought of the house like an ant hill with most of the activity below the surface.

Currently, it was quiet with only a few witches about. Elwendia went to the kitchen, knowing there was always a kettle of hot water available to make tea and some snack items. She made a cup of tea and took a dried fruit biscuit and went to the common room. She sat, staring at the stone wall, unaware when another witch sat next to her.

"You look troubled, sister."

Elwendia was startled for a moment. "I'm sorry. I didn't see you sit, brother."

"Adrian. Is there something wrong?"

"Elwendia. Brother Adrian, I'm having trouble with my conscience. My task with the Umbravox led to the death of a young man. I know I did what was right for the long term good, but my pain is for the immediate."

He nodded slowly. "The Book of Destiny tells us the journey to lifting all people will require the sacrifice of body and spirit, for the gain of wholesomeness comes with a price we must be willing to pay. The young man and you have made a sacrifice for all of us to help us obtain a greater good. Your conscience bothers you because you're a good and noble person and do not take his death easily. Sister Elwendia, please absolve yourself of the guilt which prevents you from appreciating the true path we are on."

Tears slipped from her eyes. "Thank you, Brother Adrian. I shall try and do so."

"Good. I shall let you be now, but please let me know if you wish to talk some more. Perhaps reading The Book of Destiny will help you." He stood and gestured to a book sitting on a stand near the entrance to the house.

"I will look at it later."

She watched him leave and slowly ate the biscuit and drank her tea, before walking over to the book stand. Opening The Book of Destiny to a random page, she hoped it would give her some guidance.

"We need not fear change if we trust in what we are trying to accomplish. Just as we need to prune a tree to make it stronger, on occasion we need to remove elements among us that prevent us from being stronger. This task may not be easy to face, but it is for the long term good, to help those who will be born after us."

Elwendia frowned, not sure if she really accepted the logic written in front of her. *Who decides what part of the tree needs to be removed? And how do we know what's best for the future? There's a bit of arrogance here.*

She walked back to her empty tea cup, picked it up, and briefly considered hurling it across the room, but returned to the kitchen instead. She made another cup of tea as her thoughts drifted back in time to where she was at the Claireston Terradomus.

Elwendia needed to spend time alone in her bedroom before dinner and made her way to the lower level where the rooms were located. The room was cool, and the flickering flame from the lamp gave off a soft yellow light. She sat on the edge of the bed and tried concentrating on the solitude. At first, she able to relax, but then the face of Terrowin came to her. She made her hands into fists and cried.

* * * *

After dinner, Elwendia was summoned by another witch to report to the altus rector. Without enthusiasm, she went downstairs and followed a hallway to the altus rector's chambers. Elwendia stood at the entrance and waited to be invited in. The altus rector, a small framed man in his senior years, continued to scribble in a large book.

She continued to wait with her hands clasped in front of her. She knew he had seen her when he quickly glanced at the entrance, but it seemed his writing had more importance than her requested appearance. She was not surprised by his decision, after having to appear before him on more than one occasion.

His voice was deep and flat as he finished writing. "You may enter, Sister Elwendia."

She walked slowly to the desk and sat on the chair facing it. "You sent for me, Altus Rector Brillie."

"Yes. I wish to discuss with you your last assignment. I understand you managed to infiltrate the Claireston Terradomus and have our target eliminated. That was most commendable."

"Thank you." She lowered her head, looking at the ornate carving at the edge of the desk.

"However, we are concerned. You were detected and exposed as a member of the Umbravox. Our preference would've been you continue to work within their organization. That failure may cause us some delay in our other plans."

Elwendia swallowed. "I did the best I could to hide my identity."

"That obviously was inadequate." He held up the palm of his hand to forestall her from speaking as her jaw dropped. "It may not be your fault. We should have sent you better prepared. However, you are now required to report to the altus councillium in Newharken. They will give you your new assignment."

Elwendia stood, quietly seething. "Is that all, Altus Rector Brillie?"

"Yes." He looked back at the paper on his desk with the pen poised. "Peace be with you."

"And to you, Altus Rector Brillie." She turned and hurried out of the chamber. A tear broke free and trickled down her cheek as she walked back to the stairs. A witch observed her but didn't comment as he passed her on the staircase. She continued to her bedroom, closed the door, and sat on the edge of her bed, allowing the tears to fall freely.

* * * *

Still weary after a poor night's sleep, Elwendia made her way down the road. Mayathorp was as far as she wanted travel that day and made her way to the terradomus. The Umbravox Terradomus was small. She knew it was an older terradomus, but was still surprised to see how worn and neglected it looked. Still, she was grateful for the sleeping quarters underground, and even though the room was small, the bed was comfortable. After a rest, she ventured upstairs where the kitchen was located and checked the cupboards for food. Another witch helped her find what she was looking for and sat with her at a table.

"Thank you for your help. It has been a long time since I was here last. Some of the furniture and walls look a bit worn."

"It has seen better days here. The previous altus rector was here for many years and let things slide a bit. I believe he had weak eyesight and didn't notice some of the problems. The new altus rector, when he took over, immediately had the roof repaired to prevent the rain from damaging the building further, and he had new beds and mattresses put in the bedrooms." She smiled. "Finally, my back isn't sore every morning."

"It's too bad they didn't change the altus rector sooner."

"Well, you know how they do things." The witch gave a frown.

Elwendia reflected on how the Umbravox altus councillium had established a status quo approach with many of their decisions. They promoted many of the altus rectors because of their loyalty to those above them and their unquestioning belief in the Book of Destiny. Once they were made an altus rector, there was a reluctance to change their location or to move them to a less challenging position. "Yes, it takes time for problems to be resolved."

Elwendia finished her meal and went back to her room, believing a good sleep would help her frame of mind. She saw the Book of Destiny standing on a pedestal, but feared any passage she read might raise more questions than answers.

* * * *

In the morning, she arose without feeling refreshed. Her sleep was a broken series of dreams, and although she couldn't recall anything specific, she was left with an unsettling feeling. She ate a light breakfast and started on the road to Newharken. Traffic was brisk, and she enjoyed the company, even though there was little conversation. A few passing by acknowledged her as a witch, but none seemed fearful or in awe of her.

It must be the influence of Newharken. If any city is used to witches, it'll be their original home.

The road slowly widened as she travelled. She didn't stop to eat, preferring to eat as she walked, not to sit and think. The first buildings appeared, small trading stores and gradually larger, more densely placed structures. Elwendia didn't go directly to the terradomus, but stopped at a tea house. She took a table near the far wall, away from the other patrons, carrying the pot of tea she ordered from the front counter.

How did this happen? Killing and lying is not what I believed the Book of Destiny meant when I first read it. I thought I was to help people find the true path. Now I seem to be doing what I thought I was supposed to stop. There's no peace in my heart. I thought the altus rectors were to lead by example on how to act. Half of them seem to be arrogant and no longer follow the spirit of the Book of Destiny. The altus councillium telling me to do things I know are wrong. She gave a grim smile. *I was so excited when I was first asked to approach the altus councillium. I thought they were going to make me an altus rector. Instead, they asked me to do a small special assignment. Then another special assignment. Each one a step away from what I believed was right. Now they believe they have a special tool, one they've refined for their needs. I'm no longer a witch. I'm a demon in disguise.*

Tears fell from her eyes. Suddenly she became aware of a young girl standing by her table.

"Are you all right? Are you hurt?"

Her mother hurried over. "Karline, you must not disturb strangers with questions." She looked at Elwendia. "Excuse her, please. She doesn't understand yet that it is impolite to ask witches questions."

Elwendia quickly gave a smile. "That's all right. She showed she was caring." She looked at Karline. "Thank you for asking. I hurt here." She pointed to her heart. "Someone I know died, and I grieve."

The mother gave a smile back as she took Karline's hand. "I hope you find peace soon." She hesitated and spoke again. "When my father died, I was reminded this was just our first home, and there was another home for us afterward. I believe he is comfortable and happy in his new home."

"Thank you. Peace be with you and Karline."

Elwendia finished her tea and smiled as she thought of the young girl's concern. *It's so nice someone cares how I feel.*

* * * *

The terradomus was a large square shaped building without much ornament on the stone walls. Elwendia knocked on the front door where a watcher permitted her entry. She went to claim a bedroom first, two floors below, and then sought an audience with the altus councillium one floor above. The female witch who handled appointments took her name and informed her she would be summoned in due course. Elwendia nodded without emotion and headed upstairs to the main floor for a bite to eat.

The terradomus was crowded and filled with voices. Elwendia recognized a few faces and gave a quick greeting to several before reaching the kitchen area. She waited at a counter where two witches took orders for snack items. Large pots of tea sat on a table with cups stacked next to them. Elwendia took her sandwich and tea to one of the tables in the adjoining room. Though each of the tables could hold eight there were currently only a scattering of witches. Elwendia was able to sit by herself near a wall. At first, she didn't hear the ringing of a distant bell, but quickly paid attention to their rhythm.

It's the Whiterose Terradomus signal bells, and it's an emergency. I wonder what has happened.

Elwendia just finished her tea when a gong sounded three times, the calling of an emergency meeting at the Hall of Sentential. She immediately stood and, along with the other witches in the room, made her way downstairs. She heard whispered speculation about the emergency, including it may have something to do with the Whiterose ringing of bells. The Hall of Sentential was large, but was unable to hold all the witches. Some had to stand in the hallways surrounding it, but Elwendia was able to sit near the outer perimeter of the circular hall. She watched as the altus rector stood at the podium. The older man stood straight and still sported most of his hair, although it was white. She had spoken with Altus Rector Resterra before and found him to be kind, intelligent, and calm. Those qualities certainly helped promote him to one of the most sought after positions as the altus rector in the original terradomus. Today he looked anything but calm.

He cleared his throat and looked at the other councillors seated behind him before turning his attention to the assembly.

"As some of you may already be aware, the Whiterose Terradomus has been ringing its temple bells. These bells signal an emergency that affects us as well. A terrible situation has occurred in Hardoff, the capital of Dwykath. Several Whiterose witches, including their altus rector, were abducted. King Hadrian has placed them in the castle prison where they are being tortured. He is demanding all witches leave the Kingdom of Dwykath, including the Umbravox, as a condition of their release. The Whiterose have refused to comply.

"We have offered our assistance to them, and they have accepted our help. The Whiterose want to use a spell, one that will not directly cause harm to anyone in the castle, but still force the release of the witches. Their plan will involve the use of many witches, and we hope combining our two orders will be enough. This is all I may report at this time."

He turned and left the chamber, exiting out of a side entrance.

His disappearance led to hush whispers. Elwendia listened to some of the comments, but it was clear to her it was just speculation. She wondered just what spell the Whiterose wished to use that wouldn't cause direct harm to the captors. She suspected the Umbravox wouldn't have the same restraints to obtain the release of their witches. She hoped the captured witches would survive their ordeal, knowing the torture was applied to keep the victim barely alive and conscious.

Chapter Thirteen

After their morning meeting, Willis placed Alric in charge of leading a division of men back to Dwykath. It wasn't good to have the majority of a kingdom's forces far away from the castle walls. That could invite an attack on a very defenceless castle.

Alric let his horse set his own pace as they travelled in a loose group of men on horses, not expecting any attack or meeting any difficulties. Alric allowed his thoughts to wander about Ysmay and their night together. She hadn't expressed any emotional bond between them and was satisfied with their brief encounter. It was, as she stated, just a time between a man and a woman.

Tybalt chided himself for thinking too much about one night, but Alric felt he had learned something about the witches and wanted to dissect the information. *If I ignore the superstition, witches are the same as us. Human, not demons in any way. Just because they're different, it doesn't mean they're evil, and some of them are very beautiful.*

He wondered about the Darkrose prophecy about himself after dying as a warrior, that he would become a woodworker again. It didn't make much sense to him, but he longed to be a woodworker and not as a man wielding a sword.

Midmorning of the second day brought them to within sight of the Dwykath Castle. Farms, small villages, towns, and eventually the city marked an increasing population as they followed the main road. News of their conquest and their victorious return resulted in people lining the side of the road to greet them.

Alric wondered if they knew they defeated an opposition overwhelmed by numbers who didn't want, or provoked, any war.

Tybalt spoke to him as they rode side by side.

"I believe you think too much, my friend."

Alric grinned. "Perhaps I do, but it's hard to stop my mind from wandering."

"Then I suggest you focus on the present and not what could be or has been."

"A good suggestion. You're a good friend, Tybalt. Thanks for bringing me back to the now and here."

Despite his words, Alric continued to wonder what he would do if he wasn't part of the king's army, more so when rumours of trouble quickly spread through the ranks, and a guardsman relayed the information to Alric and the other officers.

"It appears while we were away King Hadrian ordered the capture of several witches." He paused, letting the information sink in before continuing. "All the witches were tortured to death, save for a high-ranking witch he's using to convince all witches to leave Dwykath."

Alric was horrified. Witches were generally left alone by the rulers of kingdoms in large parts because it was believed their spells could bring disaster to all who lived within it if provoked. For hundreds of years, an uneasy truce had prevented any serious conflict between the two factions. He knew the king was partly mad, but was still shocked at the latest news. To kill witches put everyone at serious risk.

He and the other officers urged their horses faster to the Dwykath Castle.

It was dusk by the time Alric arrived. He didn't pause to eat or wash as he hurried down the main castle hallway. A guardian of the court confided to Alric as he approached the throne room.

"What the king is doing to the last surviving witch, an altus rector at that, could mean a disaster for everyone in the kingdom. He's torturing her, and she won't give in to his demands."

Alric entered the room as King Hadrian paused his pacing and turned to another guard standing at rigid attention at the entrance to the throne room.

"Send word to the dungeon to bring the witch up here. Make sure she's in heavy chains with iron restraints."

"Yes, my Lord." The guard immediately turned to another servant just outside the entrance and relayed the command.

Alric felt his stomach go into a knot. He knew iron was supposed to stop a witch from being able to cast spells, but having a witch that had been tortured in the same room as he was made it a cause for concern. *Who knows what she was capable of, even with iron on her?*

Alric felt for certain the king had made a serious error in judgment. *It's one thing to feud and battle with other kingdoms, but to start a war with witches didn't make any sense.*

He knew witches didn't normally make much contact with humans, and other kingdoms were quite willing to let them be. It appeared King Hadrian saw them as a threat because of their secrets and ability to use magic. He was determined to make them leave his kingdom.

Alric heard the sound of metal dragging on the floor and turned to see two guards drag in the witch by her arms. Her robe was shredded from whips she had endured, leaving her skin bloodied and blistered. She slowly lifted herself to a standing position.

King Hadrian sneered at her. "I see you can still stand. Perhaps we haven't punished you enough yet."

The witch lifted her head to look straight at him, her long blonde hair hanging limp and matted around her face. "Do what you will. I won't surrender to your demands."

"I won't have your evil spells and magic in my kingdom. Go to where other kings might enjoy your company."

"Land does not know any human boundaries. We are born of the land and return to it at death, and thus we are part of the land. Therefore, we will not do as you ask."

He thundered. "I'm not asking. I'm demanding. Leave or I'll have all witches burned at the stake."

She calmly replied, "We won't permit that to happen. King Hadrian, please stop this aggression against us before good people get hurt in the struggle."

The king opened his mouth when a messenger hurried into the chambers. He quickly dropped to one knee, waiting for permission to speak.

The king gave an impatient wave of his hand, "What is it?"

"My Lord, there's a problem around the castle, a circle of torches."

Alric followed the king to the balcony and peered into the distance. Outside the castle walls and near the boundary where the forest surrounded the kingdom, yellow and orange flames could be made out at intervals. As he watched more lighted torches joined those already there.

"What's going on there?" the king bellowed at the messenger.

The messenger's jaw quivered, but he didn't answer.

The altus rector replied. "Witches have come to set me free. Release me or be prepared for death."

"You don't scare me with this ruse."

The sound of chanting filled the air. Alric couldn't make out the words but a phrase seemed to be repeating, growing louder as more torches became visible.

King Hadrian sneered. "What's that supposed to do?"

The chanting became louder, resonating inside the room. The volume continued to increase.

The king pointed a finger at the altus rector. "Make them stop. The sound is annoying." He paused to look at his hand and a white powder on it. He quickly brushed off the residue and looked up as more powder drifted down. He stared as a crack appeared in the stone ceiling, spreading into a spider web of fine lines.

"Your castle is going to crumble into sand. Free me before it's too late."

A second messenger ran into the room, dropping to his knee.

"Excuse my interruption, my Lord, but the south tower has collapsed. It crumbled, and is no more." He stayed on one knee looking petrified.

King Hadrian stared at the witch where she stood composed while a cloud of dust descended around them. A fist size stone fell to the floor. He looked where the rock fell, seeing the floor was filled with cracks as well.

"All right! I'll let you go. Now stop this cursed spell."

She walked slowly to the balcony and raised her hands. The chanting quickly faded away.

King Hadrian pointed at Alric. "Get her out of here. Escort her to the front gate."

"Yes, my Lord." He escorted the witch to the exit, removing her restraints as soon as they entered the hallway beyond the doorway. Alric frowned as he looked at her torn robe and turned to a servant. "Get me something to cover her. Hurry."

The servant scampered away.

"I hope you're not in too much pain. I'm sorry for what was done to you."

"I accept your apology." She placed a hand on his arm to steady herself. "May I ask why you're showing such sympathy? You do not fear me, either."

He gave a small shrug. "I may be a soldier but I have no desire to see anyone in pain or stress. You're not my enemy. I've been in contact with other witches and see you as human, not demons."

She gave a fluttering smile. "You're a good man, even if you are a soldier." She clutched his arm tighter. "I fear I may not be able to walk any distance."

He looked at the floor around her and saw the bloody imprint of her footsteps. He took a blanket from the servant and wrapped it around her. "Then I shall carry you."

He scooped her up into his arms, not surprised at the lightness of her body.

Despite her weakness, she held up her head and stared at the passing walls.

"You must leave the employ of King Hadrian. He is bent on having war, and his aggression will result in many deaths, including your own. Please, you're a good man. Don't stay here under his command."

"Thank you for your concern." He nodded at two guards to open the front doors.

"What is your name?"

"Commander Alric."

"Alric? I know of you." She smiled. "I am Altus Rector Cedany. I shall remember meeting you."

He set her down where four witches waited outside the front gate. "I shall remember you as well."

"Peace be with you, Alric." With the assistance from the other witches she sat on a small horse. As he entered the castle again, she called out to give him final advice. "Two full moons. Then war and death. Decide your fate quickly, Alric."

* * * *

Altus Rector Cedany sat in her bed, slowly eating.

"It's good you have gained some of your strength back." The elderly male witch looked with concern at her bruised face. "The herbs should help you heal faster. I hope you'll be able to forget your ordeal after a while, although we shall always remember Sister Nerola and Brother Elser. Why did this have to happen?"

"There is a reason for everything, Brother Fendrel, and I believe I know what this was about. I met a guard with red hair and blue eyes. His name was Alric, and it appears he is the same man who was in contact with witches in Trontta. I advised him to leave the army as soon as possible. I believe he'll do so, for he does not have a warrior's blood."

"The prophecy about the seed of change speaks of a man like him."

"Yes. He has already come in contact with witches, enough so he does not fear us. It could be we're living in the beginning of a new era."

Fendrel slowly nodded. "The prophecy also tells dark clouds will rise first. These will be turbulent times with much death and destruction."

Chapter Fourteen

Elwendia looked up at the witch as she called her name.

"Altus Councillor Reeves will see you now. Follow me."

Elwendia trailed after the stern looking, elderly female witch. She wasn't in a mood to try polite conversation and merely followed her to the altus councillor's office.

The outer office was plain with two desks placed corner to corner in an L shape. Behind the desks was the doorway leading to the office of the altus councillor. After a few minutes, she was allowed inside to sit on a lone chair that faced an elevated table. Only one of the nine chairs on the other side of the table was being used. The large, square room had colourful stone walls and ceiling. Light came from dozens of candles inside clear crystal containers. Altus Councillor Reeves, a medium built man with thinning dark hair, locked his fingers together as he stared at her. To Elwendia, he appeared to be very ordinary in appearance for someone in such a high position. His age was hard to determine, being a witch, but he certainly didn't look much past middle age.

"Sister Elwendia, it is nice to see you again."

"Thank you, Altus Councillor Reeves." *Judging by your facial expression I don't believe you mean that.*

"I understand there were some complications with your last assignment, and the Whiterose are aware of your deception. That may not matter. I commend you for eliminating our target."

Elwendia nodded, not wanting to say thank you for the compliment of killing someone.

"I have another task for you, and as before, I depend on your upmost secrecy to carry it out. I fear the Whiterose have spies among us and will do their best to upset our plans. Do I have your solemn oath to be discreet on this?"

"Of course, Altus Rector Reeves."

"A member of the Umbravox has infiltrated the Whiterose terradomus here in Newharken. You are to give this to her and give instructions to pour the contents of this vial into the drink of the young man who was injured, Bruhamoff." He placed a clay tube with a wood seal on the table. "You will meet Sister Sybbyl at the west corner down the street from the Whiterose terradomus. She attempts to go there every day at seven in the evening for messages. You will go there tomorrow, and the day after if circumstances prevent her from showing."

Elwendia stared at it. "What will it do to him?"

Reeves glared at her. "That is none of your concern. Do your task as ordered." He stood. "I assume you have no further questions."

Elwendia took the container. "No. Peace be with you, Altus Rector Reeves."

"And to you." He turned and exited through a door behind him.

She stood for several seconds, looking at the empty table in front of her. Then she slowly made her way to her room, dropping the vial into a pocket in her skirt.

* * * *

Elwendia wasn't hungry. She heard the dinner bell, but declined to leave her room, and sat on the edge of her bed.

Is death my only solution? I cannot do harm to yet another innocent person. I know Brother Bruhamoff. Why should anyone want to bring harm to him? Of course, the same could be said about Terrowin whose death I'm guilty of causing.

She stood, making a decision to read the Book of Destiny, hoping to come across a passage that would answer her dilemma. Elwendia left her room, going to where she knew a copy of the Book of Destiny resided on the floor. There were several copies of the book in the terradomus, making it easy for the witches to seek spiritual guidance when needed.

She touched the book, closed her eyes, and opened a page at random.

One thousand, eight hundred and eighty-two pages. I just need to find one to give me an answer.

She held her breath and opened the book at random to a page, mouthing the words she read.

"Change is not to be feared but to be accepted as a natural occurrence. Change is the essence of life. Without change we do not have life. When we are confronted with an opportunity to make a change, know the refusal to do anything will still result in a change. However, by acting we can direct the change in the direction we want. Do not fear to make a change. Fear is when you fail to have control of the change. If you follow what you know to be true, then your choice will be clear and uncomplicated. Be honest to your teachings. Let your knowledge and heart guide you."

Elwendia nodded. *Time to act.*

* * * *

Time was kept by a clock that used weights attached to ropes to slowly turn large wooden spools. The spools, by a series of pulleys, eventually caused an hour hand to rotate. Elwendia knew the clock was not likely giving the exact same time as a similar one in the Whiterose terradomus and left earlier to cover the possible difference in time.

The sky still had a glow from the setting sun as she made her way down the streets. The walk wasn't far, and she carried a small lantern to help guide her steps in the shadows. There was an inherit danger for a woman walking the streets at night, but the lantern would also show her to be a witch. Those who prowled the streets at night were often more superstitious than others and fearful a witch might place a curse on them.

She waited at the appointed corner, slowly pacing as she waited in slow moving minutes. Her heart beat faster as she peered into the gloom between the buildings. Footsteps came toward her, and she turned to see the silhouette of a woman approach, transforming into a witch.

"Sister Sybbyl?"

"Yes." The voice was quiet, hesitant.

"I'm Elwendia. Altus Councillor Reeves sent me. Are you in contact with Brother Bruhamoff?"

"Yes, I have met him and actually spent some time with him."

"Do you like him?"

"Yes, he's nice and very tall." Sybbyl's voice changing slightly, with almost a giggle coming through.

"I was given a poison. You are to put it into his drink."

Seconds passed. "I'm supposed to poison him? Are you sure?"

Elwendia touched Sybbyl's arm and began walking toward the Whiterose terradomus. "It's what Altus Councillor Reeves told me."

"Why are we both going to the Whiterose terradomus?"

"It's time for a change. I cannot be part of something dark. I don't have a choice but to act against the wishes of the altus councillor."

"Sister Elwendia, I don't understand. If Altus Councillor Reeves tells us to do something, don't we have to obey?"

"We are not sheep, Sister Sybbyl. We can be the instrument of change for the good, but we have to act when we see the opportunity."

"You can't enter the Whiterose terradomus. You're wearing the Darkrose colours."

"I may not be welcome there, but I will enter. Tell me, is Sister Ululla there?"

"Yes, she introduced me to Brother Bruhamoff. Won't I get in trouble if you enter and they find out I'm from Umbravox?"

"Possibly, but that's the lesser of concern compared to what needs to be done."

Elwendia heard nothing more from the young witch as they journeyed down the street. They reached the terradomus, and as soon as Elwendia entered through the double doors, she was met by Whiterose guards. She stood just inside the doors with Sybbyl to her side.

"I wish to speak to Sister Ululla." She held her head up and spoke in a loud voice. She listened to the buzz of voices as she waited.

Presently Ululla appeared, looking surprised. "Sister Elwendia, why are you here?"

Elwendia's voice stumbled. "I've come—I want to ask for forgiveness." She pulled out the vial from her pocket. "Also, to give you this. It was intended to be given to Brother Bruhamoff, but I cannot allow this to happen."

Ululla took the vial. "Perhaps you better come with me." She looked at Sybbyl, who had pressed herself against the wall behind them. "You better come with us as well."

The guards stared at Ululla and back at Elwendia.

"It's all right. Sister Elwendia and Sister Sybbyl will be under my care. There won't be any trouble." Ululla led the way to the stairs that went to the lower levels.

Ululla spoke to Elwendia. "I'm surprised at your appearance here. You seemed so sure of your fate when I last spoke to you."

"I was less sure than I acted. I still believe in the Book of Destiny, but I'm no longer sure of the leadership of the Umbravox."

Taking them straight to Altus Councillor Alchfrid, Ululla handed him the vial. After a brief explanation of the situation and Elwendia's decisions, he turned it in his hands and looked up at Elwendia and Ululla sitting across from his desk. Beyond his office, Sybbyl waited with a guard standing by her side.

"Sister Elwendia, are you certain you wish to now join the Whiterose order?"

She nodded. "I cannot go back to the Umbravox after this."

He nodded. "I'm shocked the Umbravox altus councillor would order you to deliver a poison. We have a different philosophy than the Umbravox, but this is not what I ever expected they would do. Perhaps there's a reason they're getting so aggressive." He frowned and waited several moments before speaking again. "I will ask Sister Ululla to prepare you for our induction ceremony. Normally there is an apprentice period after a study of the Book of Redemption. However, I understand you're quite familiar with our scripture, and we can proceed without the usual indoctrination."

"Thank you, Altus Councillor Alchfrid. I feel very lost right now and believe the Book of Redemption will help me find my place again."

"Excellent. I believe it might be best if you allow Sister Ululla to show you to a guest room. You do need some rest and some time to reflect on your journey."

Elwendia stood. "Peace be with you, Altus Councillor Alchfrid."

"And to you, Sister Elwendia. Please send in Sister Sybbyl."

Ululla escorted Elwendia to one of the rooms reserved for long term guests. The room was slightly larger than the one she was using and included a larger dresser.

"Thank you for your friendship, Sister Ululla. I feel undeserving of such kindness."

Ululla gave her a hug. "Our past is behind us. It took a great deal of courage to do what you have done today. Rest. Tomorrow will see the sun shine again."

"Thank you. I feel as if a great weight has been lifted off my shoulders. I hope Sister Sybbyl isn't going to be in too much trouble. I forced her to reveal herself as a Darkrose."

"I'm sure she'll be fine. It depends on her answers to the altus councillium."

Chapter Fifteen

Alric stood at attention when the former King of Kireland was brought forth to stand in front of King Hadrian. He watched as King Briebeth, in tattered royal robes, kneeled in front of the throne with his wrists chained behind his back.

King Hadrian smirked as he leaned forward. "Now I am to decide your fate. The easy decision would be to simply have you and your family executed." He grinned. "Or I could have the lot of you rot in prison. Death might be preferable."

"Please, King Hadrian, have mercy on my family. They'll cause no harm to thee."

"You have a wife, two daughters and a boy. I must say the women are appealing to the eye. The boy is too young to have much use to anyone."

"He can learn a trade. He's smart and a willing worker."

"So, you say." King Hadrian examined his fingernails and then casually looked at the man kneeling in front of him. "You should give thanks to your God, for today is a fortunate one for you. Your former kingdom was well run and prosperous for its size. I believe you're a good administrator, and it so happens the Hexham Province is in need of a new lord to run it. Lord Andhun is in poor health and has no male heir."

Briebeth raised his head, his mouth slightly parted as he took in a deep breath.

"I shall allow you the opportunity to run Hexham. You may take your wife and your son. Your daughters will remain here, under my protection." He gave a smile. "This will help assure your loyalty."

Briebeth nodded. "Thank you, King Hadrian. You are most generous."

Alric knew Briebeth didn't have any choice but to accept. It was the only chance he and his family could remain alive, although his daughters would be little more than ladies of the court and King Hadrian's sex slaves. They were young, and Alric hoped they would understand they were being given a chance to live.

"Go." King Hadrian waved a hand at him, and two guards quickly responded by escorting Briebeth away.

Leaving as quickly as possible, Alric wasn't comfortable with the amount of time he spent near the king. It was considered a prestigious assignment to be helping protect the throne room, but Alric dislike the pompous and insane king. There was a danger King Hadrian would suddenly change his mind about Alric and have him thrown into prison on a whim.

Still, it gave him higher pay, and Willis allowed him more latitude in performance of his duties. That was partly due to Willis using Alric to inform on the latest goings on in the court. When meeting that evening, Willis took the latest information about Briebeth over a tankard of ale in one of the better taverns.

"Briebeth is the new Lord of Hexham? He might do all right there. The province has not done well with tax revenues the past few years."

"Yes, I'm sure he can improve how Hexham is run. The last lord spent more time in bed than working." Alric took a drink of his ale. "I feel sorry for his daughters. They'll have to perform duties they never expected."

"Hell, all they have to do is spread their legs. They'll get over it."

"'Tis not right."

"You, my friend, worry too much about what should be and not enough on what could be. So, they become whores in expensive clothes. They're alive and not having to fight for a bucket of drinking water. Believe me, half of the women would change their places in a heartbeat just to have a full meal."

Alric nodded. "You're quite right. I forget sometimes how difficult mere existence can be. My father told me life isn't always the choice between good or evil. It's sometimes the choice between food and death."

"You're an oddity, Alric. Too much of a philosopher for your own good, yet you survive as a soldier. A damn good one at that. I'm torn between not trusting you and making you my first lieutenant." He grinned. "I think both choices are wrong."

"I won't disagree with you. As far as philosophy is concerned, I believe our battles are only part of a larger picture and may not mean much in the long run, but you can trust me. I won't betray you."

"You see, that's where we differ. I know you'll be honest with me when I ask you a question, but somewhere in you is a man looking for a way out of this war. Come hell or high water, I think you'd turn your back on me if it means you don't have to fight anymore."

Alric nodded. "You may be right, but I assure you I'd never leave during the heat of battle. I'm no coward."

"In between battles?"

"Then I wouldn't be missed."

Willis laughed with a roar. "We're back to square one. You're slippery than a greased pig when it comes to answering a straight question." He jammed his tankard against Alric's. "May health and wealth walk the same path for you."

* * * *

Alric urged his horse through the trees to the top of the hill, where he surveyed the surrounding countryside.

"Well, Darkian, all this looks rather pleasant, but I don't see how this will aid in our escape." Alric was hoping to see a place where he could hide out from the king's army, but what he saw was still in easy reach of searchers. "I'll have to travel more than just a few miles to be safe."

A few miles behind him stood the town of Diespere. The town was surrounded by mixed farming and largely unnoticed by the rest of Dwykath Kingdom. However, it generated enough commerce to be occasionally visited by the king's men to ensure proper taxes were collected. The same men were also responsible for putting up notices for criminals, and with the inducement of rewards, towns people were quite willing to turn in a stranger. If Alric were to try to hide in Diespere, similar small towns, or the surrounding countryside, eventually he would be found out.

He made his way back to Hardoff, his mind trying to find an avenue for him to escape. Initially he thought he could leave in the dead of night and take refuge in the furtherest parts of the Dwykath Kingdom. It seemed now he would have to journey a much greater distance, making his way to another kingdom. A problem was he wasn't a low-ranking soldier, whose disappearance might be unnoticed for a few days. If he failed to show up for a morning shift, he had little doubt Willis would send out a search party for him, likely capturing him before he could cross to another kingdom.

Between the searchers and hounds, my escape would likely fail, unless they weren't looking for me. He recalled the witches' prophesy. "No, I said the soldier dies. I didn't say you did." *Perhaps there lies the answer. Pretend I'm killed in battle, but how do I do accomplish that?*

* * * *

Willis pointed to a roughly drawn map made of a dirty yellow cloth hanging on a wall. The room was also a dining room for the higher-ranking soldiers and after the food was cleared away, Willis began his plan for the next battle.

"We've Kireland secured and our next battle is going to be with the Kingdom of Fringella. They'll certainly put up more of a fight than Kireland did, but they have a weakness. They depended on Kireland for two things. One is the trade route to Styrnovo..." He pointed to the road skirting the border of Kireland to the port city of Styrnovo. "...that we can cut off very easily. The other weakness is they used to buy weapons from Billige. Kireland had a good reputation for metal works, but now Fringella will have to get weapons from another source or make them themselves."

An officer spoke up. "It'll take weeks for the effect of the closing of the trade route and the lack of new weapons from Kireland to be a factor in a battle."

"True, but we will weaken them by attacking on two fronts. First, we draw their attention by shutting down the road to Styrnovo. We will block it well away from their border and allow only small, insignificant goods to arrive to their capital, Torland. Their response will be to send a large contingent of troops to help secure safe transit of goods going to and from Torland."

A second officer questioned Willis. "Won't that tie up a lot of our men as well? Fringella has a lot of well-armed troops."

Willis smiled. "We don't need a lot of troops. First, the area of battle, if there is one, will be near Kireland. We could send additional troops easily, but we don't need to battle Fringella troops there. Merely detain them by claiming the right we have to enforce a levy on goods travelling on our road. It's nonsense, of course, but while their troops are tied up far north of Torland, we attack the city of Lorem." He pointed to a point west of Torland. "Once we have Lorem, we cut their kingdom in half."

"How well is Lorem defended? Can we take it over quickly, or will there be a prolonged battle?" Alric asked.

"It is a large city, but with only a small castle for an area of sanctuary for the population. We should be able to win the day quickly."

Alric listened to other parts of the battle plan. It was clever because Fringella wouldn't expect an attack only weeks after Kireland was absorbed into Dwykath Kingdom. Fringella was a large, low populated region. Rocky hills, swamps, and poor farmland made Fringella one of the poorer kingdoms. It was left alone by other kingdoms, largely due to the fact there was little value to adding it to their own. Alric saw the addition of Kireland and Fringella made an attack to Kingdom of Allisure possible. He also thought such attack would be foolish against the large, prosperous kingdom, but King Hadrian was power hungry. Another thought came to Alric.

A soldier could get killed there, far away from Dwykath and close to Allisure.

* * * *

Alric approached Tybalt as he readied his horse.

"Well, my friend, I hope one of us survives this upcoming battle."

Tybalt laughed. "You've a strange way of saying things. I shall miss you."

"You could join me."

"No, I'm a soldier and wouldn't know how to live without a sword in my hand. Besides, I need to make sure you're thought of as dead." He pulled the last saddle strap tight.

"True. Thanks for what you're doing."

"It's odd. You spared my life, and I'm making sure yours isn't spared as a repayment." Tybalt swung up on his horse. "You're a good man, Alric. I know you're not comfortable as a soldier, so may your next calling be more to your liking."

Alric and his men, which included Tybalt, were to attack Lorem. Most of the other available Dwykath forces were in on the same attack. However, with some of the troops being used to block the trade route to Styrnovo and other troops left behind to protect the Dwykath castle, they didn't enjoy overwhelming odds to defeat the enemy.

The day became blistering hot as the sun approached its midway journey across the sky. The horses moved slowly along the trail, and the men knew better than to try to speed up the pace. Alric knew they had some leeway when they had to attack. The blockade was likely to tie up part of the Torland troops for several days, and they would not be able to give any assistance to an attack on Lorem.

When the cool of the evening finally gave them some relief, Willis ordered them to carry on rather than taking up camp. "We need to make up for lost time. It's cooler now, and we can cover some distance in a couple of hours. That'll put us within a half-day travel to the Lorem. We can attack tomorrow, and I suspect the enemy will not be enjoying the heat any more than we are. They may be lazy with their defences, which can be a big advantage for us."

Alric urged his horse on, although he was used to stopping at dusk. Darkian wasn't happy about the longer journey and let his feelings known. Still, he listened to Alric's command and continued on the worn road. Alric thought it was odd Willis wanted to travel another two hours. Travel during the evening did bring the advantage of cooler temperatures, but it also made the horses and men even more tired.

When they did finally stop for camp, Alric entered Willis' tent. The tent was large enough to hold several men and could be used during battle as a headquarters. The bed and loosely set up furniture cast shadows from the flickering oil lamp.

"Excuse me, but I was curious why you wanted to push on today. Is there a reason why we need to attack Lorem tomorrow?"

Willis scowled. "It's not your place to ask why I do things."

"I'm not challenging you, but seeking information. You've always been careful on how you plan an attack. This seems different from your usual preparations. I'm asking because I, and my men, need to be ready for any change in battle strategy."

Willis beckoned him to close the tent flap.

"Now see here, I don't like divulging details of a battle, but this is different. And so are you." He took a long drink from a battered tankard. "I like battles. I get to use my head. I, and the enemy, understand the rules. You win or you die. Sword against sword. What I don't like are traitors or other manners of cheating. You understand what I'm saying?"

"I do. Rules of engagement. A fair fight."

"I was told we need to fight tomorrow by mid-day." He jerked his thumb in the air.

Alric nodded. He knew there were only a couple of men of higher military rank than him, and also King Hadrian. Willis could be referring to any one of them, and Willis wasn't saying who.

"It seems a spell has been, or will be, placed on Lorem. The spell will make everyone there weak and will give us a big advantage during a fight, but the spell will be gone by tomorrow evening. I don't like it, but I do as I'm told."

"Spells have a tendency to cost the user of them. Who knows what such spell will do to us? Using a spell to win this battle may have dire consequences to us later."

"I'm aware of that, but there's little I can do."

"This means we fight them with an unfair advantage." Alric shook his head.

"You're to tell no one of this. I'm only telling you this because..." He stopped, at a loss for words.

"Because you do have a conscience. I shall keep my lips sealed."

* * * *

Lorem was a sprawled-out city with the border of farm land and the urban dwellings being indistinct. As the Dwykath troops rode into the city, the outlying areas came into life, and people hurried to get out of the way.

Alric pulled alongside of Willis as they reached the outer wall. They observed civilians hurrying to safety. He saw a few witches as they walked to their terradomus. Like in other cities where battles were to take place, the witches believed they were safe in the terradomus for soldiers were known to avoid witches and were fearful to enter their sanctuary.

"The people are moving to where they feel protected."

Willis grunted. "Yeah and they don't act like they're sick. Maybe the spell didn't work."

"Or, maybe the witches used a counter spell. They are healers for the sick and injured, and if it came to their knowledge a dark spell was used, they might have decided to block it."

"You may be right there. We shall find out how healthy those soldiers are soon enough." Willis swung his arm up high, signalling the archers and those carrying the ladders to move to the outer wall. "Get your horsemen into position. It's going to be a bloody battle to get through those gates. Follow the pike men when I give the signal."

Alric nodded and turned Darkian away, back to where his men followed the main troops. He didn't envy the pike men. They were to use long pikes to force back the enemy troops from the gates, allowing horsemen and regular troops to engage in battle easier. The pike men, being the lead charge, were likely to suffer the highest rate of casualties. If successful in quickly penetrating the opposing ranks, then horsemen and regular troops would take over. The other hope was the archers could also drive back the enemy, although archers on the other side would be directing their attention to the pike men. If their charge failed, the pike men could find themselves isolated, with little chance of survival.

"Well, Alric, are you still ready to go through with your plan?" asked Tybalt.

"I am, but I shall delay until we've secured victory. It'll be a tough battle."

"Indeed, and if we lose the day?"
"Then I may die for real."

* * * *

Alric watched as the pike men charged. Just as they reached the gate, archers climbed the ladders to the top of the outer wall. The archers planted their large shields on the top of the wall, crouched behind them, and fired arrows. Arrows flew from the other direction and several archers fell. More archers took their place. To Alric, it looked like chaos. Arrows, dust, and screams combined to make it look like a war in hell.

Willis waved a red flag and gave the gesture for his men to attack. The thundering hooves tore through the narrow streets, headed to the stone gates. Darkian was a strong horse and pushed his way to the front. Alric knew it would be useless to try to slow down the big horse; it looked forward to the battle.

The pike men have done their job. We can get through the gate without a problem. Now the real fight begins.

Alric readied his sword, a heavy blade that, even if it failed to penetrate an adversary's armour, would be able to knock him down. It could also be used to block another sword without breaking. His horse leaped over two men engaged in a fight, landing and quickly turning to Alric's command.

Darkian pushed into the flank of another, smaller horse. As the horse tried to regain its footing, the rider was forced to readjust his balance on the saddle. Alric quickly took advantage, swinging his sword at shoulder level. The rider fell off his horse, and Alric moved on to his next opponent, not worrying about the man suddenly on the ground surrounding by horses. If he didn't get trampled, he was still unlikely to be able to do much harm.

Alric, being a tall man on a tall horse, took advantage of the height in any sword fight. Darkian was also a willing partner in the fight, bullying smaller horses to aid Alric. One disadvantage of being one of the tallest men on a horse was the invitation for archers on the rival side to target him. He was hit by several arrows that just failed to penetrate his armour, but he still felt their impact and knew he would have several bruises and punctures to deal with later. For the moment, he was scarcely aware of anything but the battle around him. Automatically he parried attacks and responded with an assault of his own. He didn't know if his side was winning or not, his mind focusing on only what was around him. Then he noticed they were pushing toward the castle, their opponents on a slow retreat to shelter. The drawbridge was within his sight.

Alric pulled his horse back, moving toward the outside of the conflict. He assumed the Lorem forces would retreat into the castle, and the drawbridge would be drawn up to cut off the Dwykath forces. He and other Dwykath forces knew it would be foolish to try to follow the withdrawing forces and risk being trapped inside the castle walls. The next step would be a siege. The Lorem ruler would likely try negotiations, but Alric speculated how Willis would proceed. There wouldn't be any negotiations, other than complete surrender. The siege would soon turn into a bombardment of arrows and other projectiles over the castle walls until the drawn bridge was lowered again.

Alric recognized this would be the best time to make his departure. He hoped Tybalt would be able to meet him at their prearranged location, just past the eastern gate. Alric tried to ensure his safety by placing himself near the back of the horsemen force. If Tybalt was injured or killed and unable to help him with his plan, Alric was willing to try to run away during the siege. There was a reasonable chance he might make good on his escape, but if he were to be caught, death would be the penalty.

"Alric."

"Tybalt. Glad you made it."

Tybalt grinned. "Are you ready to die?"

"As the saying goes, death will be my freedom."

Tybalt took the reins of Darkian. Alric took a quick look around to see if anyone was paying close attention to them. All other eyes were all looking toward the castle, and Alric slumped in the saddle, trying to look dead or severely injured.

Injured soldiers were taken to a common area where a surgeon would attempt to save them, or as often as not, send them to a second area. The second area was where dead bodies were placed. If time didn't allow burial, a fire was set to stop the spread of disease and the attraction of scavengers.

Tybalt led Darkian past where the wounded soldiers rested. "Okay, we're past the wall. I don't think anyone is watching us. May God guide you safely."

"Thank you, Tybalt. I shall never forget your friendship. Be safe." Alric grabbed Tybalt's hand briefly and then rode off. Deserted buildings lined the street, obscuring Alric's hurried race to one of the deserted homes. He quickly pulled off his armour, dumping the Dwykath uniform in the house. Alric kept his sword and knife, knowing he might need a weapon as he traveled. He jumped back on his horse, wearing only a leather vest, shirt, pants, and boots. As Darkian galloped to the outskirts of Lorem, he hoped anyone seeing him would assume he was a peasant trying to get out of the way of the battle. He did see a few other peasants also making a journey away from Lorem, but most of those were on foot. He also saw a group of witches, walking casually along the abandoned city. *They alone don't seem to be worried about who wins this battle or what happens next. How do their beliefs protect them so? I would like some of their calmness now.*

* * * *

Willis stood at a table in his command tent as Tybalt entered, holding his helmet in his hands.

"Speak."

"I regret to inform you Alric has been killed in battle."

"Really? You have proof of this?"

"Yes, Commander Willis, I saw his body with my own eyes. I took him to where we place our dead."

"Are you not one of his drinking friends?"

"I am."

"How fortunate it was you that had found him dead." Willis pursed his lips. "Why do I have a feeling if we went to where the dead are placed, you would not be able to find his body?"

Tybalt swallowed. "I don't know."

"Where is his horse? We should be able find such a large beast wandering loose."

"I don't know what happened to the horse." Sweat dripped from his brow.

Willis rubbed his chin as he walked up to Tybalt. "Well, if Alric were to try to establish a ruse to fake his death and to escape his duties as a soldier, what better method than to have his friend report his death? Of course, the danger is if his death was to be found to be faked, then he would be searched out and be put to death. Along with, I shall add, anyone who aided him. Am I clear?"

"Yes, sire."

"Shall I ask you to show me his body, or do you wish to change your story?"

"I can try to find his body again. I'm not sure where I placed it."

Willis smiled. "A careful answer, Tybalt. Unfortunately, I don't have time to pursue this investigation. I've a battle to prepare for. Let's assume Alric is dead. Thank you for bringing it to my attention. You're dismissed."

Tybalt let out his breath slowly as he turned to leave.

Willis spoke a final message. "Let us hope Alric's next life is more to his satisfaction than as a soldier."

Chapter Sixteen

Ululla carried two dresses, two blouses and a skirt to Elwendia's room. The door opened to her knock, and Elwendia looked surprised at the offering of clothes.

"You need to have something to wear. The Darkrose colours aren't normally worn here." She smiled.

"Thank you. Am I allowed to leave this room and look around? I wasn't sure of the rules."

"Of course. I'll show you around later. Right now, I have a meeting to attend to."

Ululla hurried to her meeting only to wait in the altus councillor's outer office until his assistant showed her inside.

"It's nice to see you again so soon, Sister Ululla."

"You as well, Altus Councillor Alchfrid." She looked around the large office which appeared smaller due to the size of his desk and the various memorabilia he had collected over the years. She knew he had an interest in wildlife, supported by small creatures preserved by taxidermy placed in various spots in his office.

"I have news about the poison Sister Elwendia gave us. The powder was examined by our elders who are experts, and they have found the poison was not designed to kill. Rather it was to render him sterile."

"Sterile? Not to kill?"

"I believe they felt killing him by poison would make it too obvious after the attempt by using a run-away horse. They wanted to conceal their intentions, but never expected Sister Elwendia's conscious would betray them. I suppose making Brother Bruhamoff sterile might be the same as killing him as he would be unable to have offspring."

Ululla pondered the information for a moment and then spoke. "Brother Bruhamoff has a greater purpose; at least the Umbravox thinks so. Do we at the Whiterose know what that is?"

He smiled. "Well, some of us do, but that brings us to our next step regarding Brother Bruhamoff. He has gained enough strength so he can travel again. Seeing how much attention he is receiving here, perhaps it's best his journey is resumed."

"I can make preparations for us to leave tomorrow morning. Is there a particular place where we should be going?"

"Jital."

Ululla nodded. "Near the capital of Allisure. Are we to go to the terradomus there?"

"Yes, but I need to explain something to you. You asked earlier if we spied on the Darkrose, and I told you we do not. That is strictly true. I also said we use honesty as a guide and implied we do our best not to deceive. In the case of Brother Bruhamoff, I regret to say we will be asking him not to divulge he belongs to the Whiterose at a later date. It is not what we want to do, but on occasion it becomes prudent to keep our calling a secret. I'm telling you this because you did ask if we spied, and by extension, if we are completely honest in what we do. We endeavour to be truthful, but because we recognize we are not perfect, we sometimes push the boundaries of honesty. In this case, it is a case of the omission of the truth."

"Thank you for the explanation. May I ask what is to become of Sister Sybbyl? It appeared to me she genuinely liked Brother Bruhamoff, and I was surprised she would be part of poisoning him."

He steepled his hands together. "This is a dilemma. Obviously Sister Sybbyl was involved in something more devious than simply spying on us. She said she had no idea about the poison, and I'm inclined to believe her. Normally, we would release her so she could return to the Darkrose Terradomus. However, as soon as she returns they will know the poison never reached Brother Bruhamoff."

"Does that mean you won't allow her to leave here?"

"Sister Sybbyl was asked to remain here for a few days and not to converse with anyone concerning the poison. She agreed and seemed relieved we weren't going to take her to a dungeon and whip her."

127

Alchfrid smiled. "I do wonder what the Darkrose says about us sometimes."

"You trust her to do so?"

"She said she would. By giving her my trust, it makes it much harder for her to decide to betray us."

Ululla smiled. "Seek to believe those around us. There are more truths than lies, and if you seek lies, then that is what you shall find."

Alchfrid replied, "Passage twelve twenty-two. The converse is true as well. We must look for truth, unless we have good reason to think the speaker is purposely avoiding the truth. I didn't know Sister Sybbyl before and thus had no reason to doubt what she said."

Ululla listened carefully to his words, to his interpretation of the Book of Redemption. *Whenever he speaks I gain more knowledge, even on something I already thought I knew and understood.* "May I ask when is Sister Elwendia scheduled to join our order?"

"Normally there is period of reflection first, even with those from the Darkrose who are already witches and understand the Cycle of Life. However, I sense Sister Elwendia would greatly appreciate you being there for her initiation and likely as her advocate. I have spoken with Altus Rector Muriel. She has agreed to have the initiation tomorrow morning."

"Thank you, I'm sure she'll be pleased to hear that."

"Perhaps you can guide her around the terradomus and allow her to be familiar with the layout and introduce her to some of the witches."

"I shall."

"Excellent." He pressed his fingers on the desk.

Ululla had studied body language enough to know he was about to broach a subject he considered sensitive.

"We may have a situation developing with the use of magic and spells from one or more new groups. When the Dwykath forces invaded Lorem, a spell was cast to make the defenders sick and weak. The Whiterose altus rector was concerned about the use of the dark spell and initiated contact with the Darkrose altus rector to see if they had any knowledge of the spell and expressed a willingness to cooperate to remove or counteract it. What they discovered was the Darkrose were as surprised as they were. As they discussed the best counter spell, and as you know two counter spells may have an unpredictable result, someone else imitated a counter spell, effectively cancelling the original spell.

"We do not know who cast the first spell or who cast the counter spell. I say this to you under strict confidence. If you detect any use of magic you cannot attribute to a user, make certain you inform me as soon as practical to do so. The altus councillium is very concerned about this latest development."

Ululla nodded. "Do you suspect the Blackrain in this?"

"Frankly, we are not sure and are merely speculating at this point. If it is the Blackrain it is a departure from their usual behaviour of not extending their influence past their own properties. If they are involved, are they the ones who cast the first or second spell? We know so little about them."

"I understand. I shall be observant of any magic or spells I come across."

Alchfrid leaned back. "Now I suppose I best tell you of your new task." He smiled as she took in a quick inward breath. "Your journey is nearly complete, and you have fulfilled your appointed tasks admirably. It is time for you to spread your wisdom more effectively. You are, I assume, familiar with the Jital Terradomus?"

Ululla spent time years ago in Jital, a growing city a few miles from Knavemire. When she was there, work was being done to expand the size of the terradomus, more than doubling the size of the original. "Yes, I suspect most of the above ground work has been completed now for the renovations."

"True, there's still much work to be done to carve out the ground underneath. However, the reason I ask is to inform you it will be your new home. They have need of a new keeper, and they are expecting you. A place for you to settle down, if you should wish."

Ululla's lip trembled for a moment. "Thank you, Altus Councillor Alchfrid. I do long to stop wandering."

"The position of keeper, in this case, is not meant to be permanent. You are to prepare to take over as altus rector eventually, when the time is right. Altus Rector Howrand is aware of your coming and the circumstances and will give you more details at his discretion."

Ululla remained silent, surprised at the offering of being an altus rector at such an important terradomus.

"Peace be with you, Sister Ululla." He stood. "May you find what you desire the most."

Ululla replied automatically to his greeting. "And to you, Altus Councillor Alchfrid." *Home. I finally have a home.*

* * * *

Sybbyl sought out Bruhamoff in the dining room, waiting for him by drinking cups of tea as others came and went to eat. She knew it was one place he was certain to go to. When he entered the room carrying a bowl and a large sandwich, she hurried to where he was about to sit at one of the long tables.

"Brother Bruhamoff, may I join you?"

He sat, refusing to look at her. "I cannot prevent you from doing so."

"Please. I ask only that I may speak to you and try to explain." Curious heads turned slightly in their direction. There wasn't any way their conversation could be kept confidential. She sat across from him.

Bruhamoff began to eat, looking past her.

"I wouldn't have put the poison in your drink, Brother Bruhamoff. I was sent to spy, that is true. I was also told to make friends with you, but I found it easy to like you, and I truly care about your wellbeing. I regret any hurt I've caused you and wish I could prove my sincerity. Is there anything I can do that will make you believe I care for you very much? Soon I'll be banished from here, and I only want you not to think badly of me."

He glanced at her, unable to miss seeing the wetness around her eyes, she was sure. He continued to eat.

Slowly she stood. "Thank you, Brother Bruhamoff, for listening to me." She turned to walk away.

"I forgive you."

She stopped, quickly looking back at him.

He spoke as he looked at her. "I'm leaving tomorrow morning. I don't want to leave you upset. Peace be with you, Sister Sybbyl."

"And with you, Brother Bruhamoff." She walked away, wiping her eyes.

* * * *

Ululla showed Elwendia around the terradomus, ending in a library.

"A most impressive collection of books and scrolls. It may be even larger than our own...I mean the Umbravox Terradomus' library." She looked around, seeing several copies of the Book of Redemption stacked as they waited to be sent to other cities. To maintain accuracy, copies were only made from books determined to be error free.

"The Book of Redemption. I shall have to study it even more now. We have a single copy of it in the Umbravox Terradomus, and I did study it briefly there. It's not left open, and one has to have permission to read it. I suppose it is felt it may contradict what the Book of Destiny has to say."

"Interesting. We have a few copies of the Book of Destiny here, and any one may read it. Actually, one of the copies we have comes from the time of the split of the Whiterose from the Darkrose. That we keep protected, but the other copies made from it are free to be used." She took Elwendia to where a copy of the Book of Destiny rested on a pedestal.

Elwendia smiled. "I believe it still to be of value, although the interpretation of it may need to be revised." She touched the book and carefully flipped through a few of the pages and read a passage. She frowned. "That's odd."

"What is wrong?"

"Believe me when I say I'm intimately familiar with the Book of Destiny. What I've read here is not exactly the same as the Book of Destiny at the Umbravox. You said this is a copy from the time of the split of our orders?"

"It is."

"If this copy is accurate, someone has made a slight change in the wording of the Book of Destiny." She looked at Ululla. "I wonder if there's an error or it was done on purpose." She placed her finger on the well-known Prophecy of the Warrior.

Ululla read the passage.

131

Change always occurs. Sometimes the change happens so slowly we are unaware of it unless we look back and see the progression. Other times, change can happen rapidly, challenging our ability to adapt.

There are events coming in the future, which, will change the world. A strong warrior, of blue eyes and red hair dies, and gives life to a man who works wood. He will be the seed of change that will unite the Umbravox, helping to bring it on the path of peace. The dark clouds will challenge us, and it will require the joining of all the houses to defeat it.

Protect the new king, though he is not of true blood. It is he that can unite all when he returns from his quest.

"What is different in your book? Ours has exactly the same wording."

Elwendia pointed to a single word. "Where this line says 'helping to bring it on the path of peace.' Ours state 'helping to keep it on the path of peace'. A minor change of one word, but it implies we have already achieved peace. Considering the attempt to harm Brother Bruhamoff, I would say peace has not been achieved yet."

Ululla put her arm around Elwendia. "I suppose the change was done rather optimistically. As you point out, we have not attained peace yet. We should inform the altus councillor of this discrepancy, but it may not mean much other than ego."

Elwendia nodded, as she stared ahead. "I feel a bit annoyed that they would change anything in the prophecy, although I suppose the words about the warrior are still there."

"I think it's the most vital part of the message, the part we need to pay heed to."

* * * *

Bruhamoff took a cup of tea to his room, preparing for a good night's sleep before his journey in the morning. To his surprise, an oil lamp gave the room a soft glow as he entered. Moments later, his eyes saw the form of Sybbyl lying under the blanket in his bed. Her shoulders were bare as she sat up, holding up the blanket to her chest.

"Sybbyl?"

"Your final night here. I was hoping I could make it memorable." She released the blanket. "I assure you I don't have any hidden poison on me."

He slowly made his way to the bed. "You have already made my stay here memorable, but this will be a special night."

* * * *

Morning came as Elwendia waited at the side entrance to the Hall of Sentential with Ululla. She looked up at the high domed ceiling, studying the intricate design of the coloured stones under the yellow light of lanterns hanging at intervals along the curved walls. She could just make out the inscription worked along the perimeter and silently read the words. Her attention was soon drawn toward the top of the dome where coloured pieces of triangle shaped glass were joined together. From there she knew light from the morning sun would cause a play of symbols on the floor. As the sun progressed across the sky, the symbols would alter, until the evening sun gave a final message. It was the symbol from the morning sun to start the proceedings she waited for. The audience in the hall was quiet, speaking in whispers, but Elwendia could tell the hall was almost filled.

"Don't be nervous. The ceremony isn't long, and you do know the words."

"I'm not worried about the words." She looked at Ululla. "Despite being a witch for many years and quite used to nudity, being naked in front of all these people gives me pause."

"I understand your anxiety."

"I guess it proves just how much I want to join the Whiterose." She gave Ululla a grin.

A spot of blue light suddenly touched the floor in front of where Altus Rector Muriel stood, quickly blossoming to a coloured pattern.

Muriel spoke in a clear voice, amplified by the shape of the dome.

"The morning sun has come in to herald in a new day. A day we can choose to do as we will, a day we can accept what happens around us, and a day we can help make better than the day before. The morning sun returns every day, reminding us of the past, but also each day is new. The morning sun gives us the promise of a new day, also gives us a chance to celebrate a new member of our order." She turned to the side entrance.

"Sister Ululla, are you willing to advocate a new member for the Whiterose?"

"I am."

"What be her name?"

"Her name is Sister Elwendia."

"If she is willing to participate in the initiation ceremony, bring her forward."

Elwendia stepped forward with Ululla gently touching her arm to guide her. She wore only a long white cloak secured at the neck by a metal clasp. Elwendia used one hand to carefully hold the middle together to stop it from billowing out, although she knew the heavy cloth resisted being opened. They reached the centre of the room, standing in front of the coloured light that separated them from the altus rector.

The altus rector spoke. "Sister Elwendia, are you certain you wish to join the Whiterose?"

"Yes, I wish to join the Whiterose."

"Will you follow the Book of Redemption as well as you are able?"

"Yes, I will follow the Book of Redemption as well as I am able."

"Do you believe and understand the Cycle of Life?"

"Yes, I believe and understand the Cycle of Life."

"Explain it to me."

"The Cycle of Life tells us there is not an end, nor a beginning of life. All life has a past longer than we can remember and will continue longer than we know. We are part of the circle. The past has placed us where we are, and what we do now will influence the future. Like a circle, the past, present, and future are all joined together."

"Sister Ululla, please remove her cloak."

Elwendia stood straight as the cloak was removed. The room was warm but goose bumps prickled her skin.

Muriel stepped forward into the light and placed a hand on Elwendia's shoulder.

"Kneel, Sister Elwendia, and accept a cleansing of your past."

Elwendia kneeled, following the instructions Ululla gave her earlier by placing her hands at the small of her back, and looked up.

The altus rector used a large pitcher to slowly pour water over her head, her shoulders, back, front, and finally her legs. When the last of the water was drained from the pitcher, she spoke again.

"Welcome, Sister Elwendia, to the Whiterose order. May peace always be your guide and follow you."

Ululla helped her rise and wrapped the cloak around her again. She led Elwendia in the opposite direction from where they entered to a small room where dry clothes waited for her. She gave Elwendia a hug.

"Congratulations."

Elwendia smiled. "When we first met, I never would have believed this was my destiny. My heart is at peace again." She laughed. "I even survived being naked in front of all those people. I'm glad the ceremony is in the morning. The light is weaker then."

* * * *

Ululla smiled as she watched Sybbyl give Bruhamoff a long kiss goodbye.

"Come on, Brother Bruhamoff. If we don't leave soon, she'll be kissing you goodbye again tomorrow morning."

He gave her one final kiss and hurried to catch up to her.

"Sorry for being late."

"That's all right. She seems very nice and quite taken with you."

He blushed. "I asked her to consider joining the Whiterose."

"What did she say?"

"She said she was thinking about it, but her family are all part of the Darkrose, and she doesn't want to leave them. Still, I know she was influenced by how Altus Councillor Alchfrid treated her."

"And by you. Maybe she won't join the Whiterose, but she has a better understanding of us she'll tell others."

"The Book of Redemption tells us the path is laid one stone at a time."

"Excellent, Brother Bruhamoff. You're showing an understanding of the scripture."

"You have taught me to not just read, but to comprehend the meaning behind the words."

Ululla smiled. "You have changed much since we left Claireston. You seem much more confident and knowledgeable. I'm very pleased to see that." *You have also changed from being a boy into a man.*

rare cases a mixture of gold, allowed a good variance of
on. Coins far from a kingdom were often devalued slightly. In
of Tumulton, trade was done with several kingdoms, and the
was usually treated as equal.

c didn't ask what the food or drink was. He wasn't offered a
nd knew it meant there was only one type of food and drink
It likely meant a stew, bread, and cheese to eat. The drink would
vine cut with water. Most travellers did not trust water by itself,
contaminated water was an easy way to get sick. The alcohol in
usually made the water safe to drink. Pure wine was preferable
ustomer, but added to the proprietor's expense. Ale could also be
t was normally provided in large barrels.

bit stew, heavy brown bread, and white cheese were placed in
him, and the server waited for him to pay before bringing him
.

ic put two coins on the table. "Some of your table and chairs are
of repair."

an't be helped. Papa ain't much good at fixing stuff. Mom and I
ave the time."

ow about for the price of a meal and room, I fix some of the
re?"

ric expected her to talk to her mother about his offer, but she
after a moment of consideration.

ure, providing you fix them good. Otherwise I'll charge for the
"

No worries. I can work wood."

* * * *

Alric worked in a corner of the tea house. By his left side sat several
hes stripped of leaves and twigs. On his right a chair lay on its side,
alized for parts. He used his knife to shape a stick into a shape
ximating a chair leg, tapering one end slightly. A shadow crossed
nt of him, and he looked up.

he server stood, evaluating his work. "Pretty good. The chairs you
are sturdy now."

Chapter Seventeen

In the early morning of the next day, Alric was making reasonable
time as he urged Darkian down the sticky mud road, despite the rain that
pelted down. He didn't know if Willis had sent a search party for him,
despite Tybalt reporting his death. As there were few serviceable roads
in Fringella it would be easy to determine his route. He had filled up his
water bag earlier, and still had a small ration of food. However, he didn't
want to use it up and then be dependent on catching game. Hunting
should be easier later as he left the low-lying areas of Fringella and to the
foothills preceding the mountains which marked the border to the
Kingdom of Allisure. As the landscaped changed, so did the creatures
inhabiting them. Certainly, his preference was to deer, rather than the
reptiles that dominated the swamp areas. Killing any of them with only a
knife and sword was a different matter.

Sheets of rain forced Alric to seek shelter among the trees. The road
quickly turned into a muddy soup and visibility made it difficult to see
more than a few feet. After several hot days, the following thunderstorm
wasn't unexpected, and now the rain promised to refill the numerous
small lakes in Fringella.

"We might as well wait it out here, Darkian."

Alric wasn't impressed by the region. There were some hardy
individuals who preferred to live in the rugged area. He had briefly
considered doing so as a way to avoid detection, but decided it was not
how he wanted to live. The swamps and small lakes ensured a steady
supply of mosquitoes and other biting insects. Giant lizards, crocodiles,
and packs of wild dogs were the common predators, and a traveller was
smart to avoid travelling at night between the small towns. Alric had

little choice. He climbed into one of the small trees and found a Y shaped branch that could support his weight. He left Darkian loose, not wanting the horse to be tied up in case it was attacked. He was confident Darkian would return on his command.

When the rain let up again, he went back on the road. Darkian plodded along slowly, sinking into the muck with each step.

"Well, Darkian, I may be slightly crazy talking to a horse, but I doubt I'm going to have anyone to talk to for a while. I hope we can reach Tumulton by sunset and take the southern road toward Allisure in the morning. We sure don't want to go through Torland and meet up with the conflict there." He patted the horse on the neck. "You're doing good. No complaining about travelling through the heat or the rain."

The sun reappeared, and soon the muggy heat surrounded them again. Alric wiped the sweat from his forehead and looked past the road into the forest. He searched for a change in the scenery of the short trees and bush dotting the uneven ground. Mud, rock, and poor looking vegetation didn't make hunting for food an enviable task. He did see small animals occasionally dart quickly from one concealed spot to another. He also saw a pair of hawks circle in the air. So far there wasn't anything to make him believe leaving the road would warrant the trouble of trying to capture food.

Patience is the key here. It's too hot to spend energy chasing down something that can outrun me. The bow and arrow is something I could really use, but there's no point in worrying about it now. I should see something soon. If not, there's always Tumulton where I can buy dinner and supplies.

Two men on horses approached him, and he casually rested his hand on his sword. The men eyed him warily and as the second one passed along his side, gave him a small nod.

They didn't look like highwaymen, but Alric was aware hunger would push some to robbing for food. Alric wondered if he was smaller or looked weak, whether they would have tried to take his meager possessions. Shortly thereafter a horse, pulling a small two-wheel cart came by. The couple sitting on the front looked young and had toughness in their faces. Eric decided they were likely farmers and not especially fond of strangers. They ignored him. Although he was tempted to ask for

food, he decided it was best to leave them reaction.

The traffic increased slightly as he approac road dried out, travel became easier and faster need to urge the horse faster. He seemed to kn allow a rest sooner.

The town was elongated, following the rive side. The opposite bank was high, making it di living there to reach the water. Alric followed th he reached near the centre of town, picked out a two-story high building with the second level con rent. Most of the buildings, and the roads, were grey rock, giving the town a unified, if dull, appea

Alric secured Darkian to a pole set at the side other horses shared the pole with him, although higher than the next biggest one. A well stood cranked a handle to lift up a bucket of water. He Darkian, letting the horse get his fill.

"I'll be back later." He patted the horse a entrance. His eyes adjusted to the dimmer light as take in the scattered tables and the long counter sep portly, dark-haired woman stirred something in a steam escaping as she wiped her brow. A younger her carried a plate to a guest sitting at a square table table and sat on the wobbly chair. He frowned when the same dance.

A few minutes later the younger woman came quick smile. "You want food or just a drink?"

"Both. How much for a room?"

"Three bronze. Either Allisure, Fringella, or Cady

"I'll take a room as well."

Alric understood the reason for the need for di Some of the smaller kingdoms, such as the former Kin didn't have their own currency but used those kingdoms. Those that produced their own coins genera sized coins to give the same approximate value. Bron

and in
nominat
the case
coinage

Alri
choice
offered.
be red
knowin
the win
to the
used, b

Ra
front o
the wir

Al
in need

"(
don't

"I
furnitu

A
replie

"
room.

"

brand
canni
appr
in fr

fixe

food, he decided it was best to leave them alone, not sure of their reaction.

The traffic increased slightly as he approached Tumulton, and as the road dried out, travel became easier and faster for Darkian. Alric didn't need to urge the horse faster. He seemed to know a quicker pace would allow a rest sooner.

The town was elongated, following the river almost entirely on one side. The opposite bank was high, making it difficult for any residents living there to reach the water. Alric followed the main street, and when he reached near the centre of town, picked out a tea house at random, a two-story high building with the second level containing a few rooms for rent. Most of the buildings, and the roads, were made of the same, dark grey rock, giving the town a unified, if dull, appearance.

Alric secured Darkian to a pole set at the side of the tea house. Two other horses shared the pole with him, although he stood a full hand higher than the next biggest one. A well stood at the back, and Alric cranked a handle to lift up a bucket of water. He carried the bucket to Darkian, letting the horse get his fill.

"I'll be back later." He patted the horse and went to the front entrance. His eyes adjusted to the dimmer light as he entered, pausing to take in the scattered tables and the long counter separating the kitchen. A portly, dark-haired woman stirred something in a pot on the iron stove, steam escaping as she wiped her brow. A younger, slimmer version of her carried a plate to a guest sitting at a square table. Alric chose a round table and sat on the wobbly chair. He frowned when he saw the table did the same dance.

A few minutes later the younger woman came over, giving him a quick smile. "You want food or just a drink?"

"Both. How much for a room?"

"Three bronze. Either Allisure, Fringella, or Cadyvia."

"I'll take a room as well."

Alric understood the reason for the need for different currencies. Some of the smaller kingdoms, such as the former Kingdom of Kireland, didn't have their own currency but used those of neighbouring kingdoms. Those that produced their own coins generally used the same sized coins to give the same approximate value. Bronze, nickel, silver,

and in rare cases a mixture of gold, allowed a good variance of nomination. Coins far from a kingdom were often devalued slightly. In the case of Tumulton, trade was done with several kingdoms, and the coinage was usually treated as equal.

Alric didn't ask what the food or drink was. He wasn't offered a choice and knew it meant there was only one type of food and drink offered. It likely meant a stew, bread, and cheese to eat. The drink would be red wine cut with water. Most travellers did not trust water by itself, knowing contaminated water was an easy way to get sick. The alcohol in the wine usually made the water safe to drink. Pure wine was preferable to the customer, but added to the proprietor's expense. Ale could also be used, but was normally provided in large barrels.

Rabbit stew, heavy brown bread, and white cheese were placed in front of him, and the server waited for him to pay before bringing him the wine.

Alric put two coins on the table. "Some of your table and chairs are in need of repair."

"Can't be helped. Papa ain't much good at fixing stuff. Mom and I don't have the time."

"How about for the price of a meal and room, I fix some of the furniture?"

Alric expected her to talk to her mother about his offer, but she replied after a moment of consideration.

"Sure, providing you fix them good. Otherwise I'll charge for the room."

"No worries. I can work wood."

* * * *

Alric worked in a corner of the tea house. By his left side sat several branches stripped of leaves and twigs. On his right a chair lay on its side, cannibalized for parts. He used his knife to shape a stick into a shape approximating a chair leg, tapering one end slightly. A shadow crossed in front of him, and he looked up.

The server stood, evaluating his work. "Pretty good. The chairs you fixed are sturdy now."

"Thanks. Not hard when you know how." He twisted the leg into place, pressing it in the bottom of the seat of the chair. "My name is Alric, by the way."

"Agnes." She passed him a tankard. "Did you travel from the west?"

"Yes."

"Did you hear of any trouble at Lorem?"

Alric quickly looked down at the chair he was working on, speaking to the floor. "No, can't say I did."

"There are rumours Lorem has been attacked by Dwykath but no word on who won."

"Sorry, I can't help you. I guess I must have already passed Lorem when it happened." He took a drink from the tankard, finding the wine was uncut.

"That's all right. Tumulton has changed hands before. We have been part Cadyvia and Kireland at one time. We've kept the same town administration. Different crests and uniforms, but the same people."

"Tell me, do you have many witches here?"

"Doesn't every town?" She sat on one of the repaired chairs. "We have two different groups. They get along okay, no arguments, but keep to themselves. They sometimes come in here for tea and seem nice enough. Rarely see the same ones twice. Funny thing is no one sees them on the road leading to or from town. I hear they use tunnels instead of roads."

"I think you're right there. Witches like to keep their secrets." He flipped the chair he was working on to its legs. "There. Another one done."

"You've earned your meal and bed. You can stop now."

"Thanks. It felt good working with wood again. What's the road to Allisure like?"

"Pretty good. Higher elevation, so it stays dryer. Just be careful about spending the night along the way. Wolves, big ones, hunt in packs as you approach the mountains. They ain't scared to take down a lone man at night. There are also cougars and bears, but the wolves are the worse. If you're in a group, they generally leave you alone."

"Then I'll get an early start. I should be able to make it to Asper before nightfall."

"I'll make you breakfast before you leave." She took his hand. "Come, I'll show you where you can sleep."

Alric followed her upstairs to a room at the end of a hall. The corner room was obviously lived in. He quickly scanned the bed, clothes hanging at the far wall, the painting on the wall of a flowering garden, a chair with clothes draped over the back, and a dresser with a wash basin in front of the lone window. Alric took a final drink of the wine, put his arm around Agnes and kissed her.

She responded enthusiastically, pushing him toward the bed. He was mildly surprised at her strength, and soon realized while her face showed years of hard work, her body had retained its youth. She sat on him, pulling off her top, kissing him. He slowly and firmly pushed her on her back, taking control of the bed. After undressing her, he set a slower pace, determined to make the evening last longer. Alric sensed her loneliness, guessing she didn't often invite men up to her room.

Afterward, he took time to talk to her before they drifted off to sleep, with her curled up against him.

"You're a good man, Alric. You can stay here as long as you want."

"Thank you, but I must be travelling in the morning."

She laughed. "You're so polite. You work hard, do what you promise, and treat women with respect. A rarity in these parts." She kissed his chest. "You be careful on your journey."

"I shall." He stroked her hair as she fell asleep.

* * * *

Alric woke alone. Stumbling in the dark, he dressed, opened the door, and headed down the hall. The downstairs was only slightly brighter, the oil lamps casting a pale light to the kitchen and dining area. The older woman gave him a studied look as she laboured in the kitchen. Alric nodded at her and sat at a table near the centre of the room where a lamp hung from the ceiling.

Alric waited, aware of the gaze from the kitchen. He turned to the noise of a door closing, seeing Agnes enter carrying in two cloth sacks. She walked past his table, placing the sacks on the counter separating the kitchen. She turned to him, smiling.

"Good mornin'. You're up early."

"I slept enough."

Agnes walked around the counter. "I'll get you breakfast."

He looked around the empty room, determining he was a bit early for their normal opening time. "Sorry, I guess I'm a bit early."

"No worries." Shortly later, Agnes placed a bowl and a mug of tea on his table.

Alric looked at the fried egg on top of the boiled oats. He pushed a spoon into the mixture, causing steam to escape. *A bit different breakfast than what I'm used to, but it should be filling.* "Thanks, it looks good."

Agnes sat at the table, watching him eat. "Are you going to be coming back this way?"

"Not likely. Going to Allisure to work."

She smiled. "As a woodworker?"

"It's what I do best."

"I've a feeling you're good at a lot of things." She stood. "I best get busy. Good travels."

Alric finished his breakfast, waved goodbye to Agnes, who was hurrying to serve customers, and headed outside. The sun was just breaking free of the horizon, warming up the pools of mist clinging to the lower parts of the street. Darkian snorted as Alric steered him back on the road. The horse acted like he wanted to gallop, but he held him back.

"Easy, big fellow. You're going to need your energy later when we climb the mountains, but first I need to buy a bow and some arrows."

Alric stopped at a shop and picked up a bow and arrows, finding the proprietor was quite willing to bargain down his selling price. The bow and arrows were better made than he expected, although he knew he could have done a superior job if he had the tools.

The road after Tumulton was dryer than the one going in. It also climbed steadily, and the vegetation changed. The trees were evergreens and the ground was covered with spruce, pine needles, and grasses. Alric looked at the passing forest, not seeing, but feeling animals around him. Darkian snorted occasionally, picking up his pace despite the hills he faced.

Alric focused on one spot, a clearing between the trees. Moments passed. A streak of black and tan fur moved past the opening. It was quick, but Alric recognized it as a wolf. *We're being paced. That was one. How many are there?*

Darkian became more agitated, and Alric allowed him to gallop for a short time. When Alric slowed down the horse, he seemed more relaxed.

"Looks like they gave up, Darkian. This is only noon. I doubt they'll do anything until dark, but I guess you never know."

The sun slowly slid across the sky. Alric reached for his bow and held an arrow in his fingers. "Okay, Darkian, let's take a break here." He pulled the reins, steering the horse to a stream flowing over rocks. He looked around for any predators and dismounted. The horse made his way to the stream while Alric quietly walked along the bank. Alric was confident enough in his ability to use the bow and arrow to at least capture some small game. If a bird or rabbit was close enough, he was sure he could hit it. *If I had a string I could tie it to the arrow and try fishing, but there's little point in losing an arrow and a fish.*

A movement of brown captured his attention. At first it was hard to see the rabbit against the scattered rocks, but a moment later, the arrow flew across the open space. Alric was pleased with his shot. *Looks like I have dinner.*

It took longer than he wanted to cook the rabbit over the small fire. Despite the warmth of the day, many of the twigs he found were slightly damp. The fire was slow to build and gave off more smoke than he liked. Still, the skinned rabbit tasted good, and he quickly consumed the meal.

Darkian seemed to know when he was finished and wandered over to where the fire was reduced to smoldering ashes.

"You're right. Time to hit the road again."

Darkian was eager to travel again, and Alric let the horse set his own pace. A short distance later, Alric spotted a large cat, staring at him from above on the ridge above the road. Moments later the cat began to follow him.

"I don't like the look of the cougar." He urged Darkian to increase his speed, and the cat soon lost interest.

Traffic coming the other way was sporadic and usually consisted of a group of riders together. A family of six riders strung apart approached him, and he held up his hand to speak to the lead rider, a man approaching middle age.

"There's a cougar up ahead. If it attacks, it'll likely be the last in line. I suggest you close ranks for a bit."

"Thanks. I'll have an arrow ready."

"How far to Asper?"

"About two hours, maybe a tad more. There's a great bear with a couple of cubs back there." He hooked a thumb behind him. "Just be careful not to get between them, otherwise its safe."

"Are you travelling all the way to Tumulton? You'll get there before nightfall."

"No, my brother has a cabin up a ways. He's a trapper. Likes the isolation I guess." He gave a shrug.

Alric nodded. "Safe travels then." He urged Darkian forward. Alric knew there were men who preferred to live in the woods, making money by selling hides and living off the land. It didn't appeal to him, but some liked it compared to the crowded conditions of living near a castle where the majority of the population lived in less than ideal conditions. The other reason for living alone was to avoid the authorities for one reason or another.

The road became dryer, although not packed hard. Alric noticed an increase in wildlife, especially in deer, rabbits, and birds. Insects constantly buzzed around as the forest became thicker with evergreens. He paid attention for signs of the great bear and her cubs. Great bears were known for their temper and their willingness to attack anything, including a horse and its rider.

The warm sun and dry air were making him thirsty, and he reasoned Darkian was feeling the same way. Alric decided to go back to the river. He couldn't see it from the road but didn't believe it would be difficult to locate if he used one of the numerous paths between the trees. A few minutes later he saw a pathway, and judging by its size and the broken branches lying about, determined it had likely been made by deer. He cautiously turned Darkian, paying attention to his reaction to possible danger. Alric wasn't too surprised at the shortness of the path, knowing the road was designed to keep close to it. The sound of the river suddenly jumped at him as he left the cover of trees. It hissed and sloshed as it tumbled over rocks on its downward journey from high in the mountains, looking fresh and appealing.

Alric jumped off Darkian and allowed the horse to wander to the river to drink. He followed, carrying his nearly empty water sack, and refilled it in the cool water. He was tempted to undress and spend a few minutes in the water, but decided if a great bear was around anywhere, it was likely near the river where fish could be caught.

His attention was drawn to the sound of a woman's laughter, and he turned to see four people around the bend in the river. There were two women, naked, in the water while a male and another woman sat eating as they watched them. A fire blazed near the shoreline. Alric stared at them, and suspected they were witches by their build and how they dressed. The man suddenly took notice of him and stood, calling out to the others in the water.

Alric waved. The fire meant they likely had stopped to eat, and he realized he was hungry. *Perhaps, they will sell me the leftovers for a few coppers.* The man slowly waved back.

He whistled at Darkian and walked to the group. The man was tall, nearly his own height, although slimmer. The two women in the river lowered themselves to their necks as the third woman shouted out a warning and stood behind the man.

Alric stopped several feet away and called out. "I mean you no harm, just a warning there's a cougar and a great bear with cubs in this area."

The man answered back. "Thank you, stranger. We have taken precautions against wildlife and are not in any danger."

"Then I wish you good day." *I think they're too fearful of me to approach any closer and to ask to purchase food.* He turned toward Darkian and prepared to mount when the woman's voice spoke.

"Wait, we have food if you are hungry."

He looked back, seeing the dried fruit, biscuits, and stew they were eating. His mouth watered as he stared.

She smiled. "We have plenty, and it is filling."

Alric glanced at the women still hiding in the water. "Are you sure I wouldn't be intruding?"

"Your company would be appreciated."

Alric slipped off his horse and averted his eyes, turning around to pat Darkian. Giving them a few moments of privacy, he waited for the two young women hurrying to put on their dresses. He had heard witches were not overly modest about the human body, but he also believed the young women were not comfortable being naked in front of a stranger. When he turned around again and strode toward the fire, they were dressed and waited behind the male witch.

They exchanged introductions, and Alric sat on the pebbled soil in a circle with the others. Leesha, the youngest looking woman in the water earlier, blushed when he caught her staring at him. He gave a tight smile as he looked at her and saw goose bumps on her slim arms. He stood, took off his vest, and passed it to her. "You can wear this until I leave. It'll warm you up."

The young witch took the vest and slipped it on, tucking her arms inside it. The vest dwarfed her. "Thank you. It's heavy."

"You be welcome. Which direction are you heading? Toward Asper?"

The man visibly relaxed after they sat to eat. He understood if Alric meant any harm, he would've done it by now. Derikson answered. "Yes, we should be there by late evening."

"I'm going there myself. Darkian will get me there a bit sooner than that though."

Mystilla, the woman who had remained on the shore asked, "You don't appear to have any fear of witches."

He looked at her face as he answered, noting she appeared to be the oldest of the four. She was also, he suspected, despite Derikson's bravado in standing up to him, in charge of the group. "I've had the opportunity to see witches differently than most."

She looked at his sword. "That's a warrior's sword you carry. Not meant for defending, but rather for attack. Your leather vest has marks on it, as if you've been in battle."

Alric was silent for a few seconds and then responded. "I was a soldier once. Now I'm leaving to live a different life."

"You say leaving. Does that mean your journey is at the beginning?"

"Yes. I left the army just a few days ago. I'm going to Allisure to live." He ate the dried fruit and a biscuit he dipped in a bowl of stew. The heavy food quickly filled him.

"That must be difficult to do, leaving a life behind."

Alric chuckled. "Actually, a witch told me if I didn't leave the army, I would die soon. Another witch told me how I was to leave. It seems a plan was laid out for me. I do regret I didn't have a chance to tell my parents I'm alive and going to become a woodworker. My father would be pleased to hear that."

"Where do they live?" asked Systalla, the older of the women bathing earlier.

"Lagary, a small town in northern Dwykath."

She nodded and reached into a backpack near her. She retrieved a piece of sharpened charcoal and a rolled up piece of parchment. In careful strokes, she began to write.

"Tell me their names and this message will be sent to them. It'll take weeks, but they shall receive the news you're alive and working as a woodworker."

Alric told her their names. He understood witches had various ways of sending information. The tunnels between the terradomus carried sounds for long distances, and the use of bells above ground could send coded messages. Paper messages were handed to witches travelling toward a destination, with the note being passed to several witches before arriving to the recipient. He was sure there were also methods they used he hadn't heard about.

"Thank you, and thank you for the food. I should return to travelling."

"Peace be with you, Alric."

"And to you." He stood. "Safe travels." He took back his vest from the young woman. "I hope you feel warm enough now."

"Yes, thank you." Her eyes focused on his, and her teeth showed as she smiled. "I hope our paths cross again someday."

Alric mounted Darkian and headed back to the road. *I sure keep running into witches. Maybe our paths are aligned as Ysmay as suggested.*

* * * *

Asper stood on a plain between two peaks, where the road from Tumulton led to Allisure. Travellers could bypass Asper via a small pathway, but most stopped at the large town. The disadvantage of stopping at Asper was higher than average prices for food and lodging, plus the fee for entering the town.

One of the two guards held up his hand as Alric approached. Asper was surrounded by a stone wall twice the height of a man with an entrance that could be closed off with an iron gate. The stone was gathered from the surrounding mountains and was loosely fitted together. It didn't appear to be meant to stop an attack by an army, but rather one to keep wildlife from entering. He halted Darkian and peered down at the guard.

"Two bronze to enter the State of Asper."

Alric understood Asper's isolation allowed its autonomy and to be called a state. The charge to enter Asper wasn't unexpected. Independent cities often had to raise additional income to provide a significant military force in relation to the population.

"Much traffic coming through?" Alric asked as he passed over the money.

"Yeah, been busy earlier today. Slowed down some now."

"Recommend a place to stay the night with decent food?"

"Harrar Inn. Turn left at the church and you'll run right into it." The guard pointed at down the street at a steeple.

Alric waved his thanks. Asper looked prosperous, with the street merchants doing a steady business. He saw three female slaves, their wide leather collars indicating their owner. He knew they also carried a tattoo on the top of their foot or hand to insure the removal of the collar wasn't going to make them appear to be free women. The fact the three slaves didn't seem to cause undue attention meant they were not uncommon in Asper and provided more proof the small city was wealthy. The church he passed looked to be in good repair, and as he left the main street, the secondary roads were also in good shape and the buildings not lacking in size.

Might be an expensive place to stay tonight.

The Harrar Inn was a three-story affair, with the upper floor set in from the rest of the building, giving a wide walkway around the entire floor.

Alric entered the inn after tying up Darkian, pushing open the large, heavy wood door. The interior was a mix of bright light coming in through the windows and dark shadows where the sun couldn't reach. To his left was a combination eating and drinking venue. His right was blocked by a wooden counter and to the side, a set of stone steps led upstairs.

The young blonde woman smiled at him as he turned toward the counter. "Are you looking for a room?"

Alric nodded as he saw the tattoo on the back of her right hand. "How much for one night?"

"Five Bronze." She saw him frown. "It's the standard rate in Asper. You may find cheaper, but not nearly as good. Clean beddings and water in each room."

"For such a price, I expect wine, not water." He placed a five-bronze coin down on the worn counter.

She laughed. "At least you didn't ask if I was included, as some travellers have."

He smiled. "Then I would have expected the price to be much higher."

She gave him a mischievous grin. "Oh, I bet you can charm the dress right off a girl." She wagged her finger at him. "But you best not waste such talent on me. I've been bought a while back."

Alric pointed to the other room. "I think I'll have a bite to eat and drink before going to the room."

The wood furniture was solid and he had a choice of two meals, opting for a bread pudding rather than the rabbit. Ale was available, and he tasted the dark brew, pleased with the flavour and the chill in it. He guessed the stone floor assured the barrels of ale never became too warm.

A short, dark skinned man walked about the room, inspecting the windows and the cleanliness of the tables. He paused at Alric's table.

"Everything to your satisfaction?"

"I might have to sell my horse to pay for the food and room, but everything is fine." He grinned at the wide shouldered man.

White teeth flashed. "Good to hear."

"You the owner?"

"I am indeed."

"Tell me, what do you do with guests having trouble affording your rates? Some families be hard pressed to afford even the entrance fee to the city."

The owner sat at an empty chair across from Alric. "Well, the truth is most people wouldn't want to sleep at night out in the open. Lots of danger there, especially for those who aren't used to weapons. That's what makes Asper such a popular spot, a nice day's journey from Allisure and Tumulton. If a person can't afford to enter Asper, or pay for room and board, we don't turn them away. It would be almost a death sentence. We let them sleep in the stables or give them odd jobs to do to earn food. I have some of the cleanest floors in Asper." He laughed.

"I noticed you have a slave girl at the front. That's not uncommon here, is it?"

"No, can't say it is. I bought her and her older sister from a merchant passing through who had too many slaves. They help do the work. Wife ain't too happy having them here, but it's less work for her." He stood. "I better get back to work. Enjoy your stay."

Alric finished his meal and went to where Darkian waited. He took the horse to a stable across the street and paid for food and water for the night. He returned to the inn where the same young woman waited at the front counter.

"I'll make use of the room now. Do I take any not occupied?" Hotel rooms normally couldn't be locked, except from the inside. When the occupant left the room, he could slide a marker to show the room was spoken for.

She gave him a smile. "Come with me. I'll take you to the best room." She walked around the counter and to the stairs.

"I heard it can be pretty dangerous outside of Asper at night."

"It can be. Wolves mostly, they're not scared of anything, even several men with horses. They prefer to hunt at dusk, so the gates to Asper are closed at evening to keep them from trying to wander the streets. The guards open them for travellers and shoot any wolves that come close. My name is Rainye, by the way."

"Alric." He continued to walk with her to the third floor where she led him to a corner room.

She opened the door to the room, entered, and gestured inside. "Best room in the inn."

Alric looked around. The room was slightly larger than average, and besides the furniture, featured a second door leading to the outside. Curious, he walked to the door and opened it, seeing mountains and forests beyond Asper and the wall protecting the city. He stepped out on the walkway. "Nice view."

"Air is fresher up here too." She spoke right behind him and put her hand on his hip.

He turned around. "Thank you for showing me the room." He put his hand on hers.

"I cannot do anything without Master Gretson's permission, but perhaps if you were to ask him..."

"He strikes me as a man who doesn't give pretty things away easily."

Rainye grinned. "There you go, charming me again." She slipped out of the room, spun around, and gave him a final wave.

Alric left his backpack in the room to wander around Asper. The mountain air in the city was a change from other urban areas, and he was impressed with the size of the stone buildings. He saw the inns, taverns, and tea houses were doing a brisk business and considered going into one of them when he saw a group of six witches walking, most of them carrying food from the market place. He recognized two of the witches from earlier in the day, Derikson and Mystilla. He raised a hand in a greeting.

Four of the witches looked at him without expression, but Derikson raised his hand in return while Mystilla gave him a smile. She stepped over to him.

"Alric, so nice to see you made it here safely."

"I've been here for a while and just having a walk about." He looked at the tea house across the street. "I was about to have something to drink. Would you like to join me? Derikson, too. I'd like to return the favour of your hospitality."

She started to laugh and covered her mouth. "I'm sorry. You've such a rough looking exterior, and then these words come from your mouth that one would expect from a scholar. You're such a contradiction." She looked at the other witches. "Please go ahead. I'm going to share some time with Alric."

Derikson looked at the group and then at Mystilla. "Perhaps I best stay with you."

Alric quickly replied. "I would enjoy your company as well."

Mystilla touched Derikson's arm. "I'll be safe with Alric and will have him walk me back to the terradomus."

Derikson nodded, looking relieved. "Peace be with you."

Alric escorted Mystilla to the tea house where he insisted on paying for the cheese and bread to go with the wine.

"Is Derikson a sort of body guard for the rest of the witches?"

"In Asper, there're a lot of visitors, and some regions don't view witches with much tolerance. Derikson, being a large man, discourages confrontation from others. That's also the reason we travel in larger groups in Asper and some other cities."

"Safety in numbers." He smiled. "It was kind of Systalla to offer to send a note to my parents."

"Witches believe doing a good deed will always benefit the giver as well the receiver. The world and beyond is interconnected. Every part is joined to the other. If you touch on anything, you're actually affecting all other parts, including oneself. For example, when you gave your vest to help Leesha keep warm, you may have a started a chain of events that will return to you in a positive way."

"She looked so chilled after being in the water and is too slim to generate much heat for herself."

"She has quite the crush on you." Mystilla smiled. "Kept talking about how big and strong you are."

Alric chuckled. "What do they say about young women turning of age? All giggles, tears, and blushes."

"That may be true, but I know Leesha. She's smart and understands people. I think she sees a good person in you." Mystilla smiled. "Besides your good looks."

Alric laughed and took a long drink.

"I'm sorry, I've embarrassed you." Mystilla reached across and touched his hand.

"I find the revelation I'm a good person at odds with being a soldier."

"You're not a soldier anymore. You're a free man with a new destiny."

"Destiny. I met a witch named Ysmay in Trontta who told me of my destiny, of sort."

"What did she say?"

"Something about having a long life and being the seed of change. She showed me the Book of Redemption."

"She took you inside the terradomus? The Hardoff Terradomus isn't open to visitors."

"No, this was a special case. They helped heal a friend of mine."

"Hmm." Mystilla stared at him. "Seed of change. There's a passage in the Book of Redemption, the same one in the Book of Destiny, which describes the red hair warrior who dies but lives again to provide the seed of change. But the prophecy is hundreds of years old, and it's hard to believe the change is occurring now. Every few years some of the witches get excited when they see a man with red hair, but so far none of them were warriors who had died."

Alric licked his lips. "I faked my death to escape from the army."

Mystilla drew in a long breath. "Interesting. Perhaps the change is really happening."

"Change is always happening. People can believe in a prophecy if they want, but it probably doesn't make a damn difference."

"True, but it's interesting how you might fit in with what's written."

"If you write something down, even something outlandish, eventually it'll come to pass if you wait long enough. That doesn't mean you actually predicted it, just it was likely to happen sooner or later."

"You're a wise man, Alric. However, a part of me wonders if you're the man written in the book."

"Can you tell me what else was written about this man?"

Mystilla smiled. "Let's just say this man's path with witches will be intertwined for the rest of his life."

After they finished, Alric walked Mystilla to the terradomus. He avoided any more talk about the prophecy, focusing on the stone work of the buildings and the cost of staying in Asper.

"It's not so bad for witches. We have our own place to stay and don't have to pay the admission fee."

"They don't charge witches?"

"No, even if we do use the road. As I'm sure you're aware, we have other methods to reach the terradomus besides the streets."

They stopped at the terradomus, the stone structure shaped like a pyramid with the entrance at the top of several steps.

Mystilla gave him a quick kiss on the lips. "Just in case you are the one, I want to be able to tell others I kissed you."

He chuckled. "I hope that's not the only reason you kissed me." He leaned down and kissed her back, extending the embrace for several heartbeats.

"Goodnight, Alric."

"And to you, Mystilla." He walked away, feeling as if he was walking down a path already laid out for him.

He returned to the hotel, acknowledging Rainye as he went up the stairs. The fresh mountain air and the wine made him tired. He quickly undressed, finding the bed comfortable. His eyes soon closed and he fell to dream where he faced two paths leading into the woods. He stood at the fork, not sure whether to go left or right.

* * * *

Alric woke, his eyes adjusting to the dark in the room. The sound disturbing his sleep repeated again. He was used to the howling of wolves, but this sound was different. Hoots and growls came from the partially open doorway to the outside. Alric rose out of bed and stepped out to the walkway outside the room. He peered into the shadowy world outside the protective wall where the hoots and growls continued.

What kind of creature produces those sounds?

Alric stood listening for a few more moments. The wolves answered the hoots with a howl. Suddenly a yelp replaced the howling and then silence. Alex returned to bed, wondering what could hurt a wolf.

Didn't sound like a bear or anything I know.

* * * *

Morning came and Alric found Rainye sweeping the floor in front of the counter. She was quick with a smile.

"Did you sleep well?"

"Mostly. I heard some strange sounds, hooting and growling."

"That would be the giant men. You can usually hear their calls at night. Sometimes during the day if you get too close to them. Last year they tore down part of the wall. It took a week to replace all the heavy stones they just tossed around."

"You mean those big hairy creatures? I thought they were a fable made up by drunks."

"They're real enough. Wolves learn to stay away from them."

Alric nodded. "You seem to be fairly cheerful. You don't mind being a slave?"

"I live pretty well here. Master Gretson is fair to us. "I'd like more company at night, but it's not my choice. His wife sometimes resents his visits to us."

Alric smiled. "I guess she would at that." He went to the dining room and received a plate of eggs with a meat from a dark-skinned woman he presumed was the wife of Gretson. He drank his tea observing the other guests in the room. They weren't a quiet group, conversing in strong voices echoing from the stone wall and floor. Still, everyone seemed to be in good spirits. That included the wife, who when she directed Rainye to sweep the dining room, did so in a reasonable tone.

Alric paid his bill and went to retrieve Darkian from the stable.

The road out of town was busy with travellers leaving the same time, everyone realizing the trip to the Kingdom of Allisure took most of a day's travel. It took most of the morning for Alric to be separated enough from the other travellers to feel alone. His thoughts returned to what Ysmay and Mystilla told him about his future.

It's like this road. I've not much choice but to follow it and see where it leads me. One thing I do know is at the end of the day, I'll be in Allisure and the start of my new life.

Chapter Eighteen

Ululla was certain of one thing. Life was likely to become less complicated after her journey with Bruhamoff and the spirit of Terrowin. Bruhamoff was turning into a man, and she felt the physical attraction between them growing stronger. She was also uncertain about her connection with Terrowin, who seemed to have an emotional attachment to her.

Still, she had to admit to herself it was flattering to have two males interested in her as she traveled on the busy road to the Kingdom of Allisure. Neither one was available to her, only reminding her how alone she was.

Ululla had been in Newharken before and knew how to navigate the docks where large number of ships came to deliver and receive goods. She noted Bruhamoff was walking slowly as he looked around at the buildings and people. Newharken was home to many different cultures, and it was reflected in the building styles and how people dressed. Some of the merchants sold specialized foods, brought in by boats from faraway places. They paused to look at some of the items, and Bruhamoff frowned at the live fist size insects kept in wire containers.

"Who would want to eat those?"

"I don't know, but insects are supposed to be nourishing." She added, "If you're hungry enough."

He pointed at some skinned animals hanging by their legs on wood poles. "I wonder what those are? Too big to be rabbit."

"I suspect you may find out someday if you journey far enough. Obviously, some people do have a liking for them."

"Why wouldn't they just eat what's available here? I don't understand the need to eat so many creatures from far away."

"Brother Bruhamoff, understand the diet for witches is different than for most people. They consume what they're used to."

Bruhamoff shook his head. "I don't understand their reasoning. The Book of Redemption tells us to eat in proportion to the land around us. If most of the land has plants, then our diet should be mostly vegetables. Farms with herds of animals for food are giving a false balance if meat is plentiful. They really don't need to consume so much meat."

"That may be true, and I'm glad you understand what the Book of Redemption is teaching us. However, the Book of Redemption also tells us to appreciate the differences in people and their needs. The path we walk is not same as a friend or stranger. They see differently than we do, hear differently, and taste differently. Be appreciative of these differences, otherwise you would be walking with a mirror without a chance to learn the beauty of a different world."

He smiled. "I guess I need to keep my mind open to the differences."

"Well said." She watched him as he peered at the wide street full of merchants and bustling traffic.

"It looks like when you open an ant hill."

"Yes, it does. Now, let's see if we can find a boat that will take us to Allisure." She gestured vaguely toward the end of the street. "This will take us to the piers. The River Basica is a big river, slow moving as I recall, but there are boats there that travel to Allisure."

Ululla wondered if Terrowin would have any difficulties being on a boat. She recalled hearing superstitious rumours that spirits couldn't travel over water, but couldn't confirm it with any of the witches she conversed with. *Terrowin doesn't feel there would be any problem. I guess we will find out for sure soon enough.*

The docks appeared at the end of the street, and Ululla took the view of a nearly a hundred-water craft. Over half were docked at one of the dozens of piers lining the river. Cranes using pulleys were in constant motion, moving goods as wagons pulled by horses rumbled by with goods. She breathed in the scent of water, fish, and nuances of a thousand different goods.

Ululla approached a dock hand holding a flat piece of wood with a paper document attached to it. The older man was eyeing cargo being unloaded and occasionally glancing at the paper.

"Excuse us. I'm wondering where we might get passage on a ship going to Allisure."

He looked at her and Bruhamoff. He gave a nod toward the far docks. "Most likely find a boat there going back to Allisure and will have some room."

Ululla quickly passed a coin to him. He smoothly slid it into a pocket, telling her, "I'd be lookin' for the Questor or the Harlot's Revenge. Neither captain minds witches."

"Thank you for your help." Ululla smiled. "Peace be with you."

Bruhamoff asked, "We have to pay for information on which boat to take?"

"Yes. Dock workers are notorious for being low paid and often make up for the loss of wages by accepting bribes to ensure goods arrive safely to their destination and in some cases to make sure some of it is diverted elsewhere. You may think it's dishonest, but this is how things are done around here."

"I see." He quoted part of the Book of Redemption. "Do not judge others with your standards, for they may be judging you. Stay true to your principles and allow them to do the same. If they are not causing you pain, then they harm you not."

"Excellent. I'm impressed how you are applying the words from the Book of Redemption to the practical world we live in."

"Thank you, Sister Ululla. You have been a good teacher and taught me how to actually read and understand the Book of Redemption."

They reached the portion of the dock where several sailboats waited, their masts down. Foot traffic was brisk as goods were loaded on carts up the ramps and disappeared into the hollow of the ships. The ship stood high in the water, and the ramp proved to be a challenge for some of the heavier goods to be rolled up. Below the main deck were cut outs for oars to reach the water. Ululla was careful to keep out of the way of the hurried workers as she made her way to a ship carrying the name Harlot's Revenge. She wondered briefly how the ship obtained such an odd name, deciding if the opportunity arose she would ask the captain or one of the officers.

She spotted a man on the deck with his arms crossed as he watched the cargo being loaded. He wore a blue arm band signifying him as the captain, and when she reached the ramp, she called out to him.

He looked down at her and Bruhamoff with a curious look.

"Are you looking to ship goods?"

"No, passage to Allisure."

"You have coins?"

"Yes." Ululla called back and held up two large bronze coins.

The captain signaled for them to climb up the ramp. When they arrived at the end of the iron reinforced wood plank, he uncrossed his arms. "I'm Captain Stavins. Which part of Allisure do ye wish to go? We stop at Ketamine, Patricide, and the port city of Giorgia."

Ululla answered with Bruhamoff standing slightly behind her. "We are going to Jital."

"Ah, the closest stop would be Patricide." He paused. "I don't mind witches, but some of the crew are a bit superstitious, so just be quiet and stay at the sides."

Ululla passed him the coins. "We will be careful not to attract attention."

* * * *

They took on five more passengers, and soon after, the last of the cargo was loaded, the ramp was pulled up and ropes securing the ship were loosened. Commands from the captain and his officers quickly had the crew dashing around to help the ship pull away from the dock.

She followed Bruhamoff as he leaned over the railing, watching the long oars reach into the water.

A short, heavy set man standing a few steps away commented. "These river ships use three methods of moving. The wind, oars, and the current in the river. We're going downstream, so we should make good time."

Bruhamoff looked at the speaker and the rest of the ship. "It sure is a big boat."

The man shook his head. "This ship is just for river transport. There're much larger ships for the seas. The problem with river ships is there are parts of the river that aren't deep, especially near the piers. So, the bottom of the ships are a bit more flat. That makes it more top heavy and so the masts can't be as high. These ships are okay on the river, but they'd have a hard time on a stormy sea."

Ululla looked at his rough hands and strong arms. "You know a lot about ships."

He smiled. "I'm a ship builder by trade. Going up to Allisure to help with the king's new ships."

"That must be interesting work."

"It is, although hard on the body." The ship jolted. "Ah, they must be trimming the sails to catch some wind. On a crowded river like this they have to be careful not to pick up too much speed. With all the weight she's carrying, the Harlot's Revenge will have trouble making quick adjustments."

Ululla asked, "Do you know why they call it the Harlot's Revenge?"

He grinned. "I heard some merchant owned this ship before and lost it in some dealings with a woman of ill repute. He was angry and called her some very unpleasant names. She renamed it as such, just to rub a bit of salt in the wound."

Silence came across as they watched the shoreline slide past them. Occasionally Bruhamoff would point out something he found of interest, such as beavers, birds, and an occasional fish jumping out of the water.

Finally, the shipbuilder chuckled. "If you truly like interesting creatures, you should go on a ship that crosses the seas. Some strange creatures, big and small abound on the far lands and water."

"You mean like sea monsters?"

"There are some of those, but not as many as sailors make it out to be. Every time a ship disappears they blame a sea monster instead of a bad storm, a poorly made ship, or the captain being too drunk to steer a ship. No, there're other creatures that are quite strange. I've actually seen big tooth cats, huge elephants with hair covering their bodies, reptiles walking on their hind legs, and heard, but not seen, the scream of true monsters. The sound made my hair stand on end. I've had my share of adventures and made up my mind I tested lady luck enough. I decided if I didn't want to sail anymore, then I'd make ships."

Ululla smiled. "You look young to have seen so much. Were you a boy when you first went to sea?"

He laughed. "My dear, I was born on a ship. I learned to swim before I could crawl. Never knew my father, and my mother died at sea before I could grow whiskers. I was raised by different crew members, and I thank every one of them for teaching me how to survive. When I build a ship, I make sure the ship will not be cause of any sailor's death. I make them strong and sea worthy as any ship you'll find. My name is Selkirk."

Ululla gave their names and watched Bruhamoff listen to him with fascination. She guessed he was imagining the seas and the creatures the ship builder was talking about. She suspected some of it was just a tall tale but with a bit of truth in it as well.

She felt a presence next to her and turned, seeing nothing. *Terrowin is letting me know he's with us on the ship. I wonder what he makes out of the shipbuilder's stories? I suspect he's like Bruhamoff in he'd like to find out for himself about those creatures.*

* * * *

The River Basica was wide, allowing a variety of ships to move past each other along the slow-moving current. It gave Ululla a feeling of contentment to watch the passing scenery and lapping of water as it pushed past the hull. *For the moment, all is well. The Book of Redemption tells us to enjoy these times and to remember them when going through difficult ones.* She recalled a passage she liked to quote to herself. *For what once was, will be again. The circle can be long or short, but always will return to the same spot it started from. If you are feeling distressed, know this will pass as the circle continues its journey and the feeling of wellbeing will return.*

The captain walked over to where she stood at the side, giving a nod to the ship builder as well.

"We'll be docking at Ketamine to do some loading and unloading of goods. Likely take at least an hour and if you wish, you can stretch your legs on shore. There's a few good taverns close by if you're feeling thirsty."

He turned and went to the other travellers, repeating the message.

Ululla suspected he was also hinting they would be in the way during the transfer of cargo and decided a walk in the town would be good way to pass some time. The crew, who for the most part were resting on the deck, sprung into life. Sails were taken down and ropes tossed over the side. She watched the approach of the ship to the dock, admiring the skill needed to gently arrive at the desired spot. A pair of anchors splashed into the water, and the ship was frozen a short distance from the dock.

"Come, Bruhamoff. Let's see what Ketamine has to offer."

The ship builder followed them, favouring his right foot with a limp. She turned back to him. "You're welcome to join us. I don't know where we're going, but I thought it would be nice to have a look around."

He smiled, showing a missing front tooth. "Thank you, miss, but I'd just be a hindrance. I'm going to head to a bar called the Maiden Head, and after you've had your look around, you're welcome to join me. I'll even do the buying."

Ululla walked with Bruhamoff through the crowded streets, pausing at different booths, filled with a wide range of merchandise, clothing, and food. She found a silver braided hair ornament interesting and held up in her hands to examine it in the sunlight.

"This is very pretty." She turned to get Bruhamoff's opinion and saw he was looking across the wide market street to an inn standing on the corner. On the lower level hung a wood carving of the top half of a nude woman, her long dark hair providing a bit of modesty. Under the figurehead was a sign proclaiming The Maiden Head.

"Why don't you go have a drink with Selkirk?" She passed him a bronze coin, not sure of his own monetary resources. As a more senior witch, Ululla was given a larger allowance than someone of Bruhamoff's years. While it was not a large amount, her expenses were small with the terradomus providing her with food, shelter, and clothing.

"Are you sure you'll be all right by yourself?" He hesitated before taking the offered coin.

"Of course. I'll join you later after I've looked around some more."
She watched him hurry off and smiled. *Now why would I think a young
man would be interested in shopping with me when he can sit down with
a man who has adventures in faraway lands?* She felt the air around with
her mind. *Terrowin is missing. I think I can assume he's with Bruhamoff.*

She decided to purchase the hair ornament and after inserting it in
her hair, continued her inspection of the market goods. Most merchants
had tables on the sidewalk with more goods inside the modest stores
lining the street. The tables took over the sidewalk, forcing pedestrians to
use the road to make their way, leaving a smaller area for horses and
carts. Whistles and shouts were common as drivers tried to maneuver
through the crowd. Ululla enjoyed looking at the items and food rare in
other parts of her travels and also the difference in dress of the
population. She did spot two Darkrose witches not far from where she
had been. After a few minutes, she began to wonder if they were
following her as they slowly closed the gap.

*I doubt they mean any harm and are perhaps curious where I might
be going. The Darkrose like to gather information about what the
Whiterose are doing.*

Ululla paused longer at a table, studying a clay pot. The Darkrose
witches arrived at the table, and one moved close to her, speaking in a
hushed tone.

"Do not react to my words. A man has been following you since you
came from the dock. He's dressed in dark clothes. Bare faced. I know
nothing about him, but he's showing interest in your movements."

"Thank you." Ululla glanced at the witch, noting signs of age in her
face which belied her fluid movements and soft voice. "Where is he
now?"

"Across the street. Is there a reason for you to suspect you may be in
harm's way?"

Ululla considered her reply, deciding to trust the Darkrose with
some information. "A few days ago, there was an incident. At the time, I
considered it an accident." She took a casual look around and saw him.
He was tall, well dressed, and with an air of confidence about him.
Something about him made her realize he meant to do her harm.

"You came from the docks. I assume you arrived by boat."

165

"Yes. The boat stopped to load and unload supplies. I'm to return there in an hour to continue on with the journey to Patricide."

"Come with us. There's a teahouse we and the Whiterose frequent." She began to walk slowly. "I am Phelia, and this is Sister Rahal."

"Ululla. I am surprised you are taking an interest in my welfare."

"I would hope you would do the same for me. This is a unique part of the Allisure Kingdom. At one time, it was the Haiedien Kingdom and was violent, uncivilized. When conflict inevitably arose with Allisure, the witches here were suddenly attacked. The two terradomus were on opposite sides of the town with secondary entrances quite far away. Whiterose witches took refuge in our terradomus, and we did the same in yours. When the conflict was finally over and Allisure was able to claim the land, our two clans were able to have a greater understanding of each other. Although it is rare for a witch to visit the other's terradomus, we have several areas, including this teahouse, where we meet." She smiled. "Along with a few romances between the two terradomuses."

"It is too bad there isn't similar harmony in other lands between the two clans."

"Sister Ululla, those feelings are ours as well. Someday we hope our clans can rejoin, but I assume you already know the philosophy of the Umbravox, that the Whiterose are simply children seeking to understand the world and will eventually come back home."

Ululla heard a hint of humour in her voice. "It is an interesting interpretation of the status of the Whiterose. I will say only perhaps the child has become an adult in its own right and may never return to home, although it will always have great affection toward it."

"Well put. Today that certainly seems true. However, in a hundred, two hundred, or a thousand years from now, who can say what will transpire?"

The teahouse was a converted home and was filled with patrons, almost a third witches. It smelled of baked breads and tea. Various clay pots and cups were on the tables with partially eaten food. She immediately felt relaxed with a feeling of belonging as she saw the two clans sharing tables. *Yes, this is the way things should be. The witches of both clans preach peace and harmony, but it seems only here do they show it to each other.*

Phelia went to a table where four witches sat, placing her hand on a light blue dressed female witch.

"Sister Marcellia, this is Sister Ululla. She is being followed by a man I can only surmise has dark intentions. I believe it would be prudent if we escorted her to safety to where her boat waits at the docks."

"Actually, I have a fellow traveller waiting at the Maiden Head Tavern." She paused and clarified. "He is also a witch and went there to listen to another man tell stories of his sea adventures."

Marcellia stood, replying. "Then we shall go there first. We will use a different route to get there to avoid being seen."

Phelia spoke to Rahal. "Why don't you wait here? It may attract attention if there are too many of us travelling together."

Phelia nodded and took Marcellia's place.

Ululla went with Phelia and Marcellia to the back of the teahouse, passing through the kitchen. A cook, rolling dough, raised her eyebrows but didn't comment. Ululla saw she was a Darkrose witch as well, but wasn't surprised as many witches had an occupation outside the terradomus.

The teahouse had a rear exit that led to a pathway between buildings. It would be just wide enough for a hand pulled cart or wheelbarrow, but Ululla judged by the height of the weeds it wasn't used very often. She brushed back the small blue flowered plants as she followed the other witches. Insects buzzed around her head, and she was glad when they reached the end of the block.

They turned around the corner with Marcellia going first as they approached the main market street again. She scanned the area and came back with news.

"I don't see any sign of him. I suspect he's still waiting by the teahouse or has gone inside and found out he's been tricked. The Maiden Head Tavern is straight across the street."

They walked quickly to the tavern, with Ululla commenting, "That's quite a decoration for the tavern."

Marcellia laughed. "Yes, I was quite annoyed they used my likeness without seeking my permission."

Ululla laughed in return, suddenly seeing the similarities between the witch and the wood carving. "It may have made you famous."

"Oh, yes. One witch started calling me the tavern sea witch, and it took a while for the nickname to disappear."

They entered the tavern, finding Bruhamoff listening to Selkirk in rapt attention. She hoped the witches with her would not detect Terrowin, and if they did, would not connect him with her or who he was. Two other seamen were at their table, one looking mildly amused at Selkirk's tales while the other was only half-listening, being more concerned with his drink.

"It was big, tall as a man at its shoulders, yellow and white fur, a long tail, and the head—big around as you could circle your arms, with teeth the length of your forearm. One bite was all it'll need to rip you in half."

Ululla stood by the table. "It's time to head back to the docks."

Selkirk shrugged. "I think we still have lots of time, but I guess we've had enough to drink."

One of the men at the table looked up at Marcellia. He grinned. "Damn, there're more witches in here than a terradomus. Isn't there any place where a man can drink in peace?"

Marcellia frowned. "You should consider yourself lucky to have us in your company."

"That's the type of luck that can sink a ship." He pulled out a chair. "Are you going to join us for a drink?"

She smiled. "Not this time. We have some work to do."

He waved her off. "Another time then."

Ululla was curious at their familiarity. It seemed to her Marcellia had visited him in the tavern before. It implied a relaxed attitude toward the witches' guidance of avoiding excessive drink. *A very different set of rules the two witch clans follow.*

The five of them left the tavern with Marcellia in the lead and Phelia at the rear. They reached the street that took a downward slant when Ululla spotted the mysterious man observing them as he stood by a doorway of a shop. Again, she felt a sinister aura come from him. Her hair at the back of her neck stood on end as they passed him.

Marcellia gave Ululla a final piece of advice as she boarded the Harlot's revenge. "Make sure you place a protective spell around

Bruhamoff and yourself. I pray neither of you come to harm, but there was evil coming from that man."

"Have you ever seen him before?"

She nodded. "Yes, and I had an uneasy feeling from him then, too. He has never used any dark magic openly before, and perhaps we have thwarted his intentions this time."

Ululla thanked her and Phelia for their help and climbed aboard the Harlot's Revenge. She quietly mouthed a spell to protect Bruhamoff and her from dark spells and tried to relax as the last of the new cargo was loaded. The captain supervised the storage of the containers to the lower levels and then walked over to her.

"We'll be leaving in a few minutes and will have you at Patricide by dinner. Hope you enjoyed the look around Ketamine. It's a very old town. Some say dating back before there was writing."

"Thank you, it was quite interesting to visit."

The boat cast off, with the usual shouting and running of crew members as they tossed ropes and raised sails. On the highest mast a sailor rang a bell, warning those nearby the boat was on the move. The sails caught a small breeze, and the Harlot's Revenge quickly moved away from the dock and down the river.

Ululla breathed a sigh of relief, glad to be away from Ketamine and the stranger watching her. She noted Bruhamoff was still asking Selkirk questions, and after carefully feeling the air around her, decided Terrowin was listening as well. *Boys do love hearing about faraway lands and adventures, even after they become men. I do not have any desire to see monsters or battle pirates.*

She turned her attention to the far shore as the boat quietly sailed on through a chorus of birds that circled above them. They passed smaller boats, some using sails and others using oars, as they followed a bend in the river.

The shout startled her.

"Kill the witches! They're demons!"

She turned to see an olive-skinned man, slim and of medium height, race across the deck toward them. He carried a fish club in one hand and a long, thin bladed knife in the other.

Ululla froze for precious moments, saw the man alter his course slightly toward Bruhamoff. She doubted she could move fast enough to help him. The charging man, with his teeth bared, raised the club. Ululla screamed. Selkirk stepped forward, blocking his path. The club came down but Selkirk blocked it with his arm. Ululla watched in slow motion as the knife plunged into Selkirk as he used his other hand to pull the assailant down to the deck.

Crew members swarmed the man, disarming him and with several punches and kicks, left him unconscious on the deck.

Ululla raced over to Selkirk and fell to her knees, rolling him to his back. Blood oozed from his side, his face pale. She lifted his head onto her lap. "Selkirk, you saved our lives."

He licked his lips and drew a ragged breath. "I don't think..."

"Shh. It's okay. Save your strength."

He looked up at her. "Born at sea, die at sea. Seems right." His smile trembled.

She stroked his face. "This circle for you is nearly complete, but a new one will start."

Selkirk took a slow breath. "Who's he?" He half-raised his arm and pointed with a finger.

Ululla looked at the empty space next to Bruhamoff. "That would be Terrowin."

"Ah, now I recognize him. Imagine that. King Terrowin himself coming to see me off."

His voice trailed off, his eyelids fluttered, and his chest fell.

"May peace guide your journey." A tear fell from her eye, and she slowly stood. "He saved our lives."

Captain Stavins crossed his arms as he looked down at Selkirk and shook his head. "He was a good man." He turned his attention to the moaning man on the deck. "Take him to the lowest level and secure him."

"What is going to happen to him?" Ululla watched as the assailant was dragged away.

"We'll hand him over to the king's authorities. I suspect he'll be in the gallows by the week's end." He looked at Selkirk's body. "I'll have his body wrapped, and when we get to Giorgia, I'll find a merchant ship

170

going out and ask for them to dispose of him at sea. It's only proper to return a sailor to where he lived his life."

"The man who attacked us, was he a member of the crew?"

"He came on board while we were loading at the dock and asked if he could work for a passage to Giorgia. I didn't really need him, but let him on anyway. An extra hand for work is always good. I know some seamen are superstitious about witches, but I've never seen one attack any before. Very odd."

Ululla wondered if a spell was used to cause him to attack them and immediately thought of the ominous looking stranger at Ketamine. *It won't matter if a spell caused him to attack us or not. The assailant's fate is doomed. The punishment for killing another man without provocation is hanging.*

She felt the presence of a spirit nearby and whispered, "Terrowin, is that you?"

Yes. The spirit of Selkirk is gone.

* * * *

Patricide appeared into view after the ship rounded a bend. The dock appeared about the same size with an equal number of boats moored as had been at Ketamine. However, the town climbed high up into the rolling hills with a light grey stone castle dominating the highest point. The massive structure had two sets of walls set into the hilly ground, making a formidable task for any invading force to capture. The docks were below a pair of towers, allowing a good vantage point for the defending army.

The prisoner was dragged out by three men, his face bloodied. Although his arms were tied by thick rope, he still struggled against his captures. Captain Stavins stood between Ululla and the escorted man. "I think he has moon madness. He has done evil, but I have pity for anyone afflicted so."

Ululla spoke her agreement with him, although she doubted the condition herself. "It is a terrible thing to happen to anyone." She had heard a full moon could change a person into another creature, such as a werewolf, but if the body wasn't able to make the change, the mind was left tormented and went insane. Moon madness was used to explain many mental problems and even sometimes for those who became too drunk. Some believed drinking strong spirits on nights of the full moon thwarted becoming a creature.

Ululla and Bruhamoff climbed up the steep incline of cobble stones and reached the main market square.

"Bruhamoff, I think it's best all we do is find the terradomus and rest here for the night."

"I agree, although I want to say a prayer for Selkirk at the chapel. He showed great kindness to me and told me much of world."

"I would like to join you in prayer."

The terradomus was a simple yellow brick structure with the entrance at the side of the rectangular building. Well placed trees limited the visibility of those entering or leaving the main entrance with two more exits well hidden some distance away. Ululla and Bruhamoff stepped past the double doors of the terradomus and were greeted by Keeper Dormus, an older, middle weight man.

"Welcome to our terradomus. It is perhaps small by some standards, but we believe you will feel comfortable here. Please allow me to show you to the sleeping quarters."

Ululla suspected Dormus was bored and was looking for an opportunity to do something. The sleeping quarters were easy to locate, four levels below the ground. The rooms were Spartan, as most terradomus guest bedrooms were, but all had a ventilation shaft to ensure fresh air was brought in. Ululla had been in few terradomuses guest rooms where the stale air had made sleep uncomfortable.

Terrowin stayed close to her and entered her bedroom.

"You must wait here until I talk to the altus rector," she told him.

I know.

"Good. I'll be back later." Ululla left the bedroom and met Bruhamoff as he left his room, located opposite from hers. They walked up the several flights of stone stairs until they reached the main level, bypassing a study centre, the altus rector's office, the Hall of Sentential, and the main kitchen. The main level was almost completely open with the dining room covering most of the area.

Bruhamoff followed her to a counter where they chose from several snack foods and then picked one of the long tables with bench seats.

Ululla soon discovered the dining room was also the conversation area for the witches. She joined in the latest theories concerning the prophecy from the Book of Redemption and listened to Sister Eileen summarize.

"Sister Mystilla spoke to him, and she said he fits the description, a tall red-haired man who used to be a warrior."

Ululla smiled, knowing how often witches had seen a red-haired man and speculated he was the one prophesied. The speculation increased on this occasion when it turned out he was also a former soldier. "Where was he seen?"

"Asper and he was heading to Allisure. Maybe he'll be coming here."

"Are you going to watch for him wandering through the town?"

Eileen smiled. "No, that may not be necessary. Apparently, he likes witches and may initiate contact with us."

Ululla raised her eyebrows. *That's different from the usual rumours. The prophecy does say he will come to the witches' home on his own accord. It would be interesting to meet him and see if he truly does match the Book's description.*

She stood as Bruhamoff finished eating. "Thank you, Sister Eileen for the information. Brother Bruhamoff and I need to visit the chapel for meditation."

As they walked down the stairs to the study area where the chapel was located, Bruhamoff asked, "Do you believe the change is really about to happen?"

"I don't know. There have been many false indications before, but this seems close to what is predicted."

* * * *

After meditating at the chapel, Ululla went to see the altus rector. She waited at the entrance of the wood framed stone entrance until she was noticed.

Altus Rector Eanfled looked up from her desk and smiled at Ululla. "Please enter, Sister Ululla."

Ululla sat across from the elder woman. "Thank you, Altus Rector Eanfled. I want to inform you I have a spirit travelling with me and waiting in my room for further instructions."

Eanfled's smile left her face. "Do you believe it is wise to have a spirit in our terradomus? I should think you should have asked permission first before bringing him inside."

"My apology if doing so is causing you any distress. However, before we arrived at Patricide, we were attacked onboard a ship. I feared someone may be still be planning to harm us, and the spirit was in danger as well. The spirit may belong to someone of great importance, and I believed it best not to delay in bringing him into the safety of the terradomus."

"I see, and what leads you to believe the spirit is of great importance? Of whom is he the spirit of?"

Ululla swallowed, taking her time in answering. "I do not wish to speculate on his exact nature, as it appears his spirit has had more than one life. However, this spirit has drawn the attention of our altus councillium, and his instructions were to aid the spirit in his quest."

Eanfled frowned. "There appears I have little say in this matter."

"The Book of Redemption tells us to not use energy on things we cannot control, for there are many other things we do have influence on. We must accept our immediate sphere of influence."

"Of course. As an altus rector, we are told the wellbeing and care of the terradomus and people inside it are our responsibility. The altus councillium sometimes instructs others to do things that appear contrary to what we would like to do."

"I am sure you were given the position of altus rector because they knew they could trust your abilities to handle difficult situations."

Eanfled gave a small smile. "Well spoken, Sister Ululla. Can you enlighten me on the rumours of the red headed warrior heading toward Allisure? Apparently, his name is Alric, and some believe he may be the one that signals the beginning of the great upheaval."

"This is the first I have heard of him. However, I have been travelling and have missed some of the news at various terradomus." *Terrowin's spirit and Bruhamoff's mission all seem to indicate something important may happen soon.*

"Very well. I have been informed you and Brother Bruhamoff are going to be travelling to Jital next, but need to leave via one of our secondary entrances. It seems the altus councillium is concerned either for your safety or a need to preserve secrecy."

"Perhaps a bit of both." Ululla stood. "Thank you for your indulgence of my special guest. May peace be with you."

"And with you."

* * * *

Ululla breathed in the damp air of the tunnel. She walked just ahead of Bruhamoff in the early morning hours, finding the silence of the tunnel in sharp contrast to the noisy breakfast in the dining room earlier. The uneven dark brick surface lining the walls showed patches of mold in the yellow light wavering from their torches as they treaded down deep below the surface. She smelled the smoke given off by the torches as it slowly drifted to small vents in the ceiling. Newer tunnels had better venting, and some even used polished metal to reflect light from the exterior to aid the torches.

Occasionally she had a glimpse of a dim phosphorous outline near her side. Ululla didn't acknowledge Terrowin as he followed them, but she considered his spirit was getting stronger, now capable of visibility in low light.

Bruhamoff finally broke the silence. "How much further is it, Sister Ululla?"

They were somewhere near the outskirts of the town and, perhaps at one time, two stories below the street level. Now the tunnel was ascending, taking them up a gentle slope. "Not much more, I believe. We are past the city now, and the tunnel takes us to the farm."

"Good. This tunnel is rather low in height, and I almost reached the top with my head."

Ululla smiled. "Sometimes height can be a cause of a minor disadvantage."

Shortly later they reached stone stairs that circled around in a tight turn. Beyond the stairs, the tunnel continued, receding into the darkness. They climbed the stairs, coming across a pair of doors lying flat above them. Ululla waited as Bruhamoff easily pushed open one of the doors, although she was sure it would have taken some effort if she had to do it.

They stepped out into the open, and Ululla quickly surmised they were in a barn. There wasn't any livestock inside, but the odour and the straw attested they were often present. The barn was strongly made, using stone walls for the bottom half of the walls and then heavy lumber for the remaining height. Interlaced wood and hay covered the curved roof. A man came running inside the barn carrying a pitchfork. When he saw them, he grinned and lowered the tool.

"Welcome. I heard the bell, and I've had to scold the kids a few times about playing with the doors. Come to the house. We'll get you fed for your journey."

Ululla wasn't hungry, but Bruhamoff was more than able to finish off a full meal.

She looked around at the full table taking up most of the floor space in the kitchen. The family included two adult men, an adult woman, and eight children of various ages. The adults were dressed as witches, and their mannerisms spoke of study of the Book of Redemption. Like many other farms where she had eaten, a healthy portion of meat was on the table. It did follow the guidelines of the Book of Redemption in taking food proportional to the land around it. The farm obviously raised several types of animals besides grain.

When it was time to travel again, Bruhamoff was given a sack of food. The woman smiled.

"That may last you until dinner. Safe travel and peace be with you."

Chapter Nineteen

Alric stopped Darkian at the top of a rise in the road. Traffic had become increasingly lighter, with an increase in wildlife and the density of the forest as he traveled downward from Asper.

"Well, we've made it to Bacatta Ridge. Officially we've reached the border of Allisure." He looked down at the steep incline that ended in a bridge over a narrow river and urged his horse down the road. The road made a series of switch backs to arrive at the edge of the river, where the wood bridge allowed one-way travel.

Like most horses, Darkian preferred to stay as close to the outside edge of the road as possible. The rocky soil didn't give plants and trees much of a foothold, and parts of the road was damaged by the recent rainstorms with silt flowing over it. Still, Darkian was surefooted and they made it to the bridge without pause. The bridge was constructed of heavy timber and sounded like it could last many years as Alric listened to the thuds of horse's hoofs. As they crossed, he felt an enormous weight lift off his shoulders. *I'm a free man again. I shall find a place to settle down and become a woodworker like my father. He would laugh it took me this long to figure that out.*

Unlike many other kingdoms, Allisure didn't put a guard post at the extreme edge of the boundary. With only one road to use through the mountains and several small bridges to cross creeks and streams, travellers had only one route to follow until they passed the foothills. At that point, several other roads appeared from different regions, and he expected to see the presence of the Allisure troops.

After he crossed the bridge, he turned back to the stream to allow Darkian to get his fill of water and to stretch his own legs. Trees and plants grew lush after leaving the stone filled ground. Alric took a long drink of water, grabbed his bow and arrow from Darkian's saddle, and followed the openings between the trees. It wasn't an actual path, but was wide enough he could make his way. He moved lightly, not wanting to scare any game before he could see them. Birds chipped and insects buzzed, but there was little sign of food. He came across a bush full of dark blue berries and paused to eat a few handfuls, recognizing them as a fruit called saskberries. They weren't a common item, and he'd had only seen them in a dried-up variety and used in biscuits and bread.

He ate what he could, moved on, and came across an actual path. Intrigued, he followed it, wondering if it would lead to a small cabin of someone who preferred to live in isolation. After a few steps, he spotted a few deer, quietly eating in a small clearing. One stared at him, not sure if he represented a danger or not. He considered the deer for a moment and decided for the amount of meat he could carry on Darkian, the majority would go to waste. *No point in killing one for a few pounds of venison when a couple of rabbits would do the same.*

Alric walked past with a buck watching him. A dozen steps ahead he saw several rabbits and moments later an arrow sailed from his bow. All but one rabbit scurried away, and he hurried with his knife to quickly kill the struggling animal impaled with his arrow. He slipped a string around the rear legs and carried it on his back.

Satisfied with his catch, he continued on the path, wondering if it went much further as it went to a fairly steep rise. Logs were set in the pathway, allowing for easier assent. At the top of the climb, he came across several large cabins, all made of dark timber.

Blackrain. I don't want to be caught here.

Quickly turning away, Alric headed back down the pathway. The rumours he had heard of the Blackrain indicated they were a cult of warlocks who used dark magic for reasons unknown. No one knew what they looked like, save for a few reports they were perhaps not entirely human.

He made his way back down the path, deciding it likely led back near the bridge. A few minutes later brought him within sight of the stream and he began to relax. *Almost there.*

A man suddenly appeared on the path and held up his hand. "What are you doing here?"

Alric took in the man, bearded, long dark hair and wearing a dark brown shirt and black pants. He stood slightly shorter than himself. In one hand, he carried a long hunting knife and in the other, a bow with arrows. He was of middle age and spoke in a clear, strong voice.

Alric stopped, resisting the temptation of holding out his arms to show he meant no harm. *I won't show him any fear. Confidence is the key in dealing with someone who is challenging you.* "I stopped to hunt for some food on my way travelling through here. Who might you be?"

The man took several moments to answer. "We own this land. You're trespassing."

"No, I'm not. This is the king's land, and I see no fence or signs that tell me otherwise."

The man nodded. "We prefer not to draw attention to our presence. Did you catch any game?"

"Yes, a rabbit. I saw some deer but let them be."

The man smiled. "We leave food for them close to our cabins. It makes it easier for us to catch one occasionally. My name is Samael, the pastor here."

"Alric. I'm travelling to Allisure to live."

"I see you're carrying a warrior's sword. Are you joining an army or leaving one?"

"Leaving. I have little blood in me for killing."

"I ask because we wish to live by ourselves and don't want to be visited by outsiders if we can avoid it. Your sword made me wonder if the king was interested in our whereabouts."

"I shall keep your location to myself. I don't wish to cause any harm to thee."

"Very well." He stepped to the side. "May the path you follow lead you to contentment."

Alric walked past him. "Peace be with you."

"Ah, you have been in contact with the witches."

Alric turned back. "It seems my journey keeps crossing theirs."

Samael smiled. "There could be worse companions." He walked away toward the cabins.

That was very odd. I've been told the dwellers of the Blackrain Cabins were evil. Samael called himself a pastor and certainly didn't appear to be a demon. Perhaps the rumours aren't true, or he was tricking me into believing he was of good intentions.

He found Darkian eating grass and quickly jumped on the saddle, deciding to eat the rabbit later rather than spending additional time near the Blackrain Cabins. The horse easily climbed the trail that went up after the bridge, and though Alric looked, he couldn't see any sign of the Blackrain Cabins. *They camouflage their existence rather well. It was by sheer chance I even found the path leading to their cabins. I wonder how many Blackrain Cabins there are and what exactly do they do?*

* * * *

Sunset was approaching with the hills promising to cut off daylight early as Alric continued along the road which had increased its width slightly. He considered it a good sign, meaning a town was likely close by. The rabbit he had eaten earlier had given him enough food to put his hunger into check at the time, but he could use a full meal and hoped the town was large enough to offer him a choice of where to eat.

Rather quickly, the road increased in traffic as it was joined by two other roads coming from a southern direction. He moved passed a couple of wagons and a group of four men on horses. Darkian quickened the pace. The horse didn't like to follow anything and had to be in the lead. He smiled at the competitiveness of his horse and felt lucky he had been able to tame him.

Traffic slowed down as he approached a pair of guard houses on either side of the road. One of the guards—Alric counted ten— approached, and Alric pulled on Darkian's reins as one raised his hand.

The guard, younger than himself, walked briskly up to Alric. Despite being smaller and standing by the side of a large horse, the guard spoke with confidence.

"What is your business here?"

"I'm seeking a place to live and work. I heard Allisure is a good place to settle down."

The guard kept his expression blank. "You're carrying a warrior's sword. Are you a soldier with another kingdom?"

"No, I've left the Kireland forces."

"Weapons, other than knives, are not permitted to be carried on one's person. You may have them attached to your saddle while journeying. Only noble men and soldiers may carry weapons inside. Is that understood?"

"Yes. I'll do so immediately." Alric removed his sword belt and attached it to the saddle.

The guard stared at the sword, frowned, and then waved him forward. "You may go now."

Alric was impressed by the guards. They certainly stood and acted with a more professional demeanor than Dwykath's forces, and there was no comparison to the Fringella ragged army.

A short distance later he arrived at the town of Orsorum, which seemed to be composed mostly of inns and places for travellers to sleep and eat. Alric passed a few places standing near the edge of town, watching the pedestrians stroll along the wood plank sidewalks along the various shops. He saw a couple of inns and picked out the Sileo Inn when he saw several patrons through the open windows in the dining area. The inn, a three-story stone building, also had a stable at the back.

The rates for a room were cheaper than Asper, and Alric was pleased he was able to get a room and a stable for Darkian for a reasonable rate. The male clerk told him which room he could use, giving him a key to unlock the door.

Alric was only slightly surprised by the key, knowing Allisure was a more civilized kingdom than the ones he had just been through. Locks and locked rooms were more common in the wealthier kingdoms. He climbed the stone steps to the third floor and dropped his backpack on the floor. He felt tempted to take a nap, but hunger won out.

The eating area had all of the windows open along the two sides facing the outside walls. Alric found a table near a window that allowed him to view the traffic along the main street. In some ways, it wasn't much different than the streets of other towns he had been in, but he began to discern some differences. For the most part, the people were dressed slightly better and moved more with a purpose. The stone road was wider than most and allowed easier movement of horse pulled wagons. The wood sidewalks were constructed a full step above the roadway and put a definite separation between foot and horse traffic. The gaps between the road and the sidewalk, he deduced, allowed rain to wash debris from the curved street under the wood planks. *That's clever. After a rainstorm, the streets are clean, and those walking don't have to step on dirt and horse manure.*

Alric also noted a few witches, identifying them easily by their dress and slim build. *Witches I can spot, but the Blackrain pastor dressed like one of the poor people here and could go unnoticed. I heard the Blackrain Cabins are inhibited by demons or semi-humans that use dark magic. Maybe that's all hogwash, and they're just normal people who use magic, white and dark. Or maybe, if they are demons, they can change their appearance to look like us.*

Alric ate his mutton stew, cheese, and bread thinking about how quickly his views about witches had changed and wondered if it was going to be true of other things as well. *I certainly have a chance to change my life to live it the way I want now. I do have to decide which place I want to settle down in. I can't live on my savings much longer. Time to make some decisions.*

He finished his dinner and went to stroll around the main street, deciding sleep could wait a while longer. At first it felt unusual to be walking around without the weight of the sword around his hip, but he gradually got used to not having the sword restrict his leg movements. *Even this town might do, although I'd prefer a larger one with a less transient population.*

Alric felt drawn to turn down a side street, narrow with an uneven covering of cobblestones. A short distance later it opened to an open courtyard surrounded by several businesses. A sparse crowd walked casually along the brick quad with several children running among them. He strode across the centre, passing by a black stone statue figure of a man wearing a crown. Two dogs eyed him curiously. Several shops had closed for the day, but a tavern and two tea houses were open. *This must be where the locals go to shop as opposed to the main street where those passing through stay and eat.*

The aroma of baked food drifted in the air, and Alric decided to venture inside one of the tea houses. It looked small on the outside, but when he entered he saw it extended deep toward the back. He wasn't hungry, but the temptation of a fresh cake square caused him to order one with strong tea. The server, an older thin woman, gave him a smile as she placed the clay cup and plate on his table.

"You're new here."

"Just a traveller. I was wandering about and came across this market area. I became curious and decided to investigate."

"Where are you going?"

"I'm not sure yet. I want to settle down in Allisure, but I'm not sure where."

"Let your heart lead you to your new home. You'll know when you arrive there. Peace be with you." She turned to leave.

Alric delayed her. "Are you a witch?"

"Yes, I practice when I can. This tea house doesn't give me much free time."

Alric nodded and noticed of the dozen patrons, four of them were witches, wearing the dark shade of clothes. "You're of the Darkrose as well?"

"Yes, though Umbravox is our preferred term."

"Sorry."

She rested a hand on his shoulder momentarily. "It's only a name."

He looked again at the witches sitting a short distance away. One turned to look back at him, and he was startled by her beauty, long dark hair framing an oval face. Her full lips smiled at him as his jaw became slack. He quickly returned her smile, and she returned her attention to her companions.

Alric slowly ate and drank his tea, finding it hard not to stare at the witch. He finished his tea and reluctantly decided he should return to his room and get a good sleep for his journey tomorrow. He stood and made his way to the exit, passing the witches as he did so. Again, the dark-haired witch looked at him, and again her smile froze him.

"I'm sorry. I didn't mean to stare so."

Her voice was gentle. "It is all right. You have harmed no one. I am Orienla."

"Alric."

"Do you live here?"

"No, I leave tomorrow morning to continue my journey." He felt flushed as the four witches, one male and three female, looked up at him.

"Where do you journey to, Alric?"

"A new home. I just don't know where that is yet."

"May God help you on your quest."

He stumbled out his thanks and left, wishing he could have talked to her longer.

* * * *

Alric dropped on his bed, feeling exhausted, but sleep initially stayed away. The sounds of the street came in through his open window, and he listened to the barking of dogs and the singing of drunks. Finally, his eyelids became too heavy, and he dropped into a dream he had before.

He walked along a path between tall weeds of green and gold, approaching a forest. He remembered walking that path before; knew it would come to a fork. The whispers of a warm wind brushed past him, and he stopped.

To his left, he could see a shadowed figure, one he had seen in his dreams before. Now for the first time he could see the colours of the robe were of a dark green, blending within the forest. He stared, realizing it was a woman. There was a familiarity about her. He knew something about her, but his memory refused to bring up the details.

Alric looked to the right. Following the path as it disappeared into the trees, he glimpsed another figure among them.

* * * *

He returned to the tea house he'd gone to last night, but while it was filled with customers, Alric didn't see Orienla among them. He headed back on the road with the memory of the dream returned to him. He pondered why the dream repeated itself several times in the past months, and each time he seemed to make more progress along the path, although he never finished the journey. He reflected it was much like his own passage, not sure of the end but making progress toward it.

His thoughts returned to Orienla, and he wished he'd had an excuse to sit down and talk to her the previous evening. The three other witches at the table made it difficult to ask to join her. Her face was easy for him to recall, and he sighed at the thought of not seeing her again.

Darkian seemed to know which route was out of Orsorum, and with a little guidance from Alric, quickly found them near the edge of town. He glanced at the passing foot traffic and noticed several witches in dark, earth tone colours.

I must be near one of their terradomus.

He looked along both sides of the street, looking, hoping, and then spotting Orienla. He quickly manoeuvred Darkian to where she was walking away from him. As he approached, she turned and looked up at him, giving a warm smile. She spoke quickly to her two companions, and they retreated a dozen steps away.

He stopped close to her, and she reached up to stroke Darkian's head.

"He's a beautiful horse." She looked up at Alric. "And rather big."

Alric slid off the saddle. "Darkian is a smart horse. A bit stubborn in what he wants but has served me well."

"Are you continuing your journey?"

"Yes. I'm going to Jital next. I heard it was a fair-sized city and perhaps a place to settle down. I'll look around there and see if it suits me."

"I think it would be a wonderful place for you to live. I happen to be travelling there myself."

"Perhaps we can meet for tea. Is there a way I can contact you?"

She bit her lower lip as she thought. "I don't know Jital very well, but there's a castle for the lord there near the river. I will be at the tea house closest to the castle's front entrance at noon in a week's time."

"Do you know the name of the tea house?"

She shook her head, causing her long hair to bounce around as she laughed. "No, I just know there can be only one tea house closest to the castle."

He grinned. "Of course. If I don't see you in the closest one, I'll check every tea house in Jital."

"I shall look out for you as well." She looked at her companions waiting for her a short distance away. "I best be going. Peace be with you."

"And to you."

Alric knew witches only rarely rode horses and usually walked to their destinations. While it wasn't uncommon to see witches leave a town, it was rare to see them on the road between towns. He accepted the widespread belief witches usually travelled underground through their tunnels. This not only protected them from the elements and possible danger, but it kept their movements and numbers a secret. No one was sure how many witches were in one place or how many there were overall.

He mounted his horse and rode on, resisting the temptation to stare at her. Alric's mind was on seeing Orienla again, and he was content to let Darkian lead the way. By mid-morning, Alric passed most of the travellers along the highway. Noon approached, and Alric considered stopping to eat. Suddenly an arrow sailed past his chest. Alric's instincts took over. He rolled to the opposite side of the saddle, clinging to Darkian as he placed his own bow and arrow into position.

"Go, Darkian, go!"

The horse bolted with Alric clinging to his side.

Chapter Twenty

Ululla and Bruhamoff had cause to spend one night in the open air on a long journey of two days. They chose a spot a short distance from the road in the forest, and though Ululla initially felt apprehensive sleeping without the protection of walls, she received one of the best sleeps she had in weeks. Terrowin assured her he would watch over them and warn of any danger, but the night remained safe and quiet.

Ululla and Bruhamoff entered the city of Jital that day, the high white walls defining the inner core. They sought out the terradomus, finding it just inside the inner wall near one of the rolling hills that dominated Jital. The terradomus was set back against the hill, showing a three-story white stone face stretching out four times its height. The roof, made of green tiles, disappeared into the hill.

Bruhamoff stopped at the brick steps that led to the entrance and looked up. "This is a very large building."

"Yes, it is. Larger than the last time I was here." She continued up the steps as she spoke. "As you may guess, the main part of the building is actually inside the hill, and the tunnel network is extensive."

"Will we be staying here long?"

"I will be. This is going to be my new home, and in the near future, I shall be the new keeper." She looked at the change in his facial expression. "You will be meeting with Altus Rector Howrand and learn of your new assignment. Don't be worried, you're ready to take your next step."

"I guess so, but I feel I have so much more to learn."

"I hope you always feel you have much more to learn. Someday soon you'll be passing your knowledge onto others, and they may say the same thing of you." She reached out and took his hand. "If the altus rector trusts you to a task, then you should trust yourself as well."

* * * *

Bruhamoff felt alone as he sat on the edge of his bed in one of the hundreds of guest rooms. He squeezed his hands together. Soon he would be meeting Altus Rector Howrand alone, and the thought terrified him. Ululla, whom he depended on for so much, wouldn't be there. He had only a moment earlier to say goodbye to her before she was taken to the third floor and given a suite for the permanent residents.

I remember the first time I entered the Claireston Terradomus. I was scared then, too, and in awe of it. Maybe this will be like that, and I just need to get used to it. Ululla said I'll be okay, and she wouldn't say that if it wasn't true. The Book of Redemption tells us we are never given more tasks than we can achieve.

He opened his hands, stretched out his fingers, and stared at them.

I believe in the Book of Redemption. I will be okay. He breathed out slowly, repeating words he read many times. *I have been placed here at this moment because I have a choice to make. Whatever decision I make, I shall accept what happens next. There is no cause to be worried about a future that has not been decided yet.*

He stood. *I'm ready for my next assignment. Right after I get something to eat.*

Bruhamoff made his way from where the guest rooms were located to the broad stone steps to the main floor. He passed by many other witches, some of them offering a greeting. He responded out of habit as he approached the dining area. There was a short lineup to the counter where food was dispensed by the kitchen staff on the other side. He was thankful it wasn't a normal mealtime. Otherwise, the wait would be much longer. He accepted a bowl of vegetable stew with heavy bread and cheese, plus a mug of tea. Bruhamoff went to a table away from the other eaters.

After his second bite, he heard a whisper. Bruhamoff quickly looked around, seeing no one. The whisper was repeated.

"Worry not. I'll be with you on your next journey."

Bruhamoff smiled. *Perhaps I'm acting a little too nervous when a spirit feels the need to help me.*

At the appointed time, Bruhamoff made his way to the second level, following the marked stones. He knew he was deep into the interior of the hill, and the presence of decorated stone walls reminded him of the strength and history of the terradomus. He reached the outer office of the altus rector where a female was busy writing on a scroll. He paused at the curved entrance and waited to be recognized.

She looked up, and he saw she was of middle age with long brown hair.

"Brother Bruhamoff, we have been expecting you. Please come in."

She smiled and offered him a tea that he declined.

"I'm a bit too nervous to hold a tea mug right now." He tried to give a small grin.

"Understandable." She led him past her desk to another doorway that opened to a larger office with a domed ceiling. To his left was a desk curved out of what looked like a single giant tree trunk of polished wood. Two other doorways were equally spaced in the room. Bruhamoff guessed they led to the council chambers and to the Hall of Sentential.

He sat in one of the two armchairs which faced the desk and looked at Altus Rector Howrand, an extraordinary tall male witch. He was slim with thinning white hair and a closely trimmed beard.

Howrand smiled. "I envy you, Brother Bruhamoff. At your age, I was barely able to stumble out phrases from the Book of Redemption. Sister Ululla has told me you already possess the ability to understand the deeper meaning of many of the scriptures. Such intelligence is not common and shall lead the way for you to offer much to the Whiterose in the future."

Bruhamoff was taken aback by his praise and stumbled out a thank you.

Howrand held up the palm of his hand. "It is all right. You need not feel embarrassed about doing well or the compliments that follow. Because of your abilities, we have a new task for you. Normally, the altus councillium in Knavemire would deliver this to you personally, but there is a concern about spies. We know the Darkrose, and perhaps others, have infiltrated our terradomus. We accept that as part of inviting all to join our order, and normally we have little to hide in our philosophy and our everyday doings."

Bruhamoff nodded, recalling Sybbyl, a Darkrose spy.

"However, in this case, we believe it would be prudent to avoid anyone seeing you talk to the altus councillium. Your visit to me would not be considered out of the ordinary, and thus I shall be informing you of a new assignment, which I shall impress upon you is not an order, and you may refuse without us thinking any less of you. Is that clear?"

"Yes, I understand."

"Excellent. Sometimes a situation arises where the altus councillium has knowledge where the right person and the right time and place can have tremendous influence of future events. Indeed, such opportunities often lay outside of the order of witches. Such is the case here." He paused, leaned forward, and clasped his hands together on the desk.

"Brother Bruhamoff, we ask you to shed the garments of a Whiterose witch and look and act like a townsperson. You are to approach the recruitment office of the Royal Guardsmen in Knavemire and seek employment there."

Bruhamoff jaw dropped. "I wouldn't be a witch anymore?"

"Yes, you would still be a witch, only you would not appear to be one."

"Then am I to be a spy?"

Howrand shook his head. "No, you would not be a spy. Simply by being a Royal Guardsman in Knavemire at this time, you could change a sequence of events in a positive way for all humans and witches. I cannot tell you anymore details than that, other than in a year's time you may return to us as a witch. I want to stress you do not need to deny being a witch if asked. Many witches live and work outside the terradomus and a few are employed within the castle itself."

Bruhamoff took in the information, not expecting to be asked to do anything but to be a witch.

"Do you wish some time to reflect on your answer?"

The Book of Redemption tells us to accept new events and tasks with the knowledge we need only try to do the best we can. There is no failure if we are sincere in our efforts. The book also tells us we should welcome new opportunities to test our skills.

"Altus Rector Howrand, I shall be glad to accept my new task."

Howrand gave a broad grin. "Excellent. I believe you will find this new task something you'll reflect upon in years to come as one of your greatest accomplishments."

* * * *

Ululla listened to Keeper Cynwise speak about her decision to remain at the Jital Terradomus.

"I had hoped I was going to be offered a position on the council, but it seems that will not happen. They did offer me the altus rector position at Secary, but at my age I don't see myself travelling that far and living in a small town. I'm happy here and shall offer my service to those in need here."

Ululla smiled. "You are making a thoughtful and wise choice." She understood how Cynwise longed to be promoted to the council, but also knew how carefully members were chosen. Long service and knowledge were not the only considerations, but also temperament, personality, health, and problem solving abilities were also key factors.

"Thank you, Sister Ululla. I am sure you will be a fine keeper, and if I ever can be of help to you, I would be happy to do so. I have shown you the office and lookout, but there is one more thing I wish to show you."

Ululla followed her down a hall on the third level, then up another set of stairs. The fourth level, which held the suites for the altus rector and councillors, had a set of wood steps at a sharp incline at the end of the hall.

The steps appeared to come to a dead end, but Cynwise pulled on a chain, tugging down several arm lengths. A rumbling and scrapping noise echoed down the shaft and light appeared at the top of the stairs, revealing a blue sky.

Ululla climbed the steps and looked around. She stood at the top of a hill and gazed at the green grass and yellow flowers around her. She took a few steps past where a half boulder had rolled away to reveal the terradomus entrance. The hill appeared to be one of the highest points around the city, and Ululla had a good view of the surrounding area. She stared at the stone and brick buildings set along the twisted streets. Cynwise came up next to her.

"This hilltop is a special spot." She pointed across the town to a dome topped, sand coloured building. "That's the Darkrose terradomus." She turned around. "Behind us is a Blackrain Cabin deep into the forest. We're directly between them."

Ululla looked at the green carpet past the edge of Jital. She didn't see the Blackrain Cabins, but believed Cynwise knew its exact location. She understood a keeper not only knew of the comings and goings of the terradomus, but also what was nearby. "Most interesting."

Cynwise continued to point out locations. "The capital, Knavemire, is in that direction and Hardoff, the source of so much conflict, lies in the opposite direction. We are also in line between Ketamine and the castle of Jital."

"It seems we are in the crossroads of several interesting places." Ululla gazed around once more. "This is a very old city. It seems to have a few secrets."

* * * *

Ululla found Bruhamoff on the third level, studying the Book of Redemption. She hesitated before interrupting him. "Are you feeling troubled, Brother Bruhamoff?"

He frowned slightly. "I'm trying to understand how one can follow the guidance of being a witch while being asked to do something that appears to be in conflict with our ideals."

Ululla nodded. "The Book of Redemption is clear in stating we all must strive to follow its guidelines. However, it also tells us we have to adjust for different circumstances, and we must not be rigid in all applications of our beliefs. Sometimes, we may have to act in ways which appear to be in conflict with the Book of Redemption, but that is not entirely true. As long as our mind and spirit is with the teachings of the Book of Redemption, we are still in harmony with its teachings."

"What if one is required to hold a weapon?"

"It wouldn't be the first time a witch has had to use force for protection. Our beliefs should not prevent us from doing what is necessary to protect ourselves and those around us. A weapon can be a deterrent against those who wish to do harm to us, and thus be a way of preserving peace."

He nodded. "The more I try to understand the teachings of the Book of Redemption, the vaguer some of the wordings become."

Ululla smiled. "Being a witch is not always easy. The teachings of peace and harmony can ironically cause inner turmoil."

Bruhamoff grinned. "Thank you for helping me with your insight. I feel better now."

"Anytime you wish to talk, I will be happy to accommodate you. Peace be with you, always."

"And to you, Sister Ululla."

Chapter Twenty-One

Alric reacted without thought. He rolled his body to the opposite side from where the arrow came, using Darkian as a shield. A second arrow flew by. "Double time!" He yelled, and the horse immediately reacted to the command, charging down the path.

Alric's warrior mind had taken over his actions. He knew a second man was no doubt up ahead in case the ambush failed. As another arrow sailed where he was sitting a moment earlier, Alric formed his next series of actions. A bend in the road took him out of sight from the first attacker. He moved back to sitting on the saddle and stopped Darkian, moving him just off the road as he readied his bow and arrow.

Moments later, a horse and rider made their presence known, first by the thud of hooves and then the appearance of a small man holding the reins in one hand and a bow in the other. Alric's first arrow didn't miss, striking the rider in the chest, easily piercing the heavy shirt.

The rider opened his mouth, although no sound came forth, and slowly tumbled to his side. He fell to the ground in front of Alric. His legs kicked several times and then lay still. The horse stopped and looked back at the dying rider. Alric turned his attention back to road and waited with another arrow poised in his bow. He didn't have to wait long.

Another rider, this one of medium height and heavy weight, came into view. He pulled his horse to a stop quickly as he spotted his dead companion and his horse. The horseman looked around frantically and began to turn his horse, but Alric's arrow pierced his leg. Moments later, a second arrow grazed the horse in its flank.

Alric watched the events unfold to his liking. The horse raised his front legs, throwing the injured rider to the ground. He rolled in agony, reaching for the arrow stuck in his thigh.

"Freeze where you are." Alric shouted. He kept an arrow drawn, aimed at the helpless man.

The man looked around as he gripped the arrow in his hand. "Please, have mercy."

"I might. Don't pull it out, or you'll bleed to death. Are there any others?"

"No, just us two."

"Why did you attack me?"

"A man paid us to kill you. He said you were carrying money as well."

"Who was this man? What did he look like?"

"Never seen him before. Tall. Black clothing."

Alric urged Darkian forward and stopped near the would be robber. He looked down as he spoke. "Get on your horse. Get a doctor to remove the arrow. Take heed the next time you attack someone. You've used up your luck."

He moved Darkian back on the road and galloped away.

Why would someone want me dead? A tall man wearing black clothes? Not anyone I know.

* * * *

Alric became aware of the increased traffic on the road since arriving in Allisure compared to Fringella and Asper. Even Dwykath didn't have nearly the movement of people and horses, and to Alric it showed Allisure had a much greater wealth and commerce.

On his arrival in Allisure, he had been quickly impressed with their road system. Most of the roads were constructed of rock supported by gravel and clay with a wide surface and could support horse pulled wagons that could pass one another easily. The Allisure road builders had gone one step further and had put a drainage system under the roadway to allow the passage of water to go underneath the road rather than washing over the top. In all, it made his trip easier as he could simply let Darkian move at his own pace, letting him think about the attack earlier. *Maybe he made up the story that someone had paid him to attack me. Certainly, there are highway men who would prey on anyone. It's hard to believe I'm someone important enough to be worth killing.*

Farm land used for both crops and livestock increased. Between the farms where trees stood, he spotted deer and other wildlife. With plenty of game available, Alric didn't worry about attacks from a hungry panther, wolves, or even bears but wondered if there were more robbers.

He stopped at an inn at the halfway point to give Darkian a rest and to eat. There were several inns in the area, and although it wasn't an actual town, a sign down the road proclaimed it to be Deyell. There was a cluster of farms in the area, plus a merchant store and the various inns. Alric suspected it may have been a village at one time and was slowly growing into a town.

At the inn, one still fairly new, he sat at one of the long tables. He slowly spooned his soup, when another man sat down opposite him a short distance down the bench.

"Travelling far?"

Alric looked up and studied the bearded stranger. His face looked relaxed, and his eyes showed years of knowledge.

"Some. Going to Jital. Thinking I might settle down there."

The man nodded with approval. "It's a good place. Not poor and like most Allisure places, well governed. Mind you, you'll need to find a place to stay. They don't allow sleeping in the streets."

"That's okay. I'm not sure I like the idea of sleeping on the ground anyway. Jital is a fairly old city, isn't it?"

He gave a smile, and Alric was under the impression the stranger was holding back some information. "Old is right. Jital is built over another ancient city, a city lost in the eons of time."

"A city over another? What was the name of this city?"

"It matters not, but Jital is located in a sacred place. There always has been a city here and always will be. Jital is its name now, but not its identity."

"What's its identity?"

"Ah, a very good question. Someday you will understand this answer better. Its identity is the push and attraction of opposite forces, like the currents in an ocean that circle each other and produce a calm.

Jital, and the cities before it, is in the middle of forces which cancel each other. It is why people are attracted to it. There is calm there, but also energy. I believe it would be a good place for you to seek a home."

"I see. How do you know this? Are you a witch?"

He smiled and shook his head. "No, my friend, witches are not fond of us. We have different concerns than they do, although our goals are more similar than they would believe." He stood. "May the path you follow lead you to contentment."

Alric watched him leave and remembered hearing that phrase before. *Blackrain.*

Alric sat after he finished his meal, wondering why the man had sought him out. *He was hinting at something concerning Jital. But why me? The witches also seem to think I am a key to something. But what? I'm a former soldier who wants to be a woodworker. How will that change the world?* He went to retrieve Darkian from where he resting.

"Come on, time to hit the road. Let's see if we can make Jital by sunset."

* * * *

The farms had become continuous, requiring fences to separate them from their neighbours. Earlier farms were usually open, bounded by a creek or where the farmer had stopped plowing the land. Wagons carrying goods were common, and Alric began to look for the first signs of Jital itself, expecting to see a gated entrance patrolled by Allisure troops.

Instead, he saw shops with merchants doing a brisk business. Many of the shops were two stories with the proprietors living up stairs. He also spotted tea houses and taverns, and the thought of an ale after the long ride proved to be irresistible.

The Huntress Tavern had low stone walls around the perimeter with the rest of the tall building made of wood. He stopped there, tied up Darkian, and pushed open the wood door. He liked the interior. It was almost full, a good sign for any traveller. Sufficient light streamed in to show off the clean interior. The chairs and tables were in better condition than most taverns, and he sat at a table where he had a view of the outside behind the building. A farm of chickens, cattle, and geese mixed together in front of a large farm house. Next to the house was a crop of grain, their golden stems waving in the light wind.

A server came up to him, carrying a mug of ale. He smiled at the middle aged, short brunette, telling her, "You read my mind."

"I assume you didn't come in here for water." She returned his smile as she put down the ale. "Are you wanting food as well?"

He saw the back of her hand, a faded tattoo of a black circle with a name inside it. "What do you have?"

"Chicken with bread."

He nodded, thankful it wasn't rabbit. "That'll be fine."

He sipped the ale as he stared at the farm, suspecting the owner also owned the tavern. They may also have made the ale that had a yeast taste to it. Like most of the ale he had, the quality varied greatly from tavern to tavern.

The server brought him a half chicken and quarter loaf of dark yellow bread. "Another ale?"

He looked at the portion of the food in front of him. "Sure." He paused before asking. "Are you a slave? I thought Allisure banned slavery."

"Our previous owner didn't know or care about that law. He took the four of us here to do some trading. As soon as we reached the gates, we asked the guards to set us free. They immediately released us from our chains."

"There were four of you?"

"Yes, one man and we three women. We decided to farm here and later built this tavern. It's hard work, but we're free. Of course, there are more of us now. There are seven adults and nine kids."

"Tell me, where are the gates to the city?"

"Not much further. Jital has grown past the original boundaries, but they still occupy the original gate house."

Alric thanked her. He admired the former slaves looking for the right opportunity to break free and then keeping together to farm and making a life together. He pulled the roasted chicken apart with his fingers and soon devoured the meal. The second ale helped to wash down the food, and he felt full and ready to finish his journey.

The server offered to bring him another ale, but Alric declined. "No, I need to find a place to stay tonight, and a few more days after that. I'm thinking of settling down in Jital. It won't be easy to find a place if I stay here and drink." He dropped several coins on the table.

"What type of work do you do?"

"I'm a woodworker." Alric felt almost like smiling as he said the words.

"Wait a moment. I may have a place for you."

A short time later, a medium height, heavily built man came to the table. He spoke in a soft voice. "You're looking for a place to stay?" He waited for Alric's nod and continued. "Our old farmhouse is empty and needs some repair work. If you're willing to fix it up, you can stay there."

"If you have tools I can use, that would be fine."

"Come with me. I'll show you the place, and then you can decide for sure."

Alric followed him out a rear exit by the kitchen and down a well-worn path along a fence. Alric gave his name.

"Fendrel. We had to move out of the old place because it was getting too small, especially with the younglings. It was supposed to be fixed up afterward, but we never got 'round to it. If you can get it fixed up, you can stay here. Plenty of space. If you want you can have a garden, but the women cook a lot of food, and you're welcome to join us for meals."

They reached the old farmhouse, and Alric could see where one part of the roof was sagging. Weeds grew next to the walls, and the wood door was ajar. Fendrel slowed his pace and frowned as he reached the door and pushed it open.

Alric was surprised the door didn't fall from its hinges and stepped inside after Fendrel. Sunlight poured in from a hole in the roof, and the sound of small animals scampering along the floor could be heard.

Fendrel spoke, "It looks worse than I remembered. Do you think you could fix it?"

Alric looked at the weathered walls supported by a stone layer. The wood flooring had gaps in areas and bowed in others. Each of the five small rooms was separated by walls where several planks had fallen out.

The silenced lingered as Alric looked at the amount of hard work it would take to restore the home to be suitable for living in again.

"Sure. I can do it, providing you have the tools to work with."

Fendrel looked relieved. "I was worried you were going to laugh at me and leave."

Alric smiled. "This is a home worth saving."

Fendrel put his hand on Alric's shoulder. "I'll take you across the road a ways. One of the family is a blacksmith. He'll make all the tools you need."

A place to live. Wood and tools to use. I think I have found my new life.

Chapter Twenty-Two

Bruhamoff sat with Ululla, eating breakfast. He knew she was curious about his appointed task, but was told to keep it a secret to protect himself and those around him.

"I wish I was allowed to tell you more, Sister Ululla, but all I can tell you is I'll be gone for a year or more."

"It is likely I'll still be here when you do return. There will be much to talk about then."

He nodded, hesitated, and then spoke in a rush. "I'll always be in your debt for the kindness and wisdom you bestowed upon me." His face felt flushed, and he reminded himself this wasn't a final goodbye.

"I gained much from you as well. Regardless when we meet again, we will always be connected to each other." She smiled. "Ironically, your journey begins here and mine ends. I shall think of you and hope you're enjoying your adventure as much as I enjoyed mine. There will be challenges for you, but they will only make you stronger and better prepared for life ahead."

After the meal, he gave Ululla a final hug, wanting to kiss her, but instead gave her a forced grin before he made his way to the lower floor. The altus rector was waiting for him and handed him a leather vest, a knife in a sheath, coins, and a silver necklace with a gem secured in the front.

"The vest and knife will make you look less like a witch and more like an ordinary man seeking his adventure. The coins should cover your needs until you receive a regular pay."

"And the necklace?" He slipped it over his head.

"It has a spell placed within it. It will aid those meeting you to believe you're an honest man and believe what you say. Now I have some information to depart upon you, and it is important you follow these instructions."

Bruhamoff listened carefully, nodding on where he was to go and the exact time. When Howrand finished speaking, he looked down the tunnel. "This goes all the way to Knavemire?"

"Yes. There are several places where you may climb stairs to the surface if you wish. I know it's nice to see the sun after a time spent in the tunnel." He placed a hand on Bruhamoff's shoulder. "Safe journey, Brother Bruhamoff. May your return here find you have grown spiritually."

A final handshake and Bruhamoff set off down the tunnel, the torch he carried making the walls appearing to close off in front and behind him.

"Fear not. I am with you."

"Thank you, Terrowin. It's nice to have company."

The dark, brick lined tunnel seemed to go on forever. His feet became sore from the hard surface. He stopped at the first set of stairs to breathe in fresh air and feel the sun. He passed the second set of stairs but couldn't resist the third set, stretching out between the trees in the forest.

This is the first time I've felt alone in years. Even when I was an orphan, I wasn't really alone. The witches were always around me. It feels nice to be alone for a change. Well, almost alone. I have a ghost with me.

Bruhamoff returned to the tunnel, closing the grass covered trap door as he lowered himself down the stairs. He continued his journey, and in the evening emerged in a field in the outskirts of Knavemire, avoiding the terradomus in the city. He understood the need for secrecy, and thus not being seen at the terradomus, but it meant he needed to find a place to sleep for the night. He made his way down quiet streets, finally entering a road with several inns and stables. He had never had to obtain a room in an inn before and was apprehensive as he entered the Townsman Inn.

The elderly, heavyweight man coughed before he spoke to Bruhamoff. "Ya want a room?"

"Yes, please. How much is a room?"

The man narrowed his eyes. "Ten bronze."

Bruhamoff stood straight. "Four bronze or I will go to the next inn."

A frown came across the innkeeper's face. "No need. Four bronze it is."

Bruhamoff nodded and passed over the coins. The room he was shown was small, but he was used to even smaller rooms as a guest in a terradomus. It was not as clean, and the thin blanket was nearly useless, but he soon fell asleep on the small cot after he ate a ration of his food.

* * * *

The streets began to fill with people and horses as the sun lifted above the horizon. Bruhamoff kept looking at the various shops while avoiding pedestrians, carts, and horses while making his way across town. The streets rarely went in straight lines, but Bruhamoff kept in an easterly direction, seeking out the castle. He passed by the outer wall as the sun crossed a third of the sky and stopped to have a bite to eat. The inn was doing a brisk business feeding travellers. Most ordered ale to go with their stew, but Bruhamoff ordered tea instead, not wanting the effect of alcohol to dampen his thinking.

He ate slowly, knowing he had sufficient time to reach the castle. He had been instructed to reach the recruitment office at just after one in the afternoon.

After the shadow from the sun reached its smallest point, Bruhamoff made his way toward the castle, hearing the bell located in the highest point of the castle ring the noon hour. He focused on his journey, ignoring the crowd of people around him. Merchants blocked the streets, calling out to offer their wares for sale, but he deftly stepped around them. *A month ago, I would have stopped at every vendor. Now it seems unimportant.*

The castle was bigger than he imagined, and he spent a minute looking at its vast expanse. The cream coloured stone glistened in the sunlight with multiple towers positioned evenly around an octagon shaped inner wall. The main castle stood several stories high with the flag of Allisure flying above the central dome. Bruhamoff walked through the gate of the inner wall. Four guards stood at attention, eyeing but not stopping those passing by. He walked the flat brick roadway that followed along the inside of the inner wall, its width sufficient for horses and people travelling in either direction. He had a glimpse of the horse stables and the barracks for the soldiers behind the castle. A smaller building was attached to the castle, and he understood it was the recruitment office. *The barracks are bigger than any terradomus I've seen. It must hold a few thousand soldiers.*

The bell chimed again, signifying it was one o'clock, and he made his way to the recruitment office. Two men left as he approached, walking toward the rear of the castle.

He entered the open doorway. The room had maps hanging from the walls and a second door Bruhamoff suspected led to the castle. The table held a dozen chairs tightly placed around it. Behind a desk a dark-haired man looked up.

"At least you don't look like you're starving like the last two." He frowned. "Do you know how to use a sword or ride a horse?"

"I can learn."

The officer grunted. "I suppose you'll have to. Either that or die." He turned as the second door opened and immediately stood for the woman who entered. She was carefully dressed in a full blue and white dress.

"Lady Asturias," he said in greeting and bowed.

Bruhamoff stood straight, wondering who she was, but supposed she ranked high in the king's court.

She looked at Bruhamoff, appraising him, and spoke to the officer. "I came to ask you for a suitable candidate for a royal guardsman. I think he will do nicely."

"Yes, my lady, although he hasn't officially joined the army yet."

"No matter." She turned her attention to Bruhamoff. "You're now a royal guardsman. Report immediately for duty." She turned and left the room, leaving Bruhamoff surprised at the sudden turn of events.

The officer sighed. "Come with me. We better get you up and ready as soon as possible."

Bruhamoff followed him down a hall to a set of stone steps to a lower level. They passed several rooms where four sets of bunk beds were jammed into a small space.

The officer gave a running commentary as they walked. "Better sleeping quarters here than in the barracks for regular soldiers. Also, you get better food. Leftovers from the kitchen, which is a darn sight better than the slop we end up with." He pointed to a room. "Go in there. They're no doubt expecting you."

The room was large, with three uniformed men in conversation in the centre, seated around a table. A cot sat in the corner and a desk on the opposite wall. The room was lit by four oil lamps located in the middle of each wall. One man looked at Bruhamoff.

"You must be the new favour. Lady Asturias has instructed us to get you prepared immediately." He stood. "Best come with me." The officer marched out of the room. "I'm Captain Hawkins."

"Bruhamoff."

"Your rank is Corporal. This puts you above the enlisted men and gives you a higher pay, among other things."

Bruhamoff followed him to another room where he was given two identical uniforms consisting of blue pants and shirt, a red vest, and black boots. A wide leather belt held a short, wide blade sword and a knife. He was handed a pike and told he would be given lessons on their proper use later. A room with eight beds was shown to him.

"Your bed is at the end, top bunk. There's a trunk at the end of the bed for you to keep personal effects. Your second uniform is kept on a hook at the far wall." He pointed at where similar uniforms hung. "Change into your uniform now, and I'll take you upstairs where you'll be reporting for duty."

Bruhamoff quickly changed as Hawkins spoke.

"You're on active duty as long as we say. A schedule is posted, and generally you will be on for a half day at a time. Sometimes you'll have a double shift, and you better learn to stay alert during that time. At our discretion, you may receive one or two days off each month. Other than those days, you're expected to be in uniform and act accordingly as a Royal Guardsman. No over indulgence in ale or wine. Women are attracted to the Royal Guardsmen, but you must act only with the highest intentions. If we receive complaints about you, there will be unpleasant consequences."

"Yes, sire." Bruhamoff walked with him to the third level of the castle.

"You are being stationed to protect the queen's quarters. I will show you the royal suites so you're familiar with their layout, but normally you do not ever enter without an invitation from the king or queen."

Two royal guards stood to the side as Hawkins pushed open one of the double doors leading to the king's chambers. Bruhamoff was impressed by the size of the room, containing an oversized bed, paintings, furniture, and a desk. One wall featured glass doors that led to a balcony. The high ceiling, with a chandelier in the centre, gave the room a spacious feeling.

Pointing to an open doorway, Hawkins didn't allow Bruhamoff to gaze around the room.

"That is where the royal bathroom is located, and next to that is the wardrobe room. Beyond are the servants' quarters. They are required to be close to the king at all times." He pointed to the far wall where a closed door stood. "That door leads to the queen's bedroom. Also to a passageway you must be familiar with." He strode across the room, opened and waited as Bruhamoff looked at the narrow hallway behind it. Past the hallway was another door.

"The passageway has a set of stairs that goes down below ground level where it continues past the castle grounds. These doors can be bolted from the inside to prevent others from following the king."

"Where does the passageway go eventually?"

"That's not for you to know, only where it is located here. If the need arises, you are to ensure his safety and then the queen's. You are to go with him only if he requests you do so. Otherwise, you are to stay here and guard against any possible intruders."

Bruhamoff nodded and followed Hawkins into the queen's bedroom. The room was slightly smaller than the king's, although it had the same expensive furnishings, wall paintings, and a balcony. He wasn't given much time to inspect the room as they went straight to the royal bathroom holding a sunken marble rectangular tub and a table full of oils and soaps. The next room held racks of dresses and several dressers. The last room was the servants' quarters with four beds and dressers. Two women were working on repairing clothing and quickly stood as they entered, looking apprehensive.

Hawkins quickly put them at ease. "Relax, there isn't any emergency. This is Corporal Bruhamoff, a new guard. Initially I will have him stationed outside these doors." He pointed to the servant's entrance to the room.

Bruhamoff gave the servants a smile, noting one was standing at a slight angle.

"Memorize their faces, Corporal. Unless you know the person, you cannot allow anyone to pass these doors."

Bruhamoff soon found himself standing on guard outside the servants' entrance with another guard.

"Corporal Harris will assist you in recognizing those allowed through these doors. Because the servants' quarters are connected to the royal chambers, we must maintain high security here. If a person wanted to do harm to the royal family, this is where they may try to gain access."

After Hawkins left, Harris turned to Bruhamoff and whispered, "Welcome to boredom."

Chapter Twenty-Three

Alric patched the roof and strengthened the timbers supporting the roof. Yesterday he'd repaired the holes on the outside walls, making the old house closer to being weather and rodent proof. Tomorrow would be a harder day when he needed to replace a support beam with one fashioned from a tree trunk. As he climbed down, he reflected the work was harder than he expected, but also going faster. *So far, I've had good fortune in my work. I hope that holds out. Good weather and good tools can shorten the labour.*

He washed up before going to the newer farm house for dinner. The home's residents had readily accepted him as part of their extended family and encouraged him to spend time with them, including meals. He didn't always go there for meals, finding the noise of children and adults around the table hard to get used to after travelling alone. He was also uncomfortable with being the centre of attention from the youngsters as they repeatedly asked him questions.

The well he used was behind the old farm house where the line of sight was blocked from the new home. The large garden at the rear was hidden by a single row of coniferous trees that provided a wind block. Satisfied with his isolation, Alric stripped off his shirt and pants, using the cool well water from a bucket to wash the sweat and dirt off his chest and back.

He didn't worry about drying off, simply putting his clothes on and tolerating the dampness. As usual when he entered the new farm house, the children quickly surrounded him, asking him questions.

Tersica, a teenage girl Alric learned was a devious planner, gave him a sly smile.

"How was work today? It must have been rather dusty work on the roof."

"It was. Thatch is hard to work with."

"Just wondering because..."

Sharron, the server he first met in the Huntress Tavern, intervened with her daughter. "Tersica, stop bothering him and help me with the potatoes."

Tersica smiled at him and sauntered over to the stove.

Alric ignored the game the eldest daughter was playing and wrestled with the younger boys before dinner. During the meal, he enlisted the help of the men to raise a beam to stabilize the roof.

"Not hard work if we do it all together. The roof will continue to sag if we don't strengthen it."

They readily agreed to assist him, and Alric filled his plate as Tersica smiled at him from across the table. *She is going to cause Sharron lots of trouble before she's grown up.*

* * * *

The next morning, Alric urged Darkian forward. The big horse dug into the ground and slowly the trimmed tree trunk pivoted from the ground up to on one end.

Around Alric other men pulled at the top of the beam with ropes to ensure it didn't fall to the side. The beam moved, wedging underneath the roof. Another man at the roof began to pound in wood spikes to secure the beam into place as Alric steadied his horse. The men holding the ropes previously quickly filled in the hole where the beam rested. A few minutes later Fendrel, wiping the sweat from his face, clapped Alric on the shoulder.

"Good work. It doesn't look like the roof is going to sag down now."

"The frame is strong now. I've patched the holes on the walls, and next I can start replacing the boards."

"You've done a lot of work. My thanks."

"I have to say it feels good to be working again and seeing the progress of my labor."

Alric joined the family at dinner, the meal a celebration for securing the frame of the old house, and Alric was happy to join in on the feast.

"What are your plans tomorrow, Alric?" Sharron asked.

"I'm going to Jital for the day. I think Darkian needs some exercise as well. He's happy being with the other horses, but doesn't like being fenced in."

"You'll enjoy going. There're some interesting sights there. If you have a chance, climb up one of the hills. You can see the whole countryside."

"Thank you, I may do that."

Alric left to sleep at the empty house, after turning down several requests from the children to take them to town the next day. *At least it doesn't feel like I'm sleeping outdoors anymore.* His thoughts drifted to Jital and the tea houses. *I hope Orienla is there.*

* * * *

The morning sun warmed the air quickly, promising a hot day later. Alric went outside to the back of the house and to the well. He looked first to see if anyone was visible from his vantage point and took off his clothes. First, he poured a bucket of water over his head before using soap. He used a second and third bucket to rinse off and quickly dressed.

Alric walked over to the tavern, stopping to pat Darkian after the horse galloped over to the fence.

"Don't worry big fellow. I'll be coming back to get you after I've had something to eat."

The Huntress Tavern was quiet with only a few guests stopping in for breakfast. Alric sat eating alone when Tersica sat across from him, smiling as she gazed at him.

Alric sighed inwardly. "Tersica, what is on your mind?"

"I'm curious about why you're going to Jital."

"Why do you ask?" He stopped eating and sat straight.

"My mother told me men go to the city for only two reasons. One is to buy supplies." Tersica licked her lips. "The other is to get a woman."

"Interesting theory."

"I know which one it is."

"You do, do you?"

"Mother saw you wash this morning. She said you used three pails of water. That would make it a special woman."

Alric chuckled. "All women are special."

Tersica stood, leaning on the table with her arms. "Including me?"

"Someday the right man will discover your charms. Right now, you should be concentrating on not giving your mother fits by growing up too fast."

Tersica grinned and waltzed away, stopping at a nearby table to collect the empty plates and cups.

Alric shook his head and finished his breakfast.

Darkian was eager to travel, and Alric allowed him to set his own pace. When they arrived at the entrance to Jital, he directed Darkian toward the city's castle. The market area in front of the castle was busy, and Alric looked for teahouses. Eventually, he determined which teahouse was the one closest to the castle and pulled Darkian to a stop.

Too early for lunch, but I might as well go in and wait anyway.

The teahouse was doing a brisk business. Alric suspected the small, closely packed, roundtables would be filled during the lunch hour. He took a table that gave him a good view of the entrance, ordered an ale, and prepared to wait for Orienla all afternoon. Alric took the first sip from the tankard, pleased with the flavour, looked up at entrance, and saw Orienla step inside to calmly scan the room.

Alric stood, raising his arm.

Smiling, Orienla reached his table.

"Alric, it's wonderful to see you again. You're here early. I thought I'd have to wait for you."

"I was here for breakfast."

Her jaw dropped for a moment until she saw him grinning.

"I just arrived here myself. How have you been?"

Alric listened to her talk about her journey, alluding to part of it being inside a tunnel. She described her visits around the city and found the buildings exotic in design with the carved symbols in the stone walls. She asked him where he was staying and listened with interest in his work restoring the old farmhouse.

Alric paid for lunch and suggested a walk. Orienla stopped to pet Darkian, telling Alric she didn't get to ride horses often.

"Witches are taught not to use animals merely as a convenience but to allow them to live as naturally as possible. We usually end up walking rather than riding."

"I think Darkian likes going for rides, although I see your point in not abusing animals."

She took Alric's hand. "Let's walk toward the castle. It looks wonderful from a distance, and I'm curious what it looks like up close."

The castle grounds were well kept with well stationed guards ensuring those going through stayed on the pathways. Alric agreed with Orienla that the castle was not only well maintained, but also designed to be pleasing to the eye.

"There is an ancient feel to it. The design of the towers looked very different." He looked at the teardrop shaped top of the tower.

Orienla replied. "I heard the design of the castle was copied from the ruins of another castle that used to be here."

"The city, in one form or another, apparently always has been here. At least that's what I've been told."

"There is a saying in Jital that two paths converge to become one, and one path will become two. So, whatever you seek, it can be found here."

"Interesting. Well, at least we did find a teahouse."

Orienla laughed. "That is true. I'm glad we could meet again, but unfortunately, I have to leave Jital soon. I received a message my father has become quite ill, and I need to return home to help my mother."

"I'm sorry to hear about your father."

"He's always been a good man, always hard working, but in the last few years his health has steadily declined. I gave him some potions that helped him, but it seems his heart has worn out."

She took his hand as they walked back, making quiet conversation.

Alric pointed at the tallest hill standing at Jital's edge. "That would be a good place to see the whole city."

"It would be, except for a small problem. The Whiterose have built their terradomus right into that hill and have an entrance at the top. Most people are afraid to get close to what is supposed to be a secret entrance."

"Witches seem to be everywhere I look."

Orienla looked up at him. "You must be treading the same path as witches in spirit then. You're in Jital, and perhaps your path and those of the witches will converge."

"Ah, but you are leaving Jital."

They reached a quiet street, and she stopped to kiss him. "I haven't left yet."

He returned her kiss, making it longer as his hands slowly pushed against her clothing, sliding up her ribcage. He heard her moan and lift up her head, exposing her neck to his lips.

"We better stop, or people will get a bad impression of witches." She gave him a hug, burying her face against his chest and turned to walk again.

"When do you need to leave Jital?"

She stopped and pointed at a large stone structure. "My terradomus." She looked down at the ground and then back at his face. "I don't wish to sound forward, but tomorrow I shall leave Jital on my journey. I will be going past the place where you are staying, and perhaps I can stop for dinner. Or the night."

"I would be honoured to serve you my best burnt chicken."

Orienla laughed. "Good thing it's not the meal I'm stopping for then."

Alric gave her a final kiss and went back toward the teahouse, his thoughts already on tomorrow.

* * * *

"The altus councillium wishes you would reconsider."

Orienla stood in front of the altus rector and crossed her arms. "I have made my decision. I'm going to be with my father during his final days and help my mother. They need me. There isn't one passage in the Book of Destiny that tells me to abandon my family and seduce a former warrior instead."

"Your decision may have long term implications when it comes to promotions."

"So be it."

"What if we were to have a special spell that could save your father?"

"I was told there wasn't any spells known that could help him."

The altus rector gave a small shrug. "We cannot reveal all we know to everyone. Otherwise, there would be other difficulties. We can possibly help him, depending on the exact nature of his illness. Will you stay now?"

She stared at him from across his desk. "First threats and now this bribe? If you can bring my father to full health again, then I will return to Jital and seek out Alric."

He frowned. "Sister Orienla, I am disappointed in your attitude. Surely you can see we are doing our best to help you."

"Save my father first. Maybe that was something that should have been offered long ago."

She left his chamber, deciding not to reveal she was going to see Alric one last time tomorrow. She was taken by surprise by the intense questioning she received since Alric showed interest in her in Orsorum. She knew of the prophecy regarding a red-headed former warrior but didn't believe Alric was actually the one, not until the altus rector himself pressed her to secure a relationship with him. Now she wondered if she had stumbled into being part of the prophecy.

It doesn't matter. My parents come before pleasing the Umbravox. If they don't like it, then maybe the Whiterose would be more understanding. Her cheeks burning, Orienla made her way to her bedroom, wanting to avoid any more confrontations.

Chapter Twenty-Four

Bruhamoff understood what the other guard meant by boredom. After three days of standing by the servants' entrance, he appreciated almost any change in the routine. He soon learned all the servants' names and faces, in particular one servant by the name of Ellyn, who was a few years older. She was the friendliest of the servants and occasionally slipped the guards a small pastry when she brought in a dessert tray for the queen. Ellyn also walked with a pronounced limp. Bruhamoff learned that when she was a child, her leg was damaged by a disease and ended up being stunted.

Today, she stopped by the door and whispered to Bruhamoff. "I heard Lady Asturias will be seeking you out for special duty tonight."

"Special duty?"

She gave him a sly smile. "You'll find out."

Bruhamoff learned of the special assignment when he was escorted by Lady Asturias into the queen's bed chambers. He stood stiffly, trying to avert his gaze from the lacy gown she wore as she sat propped up against numerous pillows in bed.

The queen looked amused at his discomfort.

"I do hope the rest of you is as rigid as your posture." She looked at Lady Asturias. "Should we assume he is not aware of his duties?"

Bruhamoff felt his face turning pink. The two ladies giggled, obviously at his expense. He had never imagined the queen acting in such a fashion and was at a loss on what to do or say next.

Lady Asturias grinned. "I think Corporal Bruhamoff will benefit from a drink or two."

When she poured him a glass and handed it to him, Bruhamoff pulled a face at the taste of the whisky. The alcoholic jolt warmed his body and slowed his heart rate. The overall effect reduced his anxiety at being nude in front of the queen. It was very clear to him what his duty was, which he performed obediently.

The guard didn't react to Bruhamoff's return to in front of the door, other than the comment, "All secure. No visitors during your absence."

Bruhamoff nodded, remaining silent for a long period of time. Finally, he whispered, "I didn't expect this to be part of the Royal Guard's job duties."

"Your duties are what anyone above you says they are. That includes just about everyone here in the castle." The whispered replied continued. "If she likes you, you may be busy on most nights."

Bruhamoff wondered why the witches would have put him in such a situation. This was not how he expected the queen to act and found it hard to believe this was part of the witches' plan. *I have no choice. I had my chance to turn down this assignment back at the terradomus. Now, I have to see this through.* He closed his eyes at the memory of the night's earlier activity. *Rather a pleasing body she has. Could be worse things to have happen.*

* * * *

Ellyn gave Bruhamoff a pastry from the tray she carried. The second guard also received one, but she focused her attention on Bruhamoff.

"Are you surviving all right as a Royal guard? I know they're making you do extra duties." She gave him a grin.

"It's certainly not what I expected." *Six times in the past three weeks. It didn't matter whether it was night or day shift.*

"You don't seem to be the usual type to be a Royal guard. Were you born on a farm?"

"I'm an orphan. I moved around as a child."

"Oh, that's so sad." She gave him a smile. "But it looks like you turned out okay."

"Thanks. I had good people help guide me."

"Talk to you again." Ellyn disappeared behind the door.

The other guard spoke quietly. "She seems to have taken a liking to you."

"Nice girl. Pleasant face and personality."

"Pity about her limp."

"None of us are perfect." *None of us are here without imperfections. When we look upon others, do we see their strengths? If we see only their weakness, is it only a reflection of our own concerns and fears? Accept who they are and trust they accept you in return.*

At the end of his shift, Bruhamoff went to his bunk to stretch out and relax, enjoying a few minutes of doing nothing. His back muscles gradually stopped aching, and he slowly sat up, nodding to the two other royal guards in the room. His stomach growled, and he made his way to the dining room reserved for the royal guards and certain other members of the royal court. That didn't include the maids and servants, and Bruhamoff briefly thought of Ellyn.

He ate his meal with several other guards along a long table, reminding him of meals in a terradomus. The conversation he shared with the other guards was far from serious, and all were careful not to divulge anything they saw during their duty. Other than extreme cases, such as a plot to assassinate, all information remained a secret. Thus, his rendezvous with the queen was not brought up.

Bruhamoff excused himself, bringing up a barb at him for being polite while off duty.

"We ain't members of the court, Bruhammy. You can save the formal talk when you're not around us."

Bruhamoff grinned, appreciating the good natured comment. The guards had become his second family, and they had shown to be a close-knit group. He strolled through the wide, hallways. Occasionally he glanced at the large paintings and statues that adorned the walls. It was impressive and a contrast to the plain walls of a terradomus.

He was shocked the queen had taken him to her bed, knowing how revered the king and queen were looked up by the population. He did understand the kingdom was the best run of any of its neighbours, and the population had received the benefits of the king's rule.

The sun peeked through the cloud cover, and Bruhamoff made his way past the vendors who set up in the courtyard. The walk was having the desired effect. His legs and back felt better after his time on guard duty.

"Bruhamoff."

He turned toward the feminine voice. "Ellyn? What brings you here?"

"I'm going to visit my mother. Are you just walking about?"

"My legs and back were a bit stiff from all that standing."

"Care to walk with me? We can stop for a drink if you like."

Bruhamoff readily agreed, and they were soon strolling toward the exit of the castle grounds.

"Did you hear about Queen Elissa?"

"No. Did something happen to her?" Bruhamoff's concern came out in his voice. Despite her teasing of his inexperience, he had become quite fond of her.

"Something happened all right. The queen is expecting."

"Expecting?" His voice went quiet.

Ellyn stopped walking and grabbed both his hands. "You must understand one thing. If the queen is pregnant, only the king can be the father. Otherwise, there would be dire consequences for everyone, including the child."

Bruhamoff was silent for several seconds, finally nodding.

Ellyn smiled. "Let's go for a drink. I think you could use one. Or two."

He agreed wholeheartedly, and Bruhamoff gulped his ale and wiped his mouth with the back of his hand. "I don't know how I feel about this."

"You shouldn't feel anything. The baby is not yours."

"But..."

"I told you already. You need to accept what has happened." She reached across the table and touched his hand. "You also need to have relationships besides royalty."

He sighed. "I know you're right. I also know I should apologize now as I plan to get drunk."

She grinned. "It'll be good for you. You have a tendency to be a wee bit too conservative."

* * * *

Bruhamoff groaned. His head hurt, and the room spun. Moments of last night came back to him of stumbling into bed and the bell being rung to announce breakfast too soon. He tried to get up, but one of the royal guardsmen pushed him back to his bunk.

"You stay there until you feel like you can stand all day. We'll cover for you."

Bruhamoff muttered thanks and fell asleep again. He was too tired to feel embarrassed at his inebriated condition. *I'm going to be a father, but not really. Strange concept.*

Chapter Twenty-Five

Orienla arrived at the edge of Jital. She looked around at the various shops and taverns, spotting the Huntress Tavern. Shifting her carrying bag from one shoulder to the other, she made her way to the tavern and pushed open the door.

A few eyes glanced at her. She was used to being noticed both as a witch and for being a young woman. Without acknowledging the stares, she proceeded to a vacant table and sat, dropping her bag on the floor.

A teenage girl came to her table, gave a quick greeting, and offered to take her order.

"Just tea and a slice of bread." She gave the girl a smile, slightly amused at how she stood and checked to see if any of the men in the tavern were watching her. *I was just like her at one time until I found the way.*

Orienla watched the server when she returned, her walk slightly exaggerated as she squeezed by tables.

"Here's your tea and bread."

"Thank you. Can you tell me if Alric lives close by here?"

The girl's jaw dropped for a moment. "Yes, in the old farmhouse." She pointed with her hand to the back of the tavern.

"I see. Is he there right now?"

"He'd be working around the yard. You know him?"

Judging by your gaze on me, I suspect you have a fancy for him.
"Yes, we're friends."

"I think he's really busy working right now. I can tell him you were here."

"Thank you, but I think it's best I said hello myself. Peace be with you."

The girl stammered out a reply and walked away, turning her head to look at Orienla once more when she left the tavern.

The well-worn path was slightly damp from yesterday's rain. Orienla saw the crops looked healthy as she approached the old farmhouse. She pulled open the door after knocking and called out. The inside looked sparsely furnished but clean. *It looks like he lives here.*

She made her way around the yard and spotted him at a fence, working a post into the ground. When she was close enough for her voice to be heard, she called out his name.

He reacted with surprise. With a grin, he ran toward her, shouting out her name.

They hugged, kissed, and both spoke at the same time. Laughing, he took her back to the old farmhouse.

"I guess I really didn't expect to see you. Hoping, yes."

"Witches keep their promises. You should know that by now." She gave him a kiss.

Orienla looked down as she sat at the kitchen table. She rubbed her hand on the smooth surface, admiring the work he had accomplished on making the table and chairs. "I guess you know I've come to say goodbye. My mother needs my help as my father's health is failing. This is a difficult decision to make as I'm really fond of you. I want to stay, but the Book tells us to put others in front of our own wants."

"You're strong to do what needs to be done. I sensed you were a determined lady when I first met you."

"Thank you. You're the type of man a determined lady is attracted to."

Lunch came, and during the afternoon sun they casually walked around the farm. Orienla stopped to say hello to Darkian as they followed the fence that kept horses and cattle.

"I met a girl in the tavern. She was rather reluctant to tell me where I could find you."

"That would be Tersica. She is causing some concerns for her mother."

"I'll bet. She has a fixation on you."

Alric frowned. "I'm aware of that. She makes me feel a bit uncomfortable, but I'm sure she will outgrow this phase."

"She'll eventually grow up, but I suspect she'll always look upon you differently." She squeezed his hand. "Just warning you. I'm not the jealous type."

"Thanks." He stopped to kiss her again. The kiss extended into a period of touching. "Let's go back to the farmhouse, and I'll see what I can rustle up for dinner."

"You can cook?"

"Some. Maybe I'll have to ask for your help."

As they approached his home, Sharron headed in the same direction carrying a basket with Tersica following her.

Sharron smiled as she handed the basket over to Alric. "We saw you had company. I hope you don't mind, but we made dinner for you. I suspect you don't have much food to cook with."

"Thank you. There's the danger of whatever food I did have might end up in smoke." He paused to introduce Orienla to Sharron and Tersica.

Sharron was all smiles while Tersica looked between Alric and Orienla. Slowly Tersica offered a flask to Alric. "Here's some wine. To go with the food."

Alric and Orienla thanked them and went inside to eat.

"That was really nice of them. The wine is a nice addition."

"It's a lot better than the water or tea I have."

"Water or wine doesn't matter. I came here to see you."

He gave her a kiss. "You say all the right things, but if it's all the same to you, I think the wine will make a difference. Let's eat before it cools too much."

After the meal, Alric took a final drink of his wine. "That was great food. I'm stuffed."

"It was, but you better not fall asleep from too much food and drink." She walked over to him and sat on his lap. "We have some personal matters to attend to."

* * * *

Orienla woke up curled against Alric with her head on his shoulder, dimly aware he was stroking her back. Her eyes fluttered open at the morning light filtering through the window.

A few minutes passed, and Orienla slid her hand across his rib cage. She murmured, "Good morning."

"Good morning, yourself."

She kissed his chest. "Did you have peaceful dreams?"

"I think I dreamed I was chasing you around the farm."

Orienla laughed. "I assume you caught me because I wouldn't try to escape." She sat up in the bed, letting the blanket fall from her top. "Now, is there any food here so I can make you breakfast?"

"I have dried bacon and potatoes in the dugout."

"All right. You get the bacon and potatoes and put some tea on. There are a lot of chickens around here. I'll ask Sharron if I can have some eggs."

Orienla walked to the new farm house and recognized a figure feeding the chickens as they scurried around their pen.

"Good morning, Tersica." She gave a broad smile.

"Good morning." She didn't smile back.

"I was wondering if I could have a few eggs to make breakfast."

"Sure." She walked away toward the hen house. "I'll get you some."

Orienla waited, observing the chickens until Tersica returned with a basket containing eggs.

"Thanks."

Tersica grunted a reply.

Orienla smiled. "Tersica, you seem to be angry. When I was your age, I too lived on a farm. I was frustrated. My day was spent doing chores, and I never had the opportunity to be with others my own age, especially boys." She saw the facial reaction on Tersica's face. "Looking back, I realized that frustration was actually something I needed. It drove me to seek my own destiny and become independent. I love my parents and my two brothers, but the farm was not where I wanted to spend my life. I sought out my own path, leaving when I was old enough."

"Where did you go?"

"I travelled from one town to another, working in taverns and other jobs. I did get into a bit of trouble now and then. It was certainly an experience. One rainy night, I had too much to drink and was staggering along the streets. I fell and could hardly stand again. A man came along and took me into this building. I remembered little from that night, except people giving me tea and making sure I came into no harm."

"Who were they?"

"Witches, it turns out. A few days later as I sat in a tea house, I came to a conclusion. In my worse moments, it was the witches who saved me from my own undoing. I returned to the terradomus and asked if they would accept me."

"My mother said you're a witch, a Darkrose."

"We call ourselves the Umbravox. It doesn't matter the name, but our beliefs. If I may give you some advice, enjoy your time here. Appreciate all that is here. When you're ready, leave with love and good memories."

Tersica nodded slowly.

"As far as Alric is concerned, he can't be more than a friend to you, or it would cause problems with the rest of your family. Understand he finds you attractive, but he knows he's too old for you."

"Are you going to stay with him now?"

"No. I came here to say goodbye. I'm returning to the farm to help my mother. My father doesn't have long to live, and I shall be fortunate to be home before he passes on."

"Oh, I..."

"We all have hopes and burdens others do not see. That is why we must all treat others with gentleness and not judge too harshly."

"You're right. Maybe I've been a bit selfish."

"It is a trait we all must resist. Peace be with you."

"To you, too."

* * * *

Alric smiled as she stepped through the door. "You do know you don't have to catch the chickens first to get eggs, don't you?"

Orienla laughed. "I took the opportunity to talk to Tersica. She's young and fast approaching womanhood. I thought she needed some advice."

"That was good of you."

Orienla cracked open an egg. "Have you ever considered becoming a witch? I think you would fit in very well."

Alric was surprised by her question. "No, never considered it. I think a man who has used a sword as much as I have is ill suited to being a witch."

"You're not that man now. Just think about it." She paused. "The Whiterose witches have an open terradomus where they give sermons. Maybe go to one or two and see if you like what they have to say. I'd prefer it if you choose the Umbravox, but the Whiterose have merits, too."

"Thanks. I'll keep it in mind."

She placed her hands on his chest. "Of course, if you don't feel like going to a terradomus to find out about witches, you could travel with me, and I would be happy to teach you."

Alric briefly considered the possibility, but even if he could simply leave, he suspected she had to focus on helping her mother. He would again have to find a place to live and work, too. "I'm sorry, but I need to stay here where I can establish myself."

"I thought that would be your answer but had to ask."

After breakfast, Alric walked her to the road, kissed her, and said goodbye.

"Someday, I'll return and seek you out. I suspect you'll be married with four kids by then."

Alric laughed. "Well, I don't know about that, but I do hope I'll see you again."

She stared at him. "I will see you again. I hope you find true love, Alric. Peace be with you."

"And peace be with you."

Chapter Twenty-Six

Bruhamoff stood stiffly with the other royal guardsmen in the grand hall. Gold, rich tapestries, and paintings decorated the walls. The king and queen stood on a high platform, preparing to announce the start of the royal ball. Bruhamoff stared at the queen's pronounced stomach.

My child. I shall never be allowed to hold it or give it a father's wisdom. It is better I leave this palace and return to being a witch. I could not stand being so close but never being allowed to acknowledge it.

The music began, and Bruhamoff crossed the floor to ask one of the ladies of the court to dance. The entire staff for the palace were also at the ball, but for most part, they huddled near the walls and didn't venture near the dance floor.

Bruhamoff asked a plump lady standing next in the line. He bowed and invited her to dance. It was one of the royal guardsmen obligations to ensure all the ladies of the court were given several opportunities to dance. Only near the end of the evening was he allowed to pick a partner of his choice.

The evening droned on for him. He stopped to have a drink and a few bites between dances, and tried to look interested in each partner he danced with. Finally, there was a slight change in the music. The up tempo was a signal he could dance with whom he wished, even though the ball was coming to an end.

He made his way through the crowd, getting inviting looks from various ladies. He smiled and passed on to where the majority of the servants huddled near a food table. He spotted Ellyn and approached her.

"Would the lady give the honour of this dance?"

He heard the gasps around her. A servant being approached by a royal guardsman was not heard of normally.

Ellyn stuttered out her reply. "I don't dance. My dress is poor. I...I..."

"You look lovely, and I will guide you through the dance." He held out his hand and bowed. "Please."

She extended her hand slowly, and he took her fingers lightly in his own. Bruhamoff led her, and she hobbled to the dance floor.

The music mattered little to Bruhamoff. He smiled at the frightened face in front of him and carefully kept her away from being bumped by other dancers. Gradually she relaxed and even returned his smile. She developed her own technique of dancing, using her strong leg to do most of the work. At the end of the dance, she accepted a second dance from him, ignoring the whispered comments.

Chapter Twenty-Seven

Alric loaded up the wagon with pieces of furniture he had made. Several merchants were happy to take his goods, and he had gained a reputation of producing quality work. With his low expenses of living at the farm, he had managed to save a good quantity of gold coins.

He checked the ropes holding a table when he heard Tersica calling him.

"Wait for me."

He turned to see her running toward him and waited until she was close. "Does your mother know you want to go to town?"

"She said I could as long as you were okay with it." She climbed into the front bench of the wagon. "You are, aren't you?" She grinned at him.

He rolled his eyes. "Sure."

"Because if you're going to town to meet women, I'll stay out of the way."

The thought had crossed his mind, but he simply smiled. "Your company will be appreciated." He did like the isolation of the farm. After being attacked on the highway a year ago, no one had shown any hostile interest in him. The farm families had taken him as one of their own, and he felt comfortable with a large group. The one problem was the lack of female companionship, and as time went on, he made more frequent trips to town to sell his furniture, hoping to meet someone. While he did have some success meeting women, few came close to his experience with Orienla.

Alric also noticed a change in Tersica. She still liked to tease him and acted like she knew more than she did, but she had stopped being angry with her mother and the others in the extended family. Alric suspected Orienla's talk with her had been the start of the transformation of her attitude but had never found out the details of the conversation.

Alric snapped the reins, and the horse started to pull the wagon. Darkian gave a look at him as they went by but didn't react otherwise. Alric was quite certain the horse wouldn't like being harnessed, and there was also the problem he didn't like to follow other horses. Alric had images of the horse pulled wagon passing other horses, making the trip to town far too adventurous.

The ride started off in quiet talk, but Alric knew Tersica liked to ask questions that put him on the spot. She couldn't help but tease him and was aware of the changes in her body that made her more attractive to men.

"What type of women are you attracted to? Dark hair?"

"As long as they have money, I don't care." He grinned as she glared at him.

"That isn't true. You really liked that witch, Orienla. I could tell, and she wasn't rich."

"I like all kinds of women. I'm looking for the right combination of looks and personality."

"Orienla was nice, and she was pretty."

"She moved far away."

"What if she hadn't moved far away? Would you have married her?"

"I don't know. I liked her."

"You just won't tell me." She grinned. "That means you really liked her."

Alric decided not to respond to her inquiries, hoping she would tire of his non-answers. Eventually she did give up prying and changed to other subjects, such as problems with various members on the farm. On this he gave some advice, trying to support her complaints while offering the possibility of another viewpoint.

"You're good to talk to." She gave him a smile. "Thanks for listening."

* * * *

Tersica helped Alric unload the furniture and was surprised over how excited the merchants were to receive his work. One commented it was the best quality he had seen in years and was fit for the castle. She saw the coins exchanged in payment and realized his own description of himself as a simple woodworker was an understatement. Her mother told her she had seen his hands and his leather vest which told her he had been in a few battles. She was of the opinion he was staying at the farm as a refuge from his earlier life, but would soon be moving on again. "He's just not a farmer and will seek a better place to do his work."

That upset Tersica, who still had feelings for Alric, although she learned not to display them openly. She did often volunteer to take him food and other items when he stayed at his farmhouse. She had also been caught hiding in the garden to watch him wash at his well. Her mother tried to be stern about it, but the lecture was weak as Tersica knew her mother had watched him as well.

The last merchant shop was owned by a couple, and Tersica had learned their dress and mannerism indicated they were witches. She was puzzled, believing witches only lived in a terradomus and had never seen them work, only travelling.

"Excuse me, are you witches?" she asked after they paid Alric.

The man smiled. "Yes, we are."

"You also own this shop?"

"Yes, we do."

"Are witches allowed to work? I thought they just studied at a terradomus."

He grinned. "We do that as well, if there's enough time in the day. Some witches only spend their time at the terradomus and study, but others are less intense. Witches can be shopkeepers, farmers, and even woodworkers. Each witch must find their level of commitment to study and a balance of other tasks they must do. Are you interested in witches?"

Tersica thought of Orienla. "Yes, a little."

"This afternoon the terradomus we are members of is open to the public for a sermon. Why don't you attend and learn a bit more about our beliefs and who we are? You will get to see the inside of a terradomus and talk to some witches."

Tersica looked at Alric. "Do we have time to go there?"

He nodded. "Sure. I think it will be good for you to understand about witches."

* * * *

The female shopkeeper hurried to the terradomus, not the normal leisurely pace most witches used. She quickly sought audience with Altus Rector Howrand. After a short wait, she was ushered into his office.

A smile came first as he gestured her to sit and speak what was on her mind.

"The red-headed man was in our shop today, the one that used to be a warrior."

"Yes, we know he lives nearby, and this isn't the first time he has visited your shop." He smiled again, trying to reassure the excited woman.

"This time it's different. He's coming to the terradomus for the sermon. He has a young woman with him. She wants to know more about witches."

Howrand sat up slightly. "That is of interest to us. Thank you for delivering the news of this."

* * * *

Standing at the front on the raised platform, Ululla faced the half-filled hall. She smiled as she prepared to speak, the nervousness she felt just minutes ago, evaporating as she considered the words in the Book of Redemption.

"Occasionally, we are asked about the word redemption and what it means to us. After all we do study the Book of Redemption, named by Altus Rector Bercthun hundreds of years ago. As the word redemption implies, we seek to rectify a wrong that was done. We are not perfect beings. We make mistakes for many reasons. Sometimes because we are angry, sometimes because we have the wrong information, and sometimes because it is always the way we have done things and never stopped to question it."

Ululla scanned the crowd, pleased they were paying attention to her words. She spotted the red-headed male near the back, and her breath caught for a moment as their eyes met. Her heart beat faster, and she forced herself to look away before she spoke again. *What if he truly is the one? Am I witnessing the prophecy becoming true? Is this now the beginning of the dark times and birth of the new order?*

"When we do make mistakes, how do we repair the damage? How do we seek redemption? Do we ask a higher power for forgiveness? According to Altus Rector Bercthun, we can achieve redemption, not by asking for absolution, but by acting better in the future. We cannot undo what we did in the past, but we can stop making the same errors.

"We are not saying there isn't a higher power that can grant us release from past sins. As witches of the Whiterose, many of us also believe in the divine being. We also follow a philosophy set out in the Book of Redemption that tells us to take responsibility for our actions. That means when we make an error, we should act to correct it. Asking for forgiveness alone is insufficient. We must make corrections in the path we follow so we don't make the same mistake again.

"This is an open terradomus. It means any of you are free to come inside this chamber. We have a copy of the Book of Redemption here, and we invite you to look at it. Read parts of it. I'm sure you will see enlightenment in the passages. Thank you for listening to me. Peace be with you."

Ululla stepped off the podium to make her way to where she saw the man who was the centre of the other witches' attention. She was stopped by several visitors who thanked her for her words. One asked her if he should forgive his neighbour for stealing one of his tools.

"Of course. It will make you feel better. Do not let a wrong against you in the past stop you from enjoying the present. You cannot change what your neighbour did, but you can stop letting a mistake continue to bother you. Forgive your neighbour and be free of that negativity."

She moved past a few more visitors and saw him again. Her jaw trembled as she gazed on him. She saw the warrior in him, and also a gentle side. A man in control of his two sides. *Am I seeing the one who is the seed of change? There is something different about him.*

Her voice stumbled as she greeted him. "He-hello. Thank you for coming to hear our words."

"It was a fine sermon. You speak well." He turned to his side. "I'm Alric, and this is Tersica. She is curious about witches."

"Thank you. I'm Ululla." She looked at Tersica, who was clinging to Alric as if he would try to leave her alone. "Perhaps you would like to have a cup of tea with me, and we can chat a little?"

Alric glanced at Tersica. "I think a cup of tea sounds wonderful."

"Follow me then." She extended her hand to briefly touch his. *Strong, working hands.*

The dining room was only open to visitors after the open sermons when escorted inside to converse with witches. Ululla chose an open spot and faced Alric and Tersica. Tea was quickly brought to them, and Ululla talked with Alric first while Tersica regained her composure.

"What type of work do you do, Alric?"

"I'm a woodworker. Tersica's family owns a farm and have permitted me to live there. They're very good people."

She saw the scars on his hands and arms and ventured out a question. "I notice marks on your arms. Have you always been a woodworker?"

He shook his head. "No, my father was a woodworker and wanted me to follow in his footsteps. But I, being young and foolish, wanted to have adventure. I joined the army. These marks came from that. I was fortunate to have been able to leave that life and return to what my father taught me."

"Are you content now, Alric?"

"I'm much better now. There's always more one wants, but my needs are fulfilled."

Ululla grinned. "It sounds like you have been in contact with witches before."

Alric laughed. "Many times. In fact, it was a witch who told me I had to leave the army or die. The truth is I had to fake my death to escape. In some respects, I became reborn as a different man."

Ululla's heart quickened in her chest. *Everything he said meets the words of the prophecy.* "Tersica, what would you like to know about witches?"

"What do witches do exactly? You don't just study."

"A good question. Witches attempt to spread peace among people. We do this by our words and actions, and offering assistance when appropriate. To do and say the right things, we study the Book of Redemption for guidance."

"What about spells? I heard witches use spells and magic."

"We have the knowledge of spells and potions, but that doesn't mean we will use them whenever we want to. Spells can often have a negative effect for the user or have undesirable consequences later. Witches also know dark spells can have long term effects, far beyond their intended target. To answer your question, we do use spells, but are very guarded in doing so."

"If I wanted to become a witch, how would I do that?"

"The first step is we have a serious talk with you to see if you truly want to be a witch and understand the path to become one. One obstacle some face is if they know how to read and write well enough to study the Book of Redemption. Some have to learn to read first before we can consider them. If we accept you for study, then we help you learn the teachings of the Book. This study never ends, but at some point, when you demonstrate you have an understanding of the basic knowledge, we invite you to join our order."

"What is the difference between the Darkrose and the Whiterose?"

Ululla smiled. "There are far more similarities than differences. The Whiterose at one time belonged to the same order as the Darkrose, but separated over differences in philosophy. Both orders want to bring peace to the world. The Darkrose use the Book of Destiny as a source of study. They believe many of our actions are preordained, while we are of the belief we have free choice."

"I'll have to think about what you said."

"Of course, but anytime you want to learn more, feel free to come here. I'm usually here, and just ask for me. Don't worry. I'll never pressure you to join." She turned her attention to Alric. "Do you have any questions?"

"Just one," he said with a smile. "Is it possible to have a tea with you sometime outside of the terradomus? I would like to talk...well, just talk."

She nodded. "I would like that, too."

Ululla made a quick decision. She suspected the conversation may become personal and didn't want anyone else hearing more. "There is a teahouse called the Crossroads two blocks west of here. Meet me tomorrow at eleven in the morning."

* * * *

Ululla sat in front of Altus Rector Howrand, her hands folded together in her lap. She heard his request, his voice sounding less sure than normal.

"These are difficult times, and we may be approaching a pivotal moment regarding the prophecy in the Book of Redemption. I trust you understand that I am not making this request lightly, but circumstances are such that I want to ask you for a special favour. I understand that you are to meet Alric, and it could be of great benefit to us if he were to see you, and by extension, the Whiterose in a positive light. Will you support our appeal?"

"I will not act anyway I do not feel comfortable. Alric invited me for tea. As a woman, I will not pretend to feel anything but my honest emotions."

"There is much at stake."

Ululla fixed her eyes on the altus rector. "It makes little difference. Do we not strive to be honest at all times? If there is so much at stake, then isn't this the time we must be especially true to the teachings of the Book of Redemption?"

Perplexed, Howrand stated, "Honesty is a good virtue."

"I agree. It's what he wants from us."

"Continue your task as you see fit then." He sighed after dismissing her.

Ululla had heard the rumours of Alric being seen in the company of a Darkrose witch earlier in the year, and there was concern he would join their order. If he was indeed the seed of change, then the change would likely follow their path and not the Whiterose.

The 'Seed of Change' was a vague line that could have different meanings. One the altus councillium favoured was him being the father to the next great leader of the witches, one that would unite all witches back to one group. There was concern the Darkrose would prevail, and the Whiterose would cease to exist as a separate identity.

* * * *

Tersica looked at Alric as the wagon headed back to the farm.

"Stop your grinning," he told her. "I only asked her out for a tea."

"I saw your eyes. You like her, really like her."

"It's still just a tea."

"No, it's not. The way you two looked at each other and how quickly she said yes, I think it won't be your last date."

"Young lady, you may keep your opinions to yourself."

"Young lady? Now I know the knife has hit a sore spot."

Alric shook his head, but knew Tersica wasn't far from the truth. From the moment he first saw Ululla, he knew he had to meet her. He had said more than he had planned but felt relief after doing so. Ululla hadn't rejected him. Their tea at the terradomus only strengthened his resolve to meet her alone.

* * * *

Alric stood as she entered the Crossroads Teahouse. She immediately saw him and walked over to him. She touched his arm and sat, watching his eyes.

Kind eyes, but one that has seen much turmoil.

"Thank you for coming, Ululla. It's good to see you again."

"My pleasure. You're an interesting man." She smiled. "Was it a long ride from the farm to come here?"

Alric grinned. "Not at all. The farm I live at is not too far away, but I left early enough to have breakfast here."

She laughed and changed the subject, asking him about being a soldier. She felt drawn to his deep voice, using words that surprised her. *Educated. Smart. I think I could listen to him speak all day.*

Time slipped by. They ate lunch at the teahouse, and she accepted Alric's insistence on paying. They walked slowly back to the terradomus.

"As the keeper, I shouldn't be away too long."

"Keeper. Is that something like a guard?"

"A little. I'm the one responsible for the terradomus security. There're others called watchers who look for suspicious activity."

"I couldn't sneak in the terradomus at night to see you then?"

"You couldn't sneak in." She paused. "You could still see me at night."

"May I see you tomorrow night then?"

Ululla licked her lips. "I would like that."

Alric stopped her at the street corner next to the terradomus. He moved slowly but with confidence, kissing her on the lips.

Ululla responded. They broke apart and returned to kiss again. They resumed their walk, and Ululla squeezed his hand.

"Just come to the front doors. They'll be expecting you and will let you in."

"I'll be there just after sunset."

Ululla stepped toward the front doors, turning around to give Alric a wave. *I suppose everyone in the terradomus has heard about my kiss with him. I'm not going to get any peace from questions for a while.*

Chapter Twenty-Eight

Bruhamoff sat across from Ellyn. He was glad she wanted to meet for lunch but now was puzzled at her demeanor.

"Is everything all right?"

"Yes, everything is fine, but I want to talk about us, before things go too far. I think I may have given you the wrong impression."

"How so? I don't understand."

"I like you. Really like you as a friend. You're a wonderful man, smart, kind, and very good looking." She gave a grin as she reached to touch his hand. "But I have a problem that prevents us from being more than just friends."

"You don't mean your leg, do you? Because..."

"No, I know that doesn't make a difference with you. The problem is I favour women to have a relationship with. I don't want you to be repeating that to anyone. I need to be discrete as some people don't understand my preference."

Bruhamoff was silent for a moment, took a deep breath, and spoke. "I know you'll be a wonderful friend. I shall keep a secret of what you told me."

"Thank you." She paused a moment. "Let's go for a walk. There's something else I want to talk to you about."

They left the dining hall, making their way through the courtyard to one of the gardens.

Ellyn spoke. "The queen is doing well with her pregnancy, although she's a bit uncomfortable at this stage. When the baby is born, are you going to be able to handle being so close to it without being allowed to show any affection? It would be dangerous if you did."

"I will be leaving shortly after the baby is born. I don't believe I could remain here and not show feelings toward it."

"A wise decision. Where will you go?"

"You told me a secret, so I shall tell you mine. I am a witch and will be returning to my terradomus."

"Why did you become a Royal guardsman if you're a witch?"

"I cannot tell you."

"I understand. Witches are known for their secrets."

"I suppose we are. In this case, I hope you understand I don't really have much more to tell you."

"I do. Do you have a girlfriend back at the terradomus?"

"No."

"I'm sure it won't be long before you meet someone. Whether you know it or not, a lot of women are attracted to you."

"Thanks. I guess I just need to be patient. Either that or have more women just as friends."

* * * *

Ululla entered her suite, preparing for her evening with Alric. She brushed her hair, and suddenly felt the presence of another person. She glanced around the empty suite. "Terrowin?"

"I've come to say goodbye."

"Goodbye? Are you leaving this plane?"

"No. I'm returning home."

"Home?"

"Yes. Thank you for your help."

"Good luck, Terrowin. It was wonderful to know you."

"Our paths may cross again."

He was gone. She smiled as a tear rolled down her cheek.

* * * *

Alric was eager to leave the farm and head to town. His lunch at the farm was highlighted by Tersica's questions about Ululla and his intentions, which he avoided by changing the subject.

He left the farm in the afternoon, deciding he wanted to avoid any more uncomfortable questions. Darkian was happy to be able to escape the enclosure, and Alric had to restrain him from galloping. They arrived too early to go to the terradomus, and Alric decided to spend time in a tavern.

He sat alone with his ale when a man in worn clothing sat across from him. At first Alric was inclined to tell him to find a different table, then hesitated when the stranger spoke.

"You have journeyed far to reach this point in your life. I urge you not to hesitate in commitment. Sometimes one finds oneself at the right place at the right time only once."

"Are you speaking of Ululla?"

"She is part of the commitment I refer to." He stood. "May the path you follow lead you to contentment."

Alric watched him leave. *Blackrain. What did he mean by commitment? If Ululla is only part of it, then he must be referring to witches.* He finished his ale and went to Darkian, his mind on his future during the hours he spent waiting.

As Ululla indicated, the witches were expecting him. He entered and stood waiting in a large entrance as several witches came and went, all of them trying to be discrete in their glances at him. Ululla entered the front hall, smiling warmly as she approached.

"I think it's best we get you out of here before every witch comes by to look at you."

"I feel like I'm wearing something odd that makes everyone look at me."

She took his arm, and they stepped outside. *I don't think it's what you're wearing.* "Witches can be rather curious about a new face in the terradomus."

"Curiosity can be a good thing." He took her hand as they walked down the streets. "I'm curious how relationships between a witch and a non-witch are viewed."

"There are a lot of couples where only one is a witch. It depends a lot on how much both sides are willing to compromise. Witches have to make a certain commitment of time to the order, and it can be a strain sometimes on relationships."

"I suppose with you being a keeper, your commitment of time to the terradomus would be fairly high."

"This is true, along with other higher rankings. A keeper and, for example, the altus rector are expected to spend most of their time in the terradomus. Emergencies and situations can arise at any time, day or night, and we should be available to make decisions."

"You need to live in the terradomus."

"True."

"And a non-witch cannot normally be inside."

She nodded. "There are exceptions. For example, small children under the care of a witch. Also, those training to be a witch but have not yet completed the induction ceremony."

"For us to spend time together, it has to be outside the terradomus."

"Yes, I'm afraid so. You're welcome to be in the front hall, but the rest of the terradomus is off limits to outsiders."

* * * *

Ululla was surprised at how fast the evening went by with Alric. They stopped at a teahouse once, but spent most of the time walking. Normally Ululla didn't like to be out along the streets at night, but with Alric she felt completely safe. On their way back to the terradomus, she insisted they said their goodnights a distance away.

"I don't want to be putting on a show for the other witches, and believe me, the watchers can see quite a distance."

"I'd be happy to kiss you goodnight anywhere. Several times, in fact."

She kissed him. "Good to know. Maybe we can stop a few times on our way back."

Alric and Ululla finally reached the entrance of the terradomus.

"Well, I have you back safely home."

"You have. You look like you want to say something to me."

"I do. Ask, really. What would it take for me to be accepted into the Whiterose order?"

"Are you serious?"

"Yes, because I'm also serious about you."

Ululla took his hand. "I'm serious about you too. Come inside. I want you to stay."

Chapter Twenty-Nine

Bruhamoff stood at attention in front of the queen servant's entrance. He was aware that the increased traffic through the doors reflected even more activity inside the queen's bed chamber. He hoped, prayed, all was well with the birth. He tried not to think of it as his baby, but the knot in his stomach indicated otherwise.

The servant's door opened and a soft voice spoke from inside. "Guardsman."

Bruhamoff turned and saw Lady Asturias beckon with her hand to follow her.

"You have been granted five minutes with the queen and her newborn. This is the only time you shall have such a privilege. It is not normal protocol, but the queen is fond of you."

Bruhamoff remembered the other times he had entered, and the drink of whisky he received during those visits. *I could use a drink right now.*

A royal blue blanket was wrapped around the baby the queen held. Slowly he approached the side of the bed. The pink face had its eyes closed. Bruhamoff peered down at it, his mouth suddenly dry.

"Would you like to hold the new prince?"

Nodding, Bruhamoff slowly reached for the child. *A son. I have a son.* He carefully held the silent baby, scared to hold it too tight. "He's a beautiful baby, my Queen."

"Yes, he is. I now have to come up with a name so he can be properly announced to the world." She smiled. "I don't suppose you have any suggestions, do you?"

Bruhamoff looked at his son. "May I be so bold as to suggest Terrowin?"

"Terrowin?" The queen paused in thought. "After the great King Terrowin. That is a wonderful suggestion. Prince Terrowin. That has a nice sound to it."

* * * *

Ululla heard the castle bells ring, and went to where a watcher was observing the streets below.

"Is there an emergency, Watcher Kerin?"

"None I can perceive. It appears to be only an announcement."

"I will be on the main floor. Inform me of any news please."

Ululla stopped on the second floor and looked in on Alric who was working on a set of table and chairs. A woodworking room had been created for him, and he produced furniture for the terradomus and others. She knew he was ready to pass the test and become a witch but he was reluctant to take the final step. She also knew the reason. He wasn't afraid of the commitment, but the thought of being naked in front of the others during the ceremony gave him pause.

"Come with me for a break."

Alric put down a chisel. "You don't have to ask me twice."

They made their way to the dining room, taking tea and biscuits to a table already holding several other witches.

Alric smiled at the others and sat across from Ululla, briefly touching her hand. He told her he had noticed a slight change in her complexion and appetite, just a few days after she confirmed to him of her pregnancy.

A witch called out from the entrance to the dining room. "King Grayson and Queen Elissa have a new son. Prince Terrowin!"

Ululla gasped. *Terrowin has made it home again.*

Chapter Thirty

Despite the warning from his advisers that such exposure was risky, King Grayson insisted on a royal parade through the provinces of the Kingdom of Allisure. He believed the stoppages in the towns and cities helped solidified support for Allisure and make resistance stronger against any attack. Although uneasy peace existed between Allisure and the Dwykath, it was expected eventually a war would come about. The when was likely when Dwykath believed its army was strong enough to overcome the well-equipped and trained army of the Allisure forces.

The king also wanted to expose his sons to the public and let them see what life was like outside the castle walls. Another part of him wanted to show off his youngest son, a surprise pregnancy considering his own age at the time of his conception.

The line of people along the main street of Drumclog went from the edge of town to the castle of the governing lord. It was the first visit from the royal family in four years, and the citizens of the town and surrounding area were happy to celebrate their arrival. The royal coaches rolled slowly past as cheers rippled along the crowd. First the king and queen rolled by, followed by the princes and princesses in order of age. Behind the last coach crowds followed, chanting the king's name.

At the castle the coaches came to a stop, and the royal family ascended the steps of a temporary platform. The crowd waved banners, cheered, and pressed in as close as the guards allowed. A shout came from one of the servants, and she chased the youngest prince as he darted toward the crowd.

"Prince Terrowin, come back here."

The servant ran after the three-year old, who was amazingly fast when he saw something he wanted. He wasn't just running anywhere, but had picked out something in the crowd. Prince Terrowin stopped as he reached the press of the people and pointed at a woman dressed in worn clothes.

"Thea." The finger moved to an older woman standing next to her. "Mama." He grinned at them happily.

The servant wrapped an arm around him, lifting him in the air. "Prince Terrowin, you mustn't run off like that." She carried him back to the platform as he curled and opened his fingers in a goodbye wave.

Thea stood shocked as the prince was placed back on the platform. People around her commented how the young prince seemed to like her, and she acknowledged their admiration. She looked at her mother and whispered. "Our Terrowin, he came back as a prince!"

Her mother nodded, tears streaming down her cheeks.

Thea listened to the king's speech, but her eyes stayed on Prince Terrowin. He seemed to have forgotten her as he studied something else on the platform floor. Still, she waved enthusiastically at him when the cheers erupted at the conclusion of the speech.

* * * *

Ululla brushed her daughter's hair, a lighter gold than her own. "Now try to stay clean, Ayleth." She smiled, knowing the words would have little effect on the two-year old. She knew her daughter—who was far too clever for her own good at times—understood, but obedience was another matter.

A male witch knocked on the entrance to her office and waited for her acknowledgement.

"Brother Drewloft, please enter."

He held up a rolled piece of paper. "This arrived for you earlier this morning. It came from a Darkrose witch."

"Really?" She took the paper. While the two orders occasionally met to discuss matters of mutual importance, it was rare for members to be singled out for communication.

She unrolled the document, reading the short request.

"Hmm. I'm being asked to meet this Darkrose witch alone on a personal matter."

"That is unusual. Are you going to do so?"

"Yes. We are to meet in a teahouse, so I don't see any danger. It may be she wants to convert to Whiterose and needs some information. I don't know what else this could be. I must make haste to be on time. Will you take Ayleth to her father, please?"

The afternoon threatened rain as Ululla made her way to the designated teahouse, located near the front entrance of the castle. She reached the teahouse, saw it was busy but quickly spotted the Darkrose witch when she stood at her table.

Ululla walked over, glancing at the young boy next to her as he munched on a cookie.

"Sister Ululla, please sit down. I'm Orienla, and this is my son, Dorian."

Ululla greeted her and ordered a cup of tea. "I'm curious why you wanted to meet me. You wrote it was something personal."

"It is. I know Alric and yourself are married with a child." She paused. "I knew Alric before you, and we enjoyed a brief time together."

Ululla remembered how nervous the Whiterose leaders were when they learned Alric had been seen in the company of a Darkrose witch. *So, this is her. Very pretty.* "You broke apart."

"True. I had to leave Jital to be with my parents. My father was quite ill, and I wanted to be with him before he passed on."

"That must have been difficult for you."

"It was." Orienla took a deep breath. "I felt Alric was a very special man, one I wanted to spend more time with, but it was not to be."

"I see. I don't wish to sound insensitive to your circumstances previously, but I don't understand why you wanted to meet with me."

Orienla looked at Dorian. "Alric and I shared a final night together. Dorian is his son."

Ululla looked at the redheaded boy and saw the similarity in the face, blue eyes, and red hair.

"The reason I asked to meet you was to ask for your help and advice on what I should do. It is wrong not to inform Alric he has a son. I also do not want to cause a problem for Alric and you. To be certain, I am quite capable of raising Dorian without Alric knowing about him, but I think Alric should know of his son."

Ululla slowly nodded. "You are correct. Alric should meet his son, and my daughter should know about her half-brother."

Orienla let out a sigh. "Thank you for your understanding. I was concerned you might deny Dorian was his son or be angry with the revelation."

"I think we need to follow the guidelines and teachings of our different orders. We will work together and find a way to unite the father and son." *Without causing a problem between Alric and myself.*

* * * *

Chilee studied the wax image on the cheesecloth. He hoped it would reveal the path, but was worried the master would heap scorn—or worse—on him if he wasn't precise. The representation on the fabric was not easy to interpret, but he eventually made out the pattern. Slowly he turned and looked up at the master.

He had learned not to use vague words or hesitate in his description. "The seed has been sown, supporting two pillars of a triangle. Another point is especially strong, a male of royal heritage. He is dominant and has the strength to be a great ruler."

"We need to eliminate him this time." The master frowned, recalling the failed efforts so far to stop him.

"There is more. The outline is distorted by other forces. I see our influence, the witches, and another force, all trying to push the pattern into a shape they want."

The master nodded, as a plan began to form in his head. So far, his efforts to cause the havoc he needed to become the ruler of all had been thwarted. The witches were a force he had underestimated, and despite managing to infiltrate part of one order, he couldn't eliminate their power. He had been able to use the Dwykath forces to his advantage, promising King Hadrian power he had no intention of granting, but the Blackrain order had shown it was capable of disrupting his spells, although they kept secretive as to their ultimate intentions.

Chapter Thirty-One

Alric rolled on the ground as Dorian and Ayleth jumped on him. Ululla let out a laugh as she stood at the edge of the field with Orienla.

"I think Dorian really landed on Alric's stomach that time."

"Good thing it was him and not us wrestling with those two. They have a lot of energy after being in a terradomus all day." She placed a hand on Ululla's arm. "I just want to say it's wonderful Alric and you have made Dorian part of your family."

"Orienla, you're part of our family, too. Ayleth really enjoys seeing her big brother."

"Thank you. That makes me feel good."

"Are you seeing anyone? You mentioned last time a man was interested in you."

"Sort of. I don't want to confuse Dorian by being too close to another man when he so looks up to Alric."

"Here they come. Alric looks like he's been in a battle with all the dirt and grass covering him."

"Once a warrior..."

Ululla grinned, "Except now his battles are slightly less life threatening."

They parted ways and returned to their respected terradomus together.

"That was a good work out," Alric told them.

"For you it was. The kids could still play."

"True. It's good Darian and Ayleth play so well together. It shows that the Darkrose and Whiterose can get along in the right circumstances."

"That's true. We will need both orders working together when the dark clouds arrive."

"Perhaps the Blackrain could help us then."

Ululla looked up at him. "The Blackrain? They may be more evil than good."

"I actually talked to them on occasion. They didn't sound evil. In fact, at one time they encouraged me to join the witches."

"Really? Tell me more."

Alric related the times when he met the Blackrain, and how his view of them changed over time.

* * * *

Bruhamoff carried his tea among the tables. He noticed Tersica sitting by herself at one of the tables, recalling her name from when Ululla and Alric introduced her to him. For a young woman, Bruhamoff was surprised at her confidence. She also implied some familiarity with Alric that made the big man uncomfortable.

He sat across from her. "Hello. I'm Bruhamoff. We were introduced a couple of weeks ago by Sister Ululla and Brother Alric."

"I remember you all right." She grinned. "You're the tall, shy guy."

"You do like to put people on the spot, don't you? I remember what you said to Brother Alric."

Tersica smiled. "I tease people I like." She tilted her head to the side slightly. "I think you're handsome."

Bruhamoff took a drink of tea, slightly shocked at her aggressive response. "The Book of Redemption teaches us to be careful how we speak to others. We should strive to make others feel comfortable when we speak to them."

"Doesn't the Book of Redemption also tell us to be honest?"

He nodded. "It does, but it also states when we speak we have to consider its effect. When we speak the truth, we must ask who gains from it. You're using the excuse of being honest to gain an advantage for yourself."

She smiled. "I didn't know about that part in the book. Maybe you can teach me more about what it says. I would like to learn more about the teachings, and you seem to know so much about it."

"Perhaps I can." He took a drink of his tea, satisfied he had taught her to be more reserved.

"Good. I'm free this afternoon and, actually, all day tomorrow. I look forward to learning from you."

Bruhamoff froze as he lifted his tea mug to his lips, not knowing how to respond to such an aggressive invitation.

* * * *

Alric sat with Ululla and Altus Rector Howrand.

"Tell the Altus Rector Howrand what you told me, Alric."

"I didn't think to mention it to Ululla before, but now I realize it may be of interest to the Whiterose. I have met those who claim to be part of the Blackrain. They seem to have knowledge of the witches, myself, and of future events." Alric went to describe his encounters with the Blackrain. "I was told Jital is far older than we believe, that it was actually built on top of another, older city. The location is sacred, for this is where opposite forces cancel each other out, producing a calm."

Howrand tapped his fingers on the desk. "Very interesting. We were of the opinion before that the Blackrain were more on the side of doing evil, and what you said about Jital is quite revealing. I shall pass this information on to the altus councillium."

Alric spoke. "I would like to meet them again. They have a cabin not far from here." He turned to Ululla. "She told me a location is known to us."

"That is true, although as far as we know none of the witches have made direct contact with them." Howrand replied.

"With your permission, I would like to travel to their cabin."

Howrand smiled. "This isn't the king's army, Brother Alric. You do not require my permission to do so, but I do appreciate knowing your intention."

* * * *

Darkian seemed to enjoy the chance to go on a longer journey. Alric had to restrain him after they left the main road, venturing into the smaller pathways.

"Ease up. I'm getting branches in my face." Alric wasn't sure where they were, but assumed the trail had to eventually lead to the Blackrain Cabins. He tried to peer between the trees for any sign of their location and caught a glimpse of faint dark smoke rising just above the trees.

He steered his horse in the direction of the smoke and discovered another path, just wide enough for a person to travel. The path twisted around trees and turned back on itself several times before it reached a clearing. Alric stopped to stare at the five dark wood cabins, surrounded by weeds and a pile of chopped wood. He sat on Darkian, waiting, unsure if he should simply knock on the door of one of the cabins, and if so, which one.

A cabin door opened on the closest cabin, and a woman in a dirty blue top and a brown skirt stepped out. She frowned as she peered at him.

"Don't just sit there. Come here if you want to talk to us."

Alric obeyed and stood outside the cabin door as Darkian grazed. The woman had disappeared back inside, replaced by an older, bearded man Alric recognized.

"I met you at Deyell."

He smiled. "You've a good memory. I am pastor Immin."

"It's not easy to forget a man who spoke about Jital as if it was an ancient mystery."

"Not far from the truth. I assume you came here to ask questions."

"I have a few. Can you tell me why the secrecy of not revealing who you are? Even the witches don't know anything about your order."

"The less our enemies know about us, the better we are able to attack them. I suspect you will say the witches are not our enemy, but the answer is the same. Information about us is hard to obtain, either from witches or anyone else."

"The witches are on the side of peace. Shouldn't you work with them?"

"Someday we may. Now is not the right time."

"Yet you tell me this knowing I'll tell the witches. So, you're giving up some of your secrets."

He smiled. "Some information can be parted with. The witches should know we are not evil. We seek peace as well, but our path is different."

"How so?"

"The witches strive to send the message of peace every day to everyone. It is commendable. However, it also leaves them exposed. It is easy to attack those who only see peace and good. Our purpose is to attack those who wish to do evil. We wait for when we are needed."

"The Book of Redemption speaks of dark clouds challenging us. Is that what you mean?"

"Yes, but the witches have misinterpreted the words. They believe the dark clouds are forming now and expect a great battle. To be sure, a great battle is going to happen soon, one that will have a profound effect on the future. Evil forces shall instigate it, and there is little we will do prevent it."

"You say will. Does that mean you can do more but choose not to?"

"That is correct. We have our reasons I cannot divulge."

Alric was silent as he reflected on the pastor's comments. "What do you mean by the prophecy was misinterpreted?"

"The dark clouds the prophecy refers to will happen decades from now, not in a few years."

"You choose not to interfere now, but will do so later."

"Essentially correct. To be more open with you, we actively used our resources to protect you. Most events can be predicted simply because circumstances force an action. Two kingdoms will usually attack one another. Those who see the future can accurately predict when that battle will occur. It doesn't have to account for individual actions. Of thousands of possibilities, nearly all of them will end up in a battle between the kingdoms.

"You, my friend, are different. You are an individual. We know, as the witches did, you would be in contact with the witches and sire offspring with them. So did the dark forces. We prevented your premature death and allowed the normal course of events to take place."

Alric remembered the arrow that missed him. "I recall being attacked on a road."

"We placed a spell on you that pushed the arrows away. We also placed an unseen spell on you which prevented others from using a spell to locate you when you lived on the farm. Earlier we prevented a spell from making the enemy soldiers ill. By making the battle more difficult, you were able to fake your death easier."

"Did you have a hand in me meeting Ululla?"

"No. You were destined to live as a witch in one of the orders. It mattered not which one. You were to also have a son in one order and a daughter in the other. You may have other children, but your role has been completed. It is your eldest son and daughter that will have a profound effect in the future. You need not worry about your safety. The dark ones know you are now, shall we say, unimportant."

"And my children?"

"We will protect them as well as the witches. They are safe, at least until they reach adulthood."

"Then what?"

"Then the true battle begins."

THE END

About the Author

J. (Jack) H. Wear lives in Edmonton, Alberta with his wife, Lorrie. They have three sons, and two grandsons. Logic notwithstanding, Lorrie blames Jack for the lack of females in the family.

Jack took up writing later than most authors. After finishing a career with Xerox, he soon felt bored and started selling beverages as a liquor agent. Over several glasses of Sauvignon Blanc, he wrote his first novel, submitted it and suddenly became a published author. This astonished everyone, especially every English teacher he had in school.

He continued with writing, adding a trilogy, along with several short stories. Most of his writing is in the fantasy and science fiction genres, although his latest novel is a murder mystery.

His current projects are a science fiction novel, a murder mystery and trying to convince his single sons their mother needs a granddaughter.

Website: www.jhwear.com

www.ingramcontent.com/pod-product-compliance
Lightning Source LLC
Chambersburg PA
CBHW020205270626
47157CB00028B/1141